Before Dorothy rightly knew what he intended, he'd heaved her over his shoulder like a sack of coal. A shoulder which she discovered had not only the width, but also the marble-like consistency of a mantelpiece. And which knocked the breath from her lungs.

He had carried her into the corridor before she regained the ability to speak. Or the wits to begin beating at his back with her fists.

"What are you doing?"

What a stupid thing to say. It was obvious what he was doing. What she ought to be doing was demanding he put her down.

"Put me down this instant," she therefore cried. To no avail. The oaf just kept on walking. Along the corridor, in the direction of the inn door.

As they reached the door, Dorothy began to get over her initial surprise at being picked up in such a cavalier fashion, and experienced a twinge of alarm.

She was being abducted.

Abducted.

But...things like this didn't happen to girls like her!

ANNIE BURROWS

His Accidental Countess

HARLEQUIN®
HISTORICAL™

Recycling programs
for this product may
not exist in your area.

ISBN-13: 978-1-335-50611-5

His Accidental Countess

Copyright © 2021 by Annie Burrows

For questions and comments about the quality of this book,
please contact us at CustomerService@Harlequin.com.

Harlequin Enterprises ULC
22 Adelaide St. West, 40th Floor
Toronto, Ontario M5H 4E3, Canada
www.Harlequin.com

Printed in U.S.A.

Annie Burrows has been writing Regency romances for Harlequin since 2007. Her books have charmed readers worldwide, having been translated into nineteen different languages, and some have gone on to win the coveted Reviewers' Choice Award from CataRomance. For more information, or to contact her, please visit annie-burrows.co.uk, or find her on Facebook at Facebook.com/annieburrowsuk.

Books by Annie Burrows

Harlequin Historical

The Captain's Christmas Bride
In Bed with the Duke
Once Upon a Regency Christmas
"Cinderella's Perfect Christmas"
A Duke in Need of a Wife
A Marquess, a Miss and a Mystery
The Scandal of the Season
From Cinderella to Countess
His Accidental Countess

Brides for Bachelors

The Major Meets His Match
The Marquess Tames His Bride
The Captain Claims His Lady

Regency Bachelors

Gift-Wrapped Governess
"Governess to Christmas Bride"
Lord Havelock's List
The Debutante's Daring Proposal

Visit the Author Profile page
at Harlequin.com for more titles.

Chapter One

Dorothy Phillips lifted her chin as she set her hand to the latch of the Blue Boar's coffee room. If she was going to become a governess, she was going to have to get used to travelling alone like this. And whoever else might be staying in this inn overnight, while waiting for their connecting stage in the morning, she was simply going to have to deal with them.

If they turned out to be the least bit unsavoury she could always treat them to the withering stare she'd honed to perfection on young Gerry Benson, the most unruly pupil in the village school where she'd been teaching until a few weeks ago. It had certainly worked earlier that day on the young buck who'd tried to talk their coachman into letting him have a turn at the reins.

Yes, she reminded herself, if she could deal with the likes of Gerry Benson, and sporting gentlemen with more money than sense, she could certainly deal with whoever might be occupying the coffee room.

And so it was with a rather determined, not to say stern expression on her face that she opened the door and stepped inside.

The young couple, who'd been sitting on a bench beneath the open window, with their heads close together, leaped to their feet. The girl shrieked, turned deathly pale and fainted.

The young man either had extremely quick reflexes, or was used to his companion fainting on the slightest provocation, because he caught her deftly, well before she could hit the floor.

Dorothy had long become accustomed to people describing her as formidable, but never before had the mere sight of her been enough to cause a total stranger to pass out completely. She had a brief, but almost overwhelming urge to apologise for scaring the slender, pale girl, before her common sense reasserted itself. All she'd done was walk into the room where the landlord had told her he would serve her, and his other overnight guests, their supper in due course. It wasn't as if she'd been brandishing a knife, or a pistol, or indeed behaving in a threatening manner of any kind.

The youth, who'd been gazing down at the pretty creature he held in his arms, lifted his head, causing one lock of silky brown hair to slide artistically across his forehead and into his eyes. Eyes that held an expression with which Dorothy was all too familiar. The expression of a male who had no idea what to do and expected her to come up with a solution.

Dorothy felt better at once. She might have, inadvertently, been the cause of the girl's fainting spell, but now she could do what she did best. She could take charge of the situation.

'Lay her down flat,' she commanded, as she briskly crossed the room.

The young man did as she'd told him, gently lowering his fair burden to the floor. Dorothy knelt down at her side and undid the strings of the girl's bonnet. Then, when the girl showed no signs of coming round, she began fanning her with it.

'I should like to remove her spencer too,' said Dorothy, who'd felt much better herself for having had a wash in cool water and changing out of her dusty carriage dress. 'It is always beneficial to loosen the clothing, in the case of a faint,' she explained, while wondering why on earth the girl was wearing such inappropriate clothing for such a hot day.

The youth blushed, and shuffled away. 'Y-you mustn't, I mean…no, not in such a public place! Anyone could walk in, at any moment, and I swore I would protect her…'

Dorothy could see his point, she supposed. After all, if she was the kind of female who fainted, she wouldn't like people to see her half undressed while in such a vulnerable condition.

'I have a room upstairs,' she said, taking the girl's hand and chafing it. 'Do you think you could carry her up there?' In the privacy of her own room, Dorothy would be able to make the girl much more comfortable, as well as preserving her dignity while doing so.

The youth straightened up, puffing out his chest. 'Of course I could. Only show me where it is.'

By the time he'd followed Dorothy all the way up to the little room under the eaves which was all she could afford, the girl was showing signs of coming round. And just as the young man was laying her down on top of Dorothy's narrow bed, her eyes flew open.

'Gregory! What is…?' She stared round wildly. 'Where have you brought me?'

'This lady,' said the youth, whose name must be Gregory since he hadn't corrected the girl for calling him that, 'has very kindly offered you the use of her room, since you swooned.'

'Miss Phillips,' said Dorothy, introducing herself, since there had been no opportunity to do so before.

'Swooned? How...humiliating,' said the girl with revulsion. 'I never swoon. Only the most chicken-hearted females swoon.'

Dorothy liked the girl much better for expressing such feelings, since they matched exactly what she would have said in the same circumstances.

'But anyone,' Dorothy pointed out, 'might be overcome by heat and exhaustion after a trying day, when perhaps they haven't eaten or drunk very much. Which is perfectly understandable, since coach travel makes many people queasy, even those with the strongest constitutions.'

'That's true, Pansy darling,' said Gregory. 'You have hardly eaten a thing all day.'

'Well, that's easily remedied,' said Dorothy. 'Young man, you can make yourself useful by going down and ordering tea and a plate of bread and butter, to start with, while I make... Pansy, is it?' The girl nodded. 'I will make you more comfortable.'

'Oh, but...' Pansy began, struggling as if to sit up.

'No,' said Dorothy firmly. 'You will feel very much better for a lie down and something to eat. And it is cooler up here than down in that stuffy coffee room. I made sure to open the window as soon as I arrived, and the door as well, to get a draught blowing through.'

'Yes, that breeze is lovely,' Pansy admitted. 'But...'

'Darling, it will be much better for you up here,'

Gregory said, in a rather pointed manner, 'out of sight, rather than down there in a public room.'

Pansy settled back on to the pillows at once, giving Gregory a worshipful look. He gazed back at her with such adoration that for a moment or two, the whole room pulsed with a kind of tension that made Dorothy rather uncomfortable.

'I... I did not think it would be so hot today,' said Pansy, sheepishly, once Gregory had left and Dorothy began to help her out of a couple of layers of her clothing. 'Or that so many things would go wrong. We had planned to get much further than this before stopping for the night, but first there was something wrong with one of the horses, then there was some difficulty replacing it, and then to cap it all something went wrong with some part of the harness, or the...the driving part of the coach,' she said vaguely. 'And then I developed such a crushing headache that Gregory refused to go one more mile, even though we are not yet truly beyond the reach of—' She broke off, with such a guilty air, that it confirmed the suspicion Dorothy had been harbouring almost from the first moment she'd seen them. If this young couple weren't eloping, she'd eat her hat.

Dorothy bit back the pithy remark she'd dearly love to make, since it was clear the girl was suffering enough already. 'You have a headache? I have something in my trunk that should help you with that,' she said, stepping across the narrow gap between the bed and the window, where her trunk sat, taking the key from her reticule and fitting it into the padlock.

'I am going away to become a governess, you see,' she explained as she lifted the lid. 'And in my experience, children are forever falling ill or scraping themselves. So I stocked up with every remedy I could lay my hands on.' She also hadn't known how easy it might be for her to summon a doctor, if she should fall ill herself. Did employers think it worth the expense of summoning a doctor for a mere governess? Probably not.

The girl meekly permitted Dorothy to sponge her hands and face with cool water, drank the herbal tea which Dorothy brewed with the hot water a chambermaid brought up, and then ate all her bread and butter.

'Try to have a nap,' Dorothy advised as she set the empty plate and cup back on the tray. 'I will go down and leave you in peace.' And get her own supper, which must surely be served soon? Her stomach certainly thought it ought.

'Oh, but Gregory...'

'I dare say he will be relieved to hear you are feeling much better,' she said firmly, 'now you've had something to eat and drink, and have cooled down.'

'That's true,' said Pansy, subsiding into the pillows.

Dorothy smiled at the girl as she made to leave. Though her smile faded as soon as she started down the stairs. If the pair of them really were eloping, then she intended to give Gregory a piece of her mind. What kind of rogue would drag a delicate, nervous creature like Pansy on such a flight when he must have known it would be too much for her? And if her parents had forbidden the match, they must have a very good reason, too. Perhaps she was very wealthy. Her clothing was certainly very modish, and of good quality, even if it was inappropriate for the season. Yes, that must be it. Gregory must be a fortune hunter. He certainly had the looks, and the caressing manner that a fortune hunter would adapt towards an heiress, if Pansy was one.

By the time she reached the coffee room, where she found Gregory pacing up and down, chewing his nails, she'd become so angry that she responded to his anxious enquiry about Pansy by informing him in no uncertain terms exactly what she thought of his conduct.

Gregory heard her out with his head bowed, then ran his fingers through his hair and totally disarmed her by agreeing that he'd behaved in a completely shabby way.

'But I am so much in love with her that I cannot bear to lose her,' he said. 'When she came to me, weeping, and begging me to save her from being forced to marry some man that her father picked out, what else could I do but promise to marry her myself? Even though it has meant adopting measures that, in any other fellow, I would denounce as being completely disgraceful?'

Dorothy's perception of the situation turned about completely. Instead of feeling indignant on Pansy's behalf, she now felt heartily sorry for Gregory. Because it was clear that, for all her air of fragility, Pansy was one of those females who used wiles to twist the dimmer sort of males round their little fingers.

'Well, I shall say no more on that head,' she said, crossing the room to pat him on the shoulder, the way she would have comforted either of her brothers after they'd confessed to falling into a stupid scrape. 'Since you already understand that what you are doing is wrong and that you are sorry.' Which was what she would have said to either of her brothers, in similar circumstances. Not that either of them was old enough to elope, nor handsome or wealthy enough for any scheming female to try to induce them to do so.

'The only thing about which I'm sorry,' said Gregory, mutinously, 'is that Pansy has fallen ill before I could get her to safety.'

'She is not truly ill. Only a little overwrought and suffering from the effects of the heat. She was looking much better when I left her. I believe, after a sufficient interval of rest, and a decent meal, she will be well enough to resume your journey.'

'Truly?' Gregory seized her hand in his own, which was unpleasantly sweaty.

'Truly,' she said, tugging at her hand, which the lad seemed reluctant to release. 'I shall return to watch over her while she sleeps—' since there was still no sign of the supper the landlord had promised '—so that you can see about the repair of your coach, which I believe is in need of some attention,' she said, giving another, futile, attempt to tug her hand from his surprisingly firm grip.

'You are an angel,' he said, raising her hand to his lips and kissing it. 'Whenever anyone speaks of angels, in future, I shall always imagine them looking just like you, towering over we lesser mortals, with bright hazel eyes either blazing with righteous indignation, or melting with sympathy for our plight. I do not know what we would have done had you not been sent to minister to us in our darkest hour. May I know your name? Your given name?'

'Dora,' she said. Then wondered why she hadn't said Dorothy. It must have been because she'd been comparing him to her brothers, who always shortened her name, in an affectionate way. And because Gregory was something of a charmer, as well as being precisely the sort of impulsive, silly boy who *would* try to elope with a girl who portrayed herself as a damsel in distress. She was starting to smile at him, in a somewhat bemused manner, when the door of the coffee room swung violently open, banging against the wall and bouncing back. Not that it could bounce far, because standing in the doorway, completely filling the frame, was the largest man Dorothy had ever seen. The effect was probably in part due to the coat he was wearing, which had full skirts and several tiers of capes about the shoulders. The drab-coloured garment reached fully to the man's heels and had mother-of-pearl buttons the size of a crown piece, which led her to assume that he was the driver of some coach who had drunkenly staggered through the wrong door. But that assumption lasted only as long as it took Gregory to drop her hands and gasp out one word.

'Worsley!'

The giant of a man had to duck his head to enter the room, which he did, pulling the door shut behind him. As he did so, the coat, which was undone, billowed out, revealing the kind of serviceable waistcoat a coach driver really might wear, as well as heavy buckskin breeches and wrinkled buff top boots that had clearly seen better days. She'd heard from her horse-mad brother Paul that some men, who really ought to know better, aped the attire of coach drivers. And since Gregory had addressed this one by name, with a look of guilty defiance, he must be one of that breed.

'I need not ask,' said the man, with a sneer, 'what you are doing here, I suppose?'

'It is not,' said Gregory, 'what you think.'

'It is precisely what I think,' growled the man, removing his hat to reveal a thatch of wildly untidy, straw-coloured hair. He turned his eyes upon her. Eyes which were of a piercingly vivid shade of blue. 'Although I suppose, now that I have finally met the jade, I can see exactly how she succeeded in making you take leave of your senses and beguiled you into eloping.'

Goodness. This man seemed to think that she was the girl with whom Gregory was eloping. How on earth could he really think that she, dressed as she was in the sombre garb of a governess, and at the age when everyone believed her to be firmly on the shelf, had somehow beguiled this boy to elope with her? The very idea was so ridiculous that a short bark of laughter escaped her mouth.

'You think this is funny?' Worsley took a step in her direction and glared down at her. 'To ruin my ward's life by not only making him wish for such a mismatch, but also to go about it in this clandestine fashion? By making him take a step that will ruin him in just about every way?'

'I am doing no such thing,' she began, intending to explain that she'd only met Gregory less than an hour ago and disapproved of the step he was taking just as much as he did.

But Worsley gave her no chance to finish.

'I wasn't born yesterday,' he snapped. 'Nor am I the kind that your type of female can manage. I am well up to your weight, even if my ward isn't.'

His comment drew her attention, once again, to his stature. Because of her height, most men scarcely reached up to her chin. This man, on the other hand, not only topped her in height by several inches, but had shoulders the width of a mantelpiece.

'So hold your tongue,' he said. 'And accept the fact that I have thwarted your plans.'

He might be larger than most men, but he was no more intelligent, she promptly decided. What was more, he was the type who thought he knew better, simply because he was a man, even when he was plainly in the wrong.

Well, let him make an ass of himself. This was nothing to do with her.

Lifting her chin, she gave him the withering look she had already used to such good effect once that day and ceased attempting to explain what was really going on. It wasn't her place, after all. The argument was really between Worsley and Gregory.

As if coming to the same conclusion, Worsley turned his attention to Gregory.

'As for you,' he snapped, 'you ought to know better. Didn't I warn you to beware of women like this?' He waved one arm in Dorothy's direction. 'Women who will do just about anything to get their hands on a title? To worm their way into society?'

'Now see here,' said Gregory, rather pale-faced, and giving the appearance of girding up his loins, as though he had never attempted to stand up to the larger, older man before. Which, since Worsley had revealed he was Gregory's guardian, was likely to be the case. 'You are making a mistake…'

'No. I am merely making sure that you do not,' said Worsley. 'It is not too late to undo what this creature has tried to make you do. You will return to London with me, now, and I will…'

'No!' Gregory shook his head. 'I cannot possibly leave a gently reared female alone and unprotected in an inn. Miles away from anyone she knows. And if you were half the gentleman you keep saying you want me to be, you wouldn't suggest it!'

Worsley blinked. Appeared to consider Gregory's argument. And gave a brief nod.

'You are correct. Much better if I return the hussy to her family instead.'

So saying, he sort of swooped on Dorothy and, before she rightly knew what he intended, he'd heaved her over his shoulder like a sack of coal. A shoulder which she discovered had not only the width, but also the marble-like consistency of a mantelpiece. And which knocked the breath from her lungs.

He had carried her into the corridor before she regained the ability to speak. Or the wits to begin beating at his back with her fists.

'What are you doing?'

What a stupid thing to say. It was obvious what he was doing. What she ought to be doing was demanding he put her down.

'Put me down this instant,' she therefore cried. To no avail. The oaf just kept on walking. Along the corridor, in the direction of the inn door.

Until the landlord stepped in his path.

''Ere,' he protested. 'What be you doing?'

Hurrah! Even if Gregory didn't have the spine to stand up to Worsley, it appeared that the landlord, at least, was not afraid of him.

'I don't hold with this sort of thing going on in my ken...'

'Out of my way,' growled the walking mantelpiece. 'Unless you want me to blacken your reputation by letting it be known you have aided and abetted in the elopement of a minor.'

'I'm not a minor,' Dorothy protested to the landlord's knees, which was all she could see of him when she tried to raise her head. 'Landlord, you know I am not. This is all a dreadful mistake!' But the landlord's knees moved out of her line of vision as Worsley carried on walking.

As they reached the door, Dorothy began to get over her initial surprise at being picked up in such a cavalier fashion and experienced a twinge of alarm. And made her first real attempt to wriggle out of his hold. His arm came down like a band of steel, making her realise that until now, he'd only been utilising a fraction of his strength.

'If you don't stop trying to thwart me,' he growled, 'I shall bind and gag you. Because return you to Coventry I shall. And nothing you do or say is going to stop me.'

'You cannot return me to Coventry,' she protested. 'Since I've never been there in my life! Oh, won't you stop and listen to me, you great…oaf!'

'Hah,' he grunted, as he strode across the inn yard. 'Listen to lies from the likes of you? What do you take me for?'

'One of…the biggest idiots… I've ever had…the misfor…tune to come…across in my…whole life,' she panted, since the combination of hanging upside down while being clamped to a marble mantelpiece by a bar of steel was making her a bit breathless.

'I cannot…go to Cov…entry,' she pleaded. She had a seat booked on the Edinburgh stage the next morning. And what would happen when she didn't arrive to take up her new post? And how on earth was she going to recover her trunk, which contained all her worldly goods? Although it probably wouldn't, for long, since she'd carelessly left it unlocked when she came down to speak to Gregory, thinking she wouldn't be long.

'You...idiot...man,' she panted. 'You are g...going to ru...in every...thing!'

She then went a bit dizzy, as Worsley swung round a couple of times while he opened the door to a carriage. And then really dizzy when he flipped her the right way up before tossing her inside.

'To Coventry you will go,' he growled, as he straightened up and backed away. 'So you may as well stop trying to pull the wool over my eyes. I am not some green boy like Gregory, to be taken in by an older, more experienced woman.'

She opened her mouth to protest that she'd never tried to pull the wool over anyone's eyes. But all that came out of her mouth was a gargling wheeze. And then, as she sat up, her head went all floaty and a crowd of black spots began dancing before her eyes. In the few moments it took for her to regain the ability to breathe in the normal manner, and for her head to stop spinning, Worsley had slammed the coach door, and, to judge from the way the whole equipage rocked, climbed up on to the driver's seat.

She inched to the door and laid her hand on the release catch.

And then she imagined the scene in the inn yard should she explain that she was no temptress, but a governess who'd only stumbled across the eloping couple he was hunting down, by the merest chance.

With the passengers of who knew how many stagecoaches watching with interest, what a spectacle she would make, with no coat, or hat, and her hair straggling down all over the place, since his method of seeing her into his coach had dislodged most of her hairpins.

And then she thought about what would happen should she finally persuade him he'd made a mistake. And how he would march straight back into the inn and up the stairs, and subject that poor, silly girl to the same Turkish treatment he'd used on her.

And what it would do to a delicate creature like that, who had already been reduced to a state of nervous collapse by the fear of him, never mind the actual presence of him. Because that was why the girl had started up and fainted when Dorothy had walked in, wasn't it? Yes, because she had suspected that Worsley was pursuing them.

But then she reminded herself that it was her duty to prevent an elopement, if she possibly could, that she ought not to consider her dignity and that even though she didn't like the methods Worsley might employ, *somebody* really should return that girl to her parents.

And by the time all those conflicting thoughts had gone through her head, the coach was moving.

She could still leap out and run back to the landlord, enlist his aid and perhaps mount some sort of defence before Worsley could really frighten the Pansy girl...

But even as she considered it, she heard Worsley whip up the horses and put them to a gallop.

And she'd lost her chance of escape.

She put her hands to her mouth as the awful truth hit her squarely in the pit of her rather sore stomach. She was being abducted.

Abducted.

But...things like this didn't happen to girls like her.

Things like this only happened to heiresses, or pretty girls. And that only in stories.

But that was what *had* happened. Worsley had mistaken a plain, spinster governess for the pretty, flighty young girl with whom Gregory had been attempting to elope. Which was absurd. So absurd that suddenly, she couldn't help seeing the funny side of it. Which was just as well, or else she might have succumbed to the temptation to cry. Just the thought of crying caused a tear to threaten. Which was always the way, wasn't it? If you thought about crying, in response to difficulties, that was exactly what you ended up doing. And what good did it do? What did it achieve? Nothing.

She sniffed and reminded herself that she'd been through far worse than this without turning into a watering pot.

Besides, she wouldn't give that great bully the satisfaction of thinking he'd reduced her to tears. She wasn't some feeble, nervy creature who could think of nothing better to do than weep and wail, because some idiot man had taken one look at her and decided she was preying on a green boy—and how on earth could he think Gregory was her slave when the lad had made no attempt to defend her? Why, even the landlord had put up more of a protest than he had, when he'd seen Worsley carting her out of the inn.

She dashed away the single tear that had trickled down her cheek while she was giving herself a stern talking-to. And forgave herself for being a bit emotional. After all, it wasn't every day a girl got thrown over a man's shoulder and tossed into a coach like a sack of potatoes. Being a bit shocked and upset was perfectly forgivable, providing she didn't give way to the extent that she ended up having the vapours.

Anyway, she, Dorothy Phillips, was absolutely not the kind of female who would ever have the vapours. She was made of sterner stuff than that.

And so she would jolly well show him.

The moment he let her out of this coach.

Chapter Two

'No need to look at me in that tone of voice, Pawson,' said Lord Worsley to his stony-faced groom, once they'd cleared the inn yard. 'I only sprang 'em to dissuade our passenger from jumping out before we'd got her far enough from the Blue Boar to think of running back and making me have to repeat the process of separating her from young Gregory all over again.'

'Hmmph,' was the eloquent reply.

Worsley ground his teeth. Pawson ought to know him better than to think he'd drive his horses too hard. Now that he'd achieved what he'd set out to do, which was to prevent his ward eloping, he could take his time returning the girl to her family.

He just needed to get far enough from the Blue Boar to make her think twice about trying to escape, before slowing down. Fortunately, as was so often the way during an English summer, the wind, which had been picking up ever since he'd spotted Gregory's distinctively fashionable curricle in the yard of the Blue Boar, veered round to the east, turning the air chilly and producing a bank of threatening-looking clouds.

Before much longer it would be raining in earnest if he knew anything about it and then she'd definitely not try to venture from the confines of his carriage. Especially without the protection of a coat or bonnet. He didn't normally enjoy driving in the rain, but tonight, its advent brought a grim smile to his mouth. Things couldn't have been going better if he'd planned this sudden squall. Now that Miss Watling was unlikely to try to run off, it meant that he could stop to change his horses, which really shouldn't have been pressed into taking him further than the Blue Boar.

It wasn't long before he spotted a reasonable-looking inn.

'You may as well light the carriage lamps, Pawson,' he said as he drew his team to a halt. Although it might stay light until almost nine o'clock at this time of year on a fair night, this was not a fair night. After glancing at the sky, the groom gave a nod of agreement. But the taciturn old fellow's eyes slid to the door of the carriage itself.

'Yes, I know, I'd better check on her as well, since we're stopping anyway.' She'd gone very quiet, very quickly. And while that had made things easier, it was also, now he came to think of it, a trifle disconcerting. He'd expected her to make much more of a fuss. But she hadn't screamed and kicked at the doors to make her feelings plain, or even cried noisily to try to make him feel sorry for her. Though that was what any of his sisters would have done, had anyone attempted to thwart any of their plans so ruthlessly. Not that he would allow anyone to get away with treating any of his sisters this way. Not that anyone would dare. Most people knew better than to try to cross him, or anyone connected to him.

Perhaps that was why she'd finally started behaving herself. Gregory must have told her a little about him, or she wouldn't have been so sure he would never have granted his permission for a marriage. Even now, when they'd drawn up in an inn yard, where she might have been able to persuade someone to come to her aid, by creating a scene, she was doing precisely nothing.

She hadn't tried to open the door and run away. She hadn't even lowered a window and poked her head out to see how the land lay.

All of a sudden, a horrible fear took hold of him. Had he gone too far, threatening to bind and gag her? Had he frightened her out of her wits? Dear God, he hoped she hadn't fainted. What on earth would he do with an unconscious woman? How the hell could he return her to her parents in such a state?

He suffered a strong sense of ill usage. Surely she must have known he'd never have carried out such a threat? He would never use violence against a woman. He'd only said it to make her think twice about opposing him. His size alone ought to have done the trick. It was sufficient to see off most adversaries without having to resort to any real action.

But this situation wasn't like most, was it? Feelings had run high. She'd been furious that he'd caught up with them and thwarted her plans. *He'd* been furious that she'd got Gregory twisted so far round her fingers that the lad had abandoned every principle he ought to have held dear. And, as a creature who had demonstrated a complete lack of scruples, she could well have assumed others, him for instance, were just as capable of going to any ends to achieve their aims.

But he wasn't…

He hadn't…

He wouldn't…

No, all he'd done was demonstrate that he was not the kind of man she could trifle with. And, yes, perhaps he shouldn't have made those threats, especially when he'd had no intention of carrying them out, but in the heat of the moment he'd felt as if he'd do anything to bring this sordid episode to an end. He simply couldn't have stood back and let Gregory ruin his life by running away with a girl who was unsuitable in just about every way there was.

He'd done the right thing. He was *doing* the right thing. Even if his methods were a bit…

Telling his conscience to take a damper, he gritted his teeth, pulled open the carriage door, and leaned inside, half expecting to see an inert body sprawled across the floor.

Far from it. The Watling wench was sitting bolt upright, her reticule on her lap, her arms wrapped round her middle.

'Don't even think about trying to escape,' he warned her.

She glared at him. 'I am not an idiot. Without a coat, or bonnet, or any luggage, and with my hair resembling a bird's nest, nobody would give me the time of day. Besides, you were the one who decided you knew what to do with me. So my welfare is your responsibility. And while we are on the subject, do you think you could find me a blanket of some sort? It is getting rather chilly.'

A prickle of shame made him flex his hand on the door latch. He hadn't given the girl's welfare a single thought. All he'd been thinking of was rescuing Gregory. If he'd thought of her at all, it was merely as an obstacle to be removed from the lad's path.

But she was just a girl, after all. And she was shivering. And in spite of putting on a brave face, now, he could see a track down one rather grubby cheek that revealed that, at one stage, she had been crying.

She hadn't given way to self-pity, though. By God, but at moments like this he could see *exactly* why Gregory had fallen so hard for her. She was rather magnificent. He'd thought so the very first moment he'd seen her, with Gregory bending over her hand in an attitude of worship. And he'd understood, right then, how she'd managed to get him in her toils. As a lad, he'd come across many such older, experienced women. Women who'd delighted in taking a young lad in hand, both figuratively and literally, and making a willing slave of him for a while. Toying with him until they felt they'd taught him all they could, at which point they grew bored and went on to lure another green, impressionable lad into their bed.

He knew how powerful a lad's feelings could run while in the throes of such a relationship. But you didn't marry such women. And Gregory was going to have responsibilities when he inherited the title. He'd need a wife at his side who would have been educated from birth to move in that sphere. And Pansy Watling was simply not up to the task. She was from entirely the wrong background. Society women would shun her and Gregory would have to side with his wife. Which would mean he would no longer attend all those frippery functions he enjoyed so much.

Pansy. The name didn't suit her. It was what had led him to think she'd be some shrinking violet, though, when Gregory had started talking about her in such nauseating terms. He'd pictured one of those tiny, fluttery females who looked up at a man as though she needed him to protect her. But the reality was that she didn't need anyone to protect her. This Amazon would look any man who dared suggest it straight in the eye and probably spit in it rather than show any weakness.

He really ought to have known that she'd be more strong-willed than her name suggested, or she could never have overridden Gregory's sense of honour and persuaded the lad to run off with her.

Lord, but it was just as well he'd put a stop to her plans. She'd have made Gregory's life an utter misery. While Worsley was the sort of man who'd much rather have straight dealing with a woman, even a virago like this one, and disliked a watering pot above all else, Gregory preferred his women weak and clinging. Women who made him feel strong and powerful by comparison.

This woman appeared to take pride in doing exactly the opposite. With one scornful remark she'd made him examine himself, in a way he very rarely did, and see that he was not behaving well. And also that none of his sisters would ever have set foot in a carriage, which was going to travel any distance, without expecting all sorts of things to be provided for their comfort, never mind a blanket.

But then he hadn't *planned* to take her up in his carriage, had he? He'd set off in hot pursuit of Gregory, the moment he'd read the sickeningly sentimental note he'd left, determined to stop the elopement. By hook or by crook. And by the very definition of that term, he couldn't afford to succumb to scruples, just because he could see she'd been crying and looked bedraggled, yet defiant, in a way that would no doubt tug at a softer man's heartstrings.

'I will see what I can do,' he said, before shutting the door, going to the boot and digging out a horse blanket he kept there just in case he ever needed to stable any of his own cattle in an inn where he wasn't convinced they could provide acceptable conditions. It wasn't what any of his sisters would consider accept-able, he reflected as he picked the worst of the straw from it, but then it was better that the Watling wench experienced a little discomfort than for Gregory to suf-fer a lifetime of misery at her hands.

She took the blanket from him without uttering a word. She didn't need to. Her disdainful expression spoke volumes.

Because he wasn't all that familiar with the route to Coventry and because night was now very definitely drawing in, he had to set a pace that didn't tax the horses, or his skills as a driver overmuch. Which per-haps accounted for the way he slipped into a mood of self-examination. Again.

Where had he gone wrong, with Gregory, for the lad to consider eloping preferable to…to the alterna-tive? He'd always done his level best to steer him right, from the moment the orphaned lad had been put into his sole care. Perhaps he should have kept him at Brinkley Court and hired tutors for him, rather than sending him to school. Or allowed one of his sisters to take him into their households, as they married, so they could bring them up with their own families.

But he'd felt it was *his* job to guard and guide the lad, because he was the next in line to the earldom. So he'd had him home to Brinkley Court every school holiday. And stayed there with him, what was more, so that he'd become familiar with the land and the people that he might, eventually, have to govern. He'd taught him the rudiments of estate management, explained the complexities of county politics and made sure he could ride and shoot well.

Eventually, when he'd been old enough to go up to London for a Season, Worsley had introduced him to the people that mattered, warned him off the worst sort of gaming hells and given him a bit of advice about women. Not enough, clearly, or the lad wouldn't have fallen victim to a grasping, scheming one like the one who was now travelling in the carriage behind him, plotting who knew what vengeance, to judge from the venomous look she'd given him as he'd shut her in again.

If only he understood women better. Or people in general, come to that. He had been raised in such strict isolation, as the only surviving male offspring and heir to all his father's wealth, that as a boy he'd only ever felt at ease in the stables where the grooms accepted him on his merits as a rider. *They* weren't disappointed in him for not being a scholar. Nor did they care that he had no wish to become a statesman, like his father, if it meant he'd have to behave in the scaly fashion that most politicians appeared to consider a perfectly normal means of climbing to the top of the greasy pole.

He'd wanted Gregory to be able to develop in his

own way, rather than cram him into the mould labelled 'Earl of Worsley', and not end up as awkward around people as *he* was. And this was the result.

Which, actually, just went to prove the point. He just *didn't* understand people. Not that it bothered him as a rule. His wealth and position meant that he never had any need to apologise for being rude.

Yes, he was perfectly content.

Except…

As if to echo the direction of his thoughts, the sky was growing steadily darker. It didn't look as if they'd be able to make it to Coventry without changing the horses again.

'Know of any decent stables,' he therefore asked, 'along this route, Pawson?'

Pawson grunted. Tugged at his earlobe. 'Never had any call to travel along this road afore, my lord. You'll have to take your chances, I reckon.'

Worsley made a point of not reacting to the tone of censure in which Pawson delivered that statement. The man might feel he had the right to speak his mind, upon occasion, but at least he only ever did so to Worsley's face. He was utterly loyal. Which was why he'd been the only person he'd taken into his confidence when he'd discovered Gregory was eloping. Pawson would never breathe a word of this day's work to another living soul.

It had been well past midnight before they found a coaching inn where there were ostlers who looked as if they knew their business. And dawn was breaking before they reached the outskirts of Coventry itself.

Worsley brought the carriage to a halt in a passing place, got down and opened the door.

'I need directions to your parents' house from here,' he said, without preamble.

'How interesting,' she said, tartly. 'I hope you manage to find some.'

'It will be much better for you if you just give them to me yourself.'

'Is that what you think?' She shook her head.

'Yes. Because if you won't tell me I shall have to ask some passer-by, which will create talk, which I should think is the last thing you want.'

She glared at him. 'It won't be talk about me, so why should I care? Look, Mr Worsley—'

'Lord Worsley,' he corrected her, irritated by her continued defiance.

'Oh, I do beg your pardon, my lord. Would you like me to get out and curtsy?'

He was getting nowhere with her. Would get nowhere with her.

'On your own head be it,' he said and shut the door.

Since a few people were already up and about, it wasn't much longer before they found someone who could give them directions to her parents' house, though it was full daylight by the time they reached the building of generous proportions which proudly proclaimed the prosperity of its owners. His hopes that he would be able to return her to safety under cover of dark, thereby keeping her escapade hidden, were dashed. But that was entirely her own fault.

He handed the reins to Pawson, who took them with a grunt. Worsley didn't care. He was about to wash his hands of the tiresome chit, for good. He'd put a stop to the elopement, saved Gregory from making a grave mistake and returned a silly female to the safety of her family home before any real harm had been done to her virtue. As for her reputation…well, she'd done nothing but defy his attempts to protect it, so if she did suffer for this night's work, that was hardly his fault, was it? The only other people who knew of her escapade would say nothing. He could trust Pawson to keep his tongue between his teeth about family business. And if Gregory really cared for the girl he would never say anything that might cause her name to be bandied about.

So he opened the carriage door with what felt almost like triumph, knowing that in a few more moments he was going to be able to put the whole sordid episode behind him. What's more, he could go back to the inn from which he'd hired his current team, which had looked pretty reasonable, if not used to catering to quality, take a room and order a slap-up breakfast, before taking a well-earned rest. Chasing down eloping youngsters, and subduing rebellious females, it so happened, was tiring and hungry work.

'Out you get,' he said cheerfully, since he was looking forward to the inn, the breakfast and a sleep.

She got out and stood for a moment on the pavement, looking at him with a worried expression.

'Look, before you make an even bigger fool of yourself than you already have done, I think I ought to warn you…'

'You can save your warnings for someone who might heed them,' he said, his mood diving.

She gave him what he supposed she thought was a withering look. The effect was ruined, however, by the fact that she was clutching a blanket that had clearly last been used for a horse round her shoulders, and the way her hair was straggling halfway down her back.

'Come on,' he said, taking her by the elbow, which he could just make out through the enveloping blanket, and marching her up the front steps.

He rapped on the door with the butt of his whip.

'You will not, later, be able to accuse me of not trying,' she remarked cryptically, as the sound of footsteps approaching the door came from the inside.

The door opened, and a rather irritated-looking elderly man, with a nightcap on his head, and a frock coat pulled hastily over his nightgown, peered out.

'The master won't take kindly to the likes of you,' he said peevishly, 'bothering him at this hour of the day. I'd advise you to take yourselves off.'

The likes of…? Worsley was not normally a man who insisted on people taking note of his rank, but he'd had a long and tiring day. And night.

'Just tell him that I have his daughter in my charge,' he retorted. 'I should think he'd want to hear that.'

'Miss Watling?' The man in the nightcap opened the door a bit wider. 'You had better come in, I suppose. I will go and rouse the master and mistress,' said the butler, as they went into the impressively large but sparsely furnished hall.

'Wait,' said Worsley, 'I…' But before he could wash his hands of the Watling girl, the elderly retainer had shuffled off up the stairs at a surprisingly quick clip for a man in slippers and a nightgown.

Worsley toyed with the idea of just leaving her in the hall to face the wrath of her parents on her own and going home. But there were things that needed saying to the parents of this hussy. And it would be better to say them now, so that he'd never have to set eyes on any of the family again.

'You are going to be *so* sorry,' she murmured, with what looked like a gleam of amusement in her eyes.

'No, I'm not,' he retorted, folding his arms across his chest. She flinched, but he didn't think it was due to anything he'd done. No, he rather suspected it was a reaction to the barrage of bad language exploding from one of the upper rooms.

The girl's father, he had to assume. It was the kind of language any father might be forgiven for using, upon hearing that his errant daughter had finally come home. His assumption was confirmed not two seconds later, by the appearance, at the head of the stairs, of a bullish-faced man in a florid velvet dressing gown.

'You dare to come to my house,' the bullish man roared, 'telling me that you have my daughter in your keeping?' He started down the stairs. Behind him, a middle-aged woman appeared, clutching an equally tasteless dressing gown to her throat.

'Pansy?' The woman began coming down the stairs. 'Where is she? Have you found her?'

The couple must both be in need of spectacles. Although their daughter was, he discovered on looking round, cowering behind him, her face flushed with the first signs of embarrassment he'd seen her display.

A less tired and harassed man might have felt some sympathy for the dressing down she was about to receive, even though she deserved it. But he wanted nothing more than to be done with her. And so he stepped to one side, leaving her nowhere to hide.

'Here,' he said, gesturing to her with a broad sweep of his hand, 'is the woman responsible for it all.'

The bullish man peered at her. 'You? You have kidnapped my daughter, have you?'

Kidnapped his daughter? Where were the old man's wits? This *was* his daughter.

'I suppose,' Mr Watling continued, 'you have come to demand a ransom. I told you, didn't I,' he said, whirling to the woman hovering anxiously halfway down the stairs, 'that it was something of the sort. Belling,' he bellowed at the retainer in nightshirt and cap, who was coming down the stairs at a far more leisurely pace than he'd gone up them. 'Fetch a constable. I shall ensure this pair of rogues do not escape.'

A constable?

Worsley felt as though the ground beneath his feet had shifted. A man would not send for a constable unless...

'No, no,' said the woman who, until this moment, he'd believed to be Pansy Watling. 'We had nothing to do with her running away. But I am afraid she has eloped with this man's ward,' she said, gesturing at him.

When Worsley had been about seven or eight, he'd fallen out of an apple tree he'd been plundering and landed on his back. The fall had knocked all the breath from his lungs and for a moment or two he hadn't been able to breathe. And that was just how he felt now. As though all the breath had been knocked from his lungs. He couldn't have uttered a word to save his life. For everything he'd thought he knew was false. This woman was not Pansy Watling. She hadn't been eloping with Gregory.

He had no idea how she'd come to be in the parlour with his ward, or why Gregory had been kissing her hand, but one thing he did know, and the horror of that knowledge was the thing that was robbing him of the power of speech.

He could no longer tell himself that he'd acted decisively to prevent a younger, gullible male from ruining his life, by returning a silly girl to the home of her parents.

The truth was that he'd just abducted, forcibly abducted, a totally innocent woman.

Chapter Three

Dorothy had the satisfaction of witnessing the exact moment when the truth hit Worsley right between the eyes. When he realised that he'd abducted completely the wrong woman. He flinched, then tensed, his face and lips turning white.

It should have been her moment of triumph and she might well have yielded to the temptation to rub his nose in it, a little, if it wasn't for the fact that Mr and Mrs Watling were so upset and more in need of an explanation, and reassurance, than Dorothy was of hearing him make a grovelling apology.

'How is she?' said the mother. 'Have you seen her?'

'And has the rogue who enticed her to leave her home and family,' demanded the father, 'actually married her?'

'Um, I don't think so, yet,' Dorothy began, making the mistake of answering the father first, rather than reassuring the mother.

'And you are responsible, are you?' said the father, echoing Worsley's rash and inaccurate statement, and advancing on her with a ferocious glare.

'Um…no…' Dorothy began. But he didn't give her time to explain.

'You aided and abetted her leaving my house, when you must have known what I thought of her throwing herself away on some idle, spendthrift sprig from some lesser branch of the parasites that term themselves aristocracy? When she could have married my partner's son? A hard-working, enterprising youth who is already making something of himself?'

Oh, so it wasn't just a question of him objecting to Gregory's suit. Mr Watling had wanted his daughter to marry someone he'd already picked out for her. For financial gain, by the sound of it.

'Look,' she began, 'I—'

'Well, if he thinks he can get his hands on her fortune he's very much mistaken. I warned her that I'd cut her off without a penny if she defied me and that's what I shall do.'

Oh, dear. No wonder the pair of them had felt they had no option but to run off. What with the father practically forcing her into marriage with a man of his choosing and Worsley here forbidding Gregory from marrying beneath him, socially, they'd probably got it into their heads that they were a modern-day Romeo and Juliet.

'And you, too,' he said, rounding on Worsley, who was still giving the impression of having turned into a waxwork model of himself. 'If I can find a way to ruin you, I shall do it! Don't think I can't! And as for you, miss,' he said, turning back to Dorothy 'if you are not out of my house by the time Belling has returned with a constable—' which was extremely unlikely to happen, since the elderly retainer had looked appalled at the order to leave the house, clad as he was in his nightshirt, and had not made a single sign of being about to obey it '—I shall have you charged with kidnapping.' He took a step closer, thrusting his face into hers. 'Extortion,' he breathed into her face. 'Trespassing,' he added, clenching his fists and raising his arm as if to strike her.

This was all it took to jolt Worsley out of his stupor. As Mr Watling's arm began to come down, Worsley's came up to block him.

'That's enough,' he said grimly. 'We are leaving.' So saying, he got himself between Dorothy and Mr Watling. It might still have descended into an unseemly scuffle had not Mrs Watling uttered an anguished cry, then sort of folded in on herself. It occurred to Dorothy, as Worsley made use of the distraction to bundle her in the direction of the front door, that fainting must be something that ran in this family. If fainting could be described as something that ran. Still, it certainly made the menfolk around the fainting women run, especially when the woman doing the fainting was halfway up a staircase. She would never have guessed that a man as portly as Mr Watling could have produced such a turn of speed. Her last glimpse of him, as Worsley pushed her outside and on to the pavement, was of him catching his wife in his arms, with far less grace than Gregory had demonstrated, and sitting down heavily, on the bottom stair, with her sprawled across his lap.

She saw no more, for, far from running out into the streets in his nightshirt and slippers, the butler decided the best way to serve his employers was to slam the front door shut in her face.

Worsley cleared his throat, which prompted her to look up at him.

'You are not Miss Watling,' he observed.

'No.'

'Why,' he said irritably, 'did you not tell me so before?'

'If you recall,' she said tartly, 'when I tried to explain your mistake, you threatened to tie me up and gag me.'

He made a dismissive motion with his hand. 'I would never have done such a dastardly thing. You should have *made* me listen.'

Perhaps she should have. Because she hadn't really believed he'd meant the threats, somehow. They'd struck her as being the kind of empty threats one made to naughty children, to frighten them into doing as they were told. But there had been that rather pathetic, wilting girl to consider.

A girl who must have been at her wits' end to embark on an elopement when she was obviously nowhere near robust enough to withstand the rigours of such a venture. Why, she'd been almost prostrate with nerves by the time Dorothy had walked into the Blue Boar, a hostelry hardly any significant distance from London, not when one considered how much further they had to go to reach the border.

Dorothy had, uncharacteristically, dithered instead of taking action, as she'd imagined what effect this forceful man would have upon poor Pansy. And then the choice had been taken out of her hands. She would have been foolish in the extreme to have attempted to jump out of a speeding coach. Apart from risking breaking a limb, what would it have achieved? He would only have chased after her, scooped her up and tossed her back into the carriage.

But…why was she standing here thinking about what *she* ought to have done, or why she hadn't done a number of equally reckless things? None of this was her fault. If *he* hadn't behaved in such a high-handed, not to say outrageous manner, they would not now be standing in this particular spot at all.

'How typical of a man,' she said scornfully, 'to insist the mistakes he has made are the fault of the nearest female.'

He clenched his jaw. By the rather anaemic sunlight which was making a weary attempt to push through the rolling clouds, she could actually see the muscles working as he swallowed whatever retort had first sprung to his mind.

'Never mind that,' he finally bit out. 'If you are not Miss Watling, then who are you? What is your name?'

'Miss Phillips,' she said, dropping him the curtsy that it was second nature for her upon making an introduction.

'Lord Worsley, at your service,' he said, making her a correct bow, which struck her as rather ridiculous under the circumstances.

Although on second thoughts, perhaps falling back on etiquette was the only thing that could help them to brush through the awkwardness of the situation.

'And just how did you come to be in that inn with Gregory?' He looked round, then, as if suddenly remembering they were standing outside the house of a very angry man, who might at any moment burst out and start breathing threats again.

'Though this is neither the time nor the place for

that conversation,' he said, taking her by the elbow and steering her back to his coach. Which, she noted for the first time, had a team of four horses in harness. And a groom perched up in front, holding the reins, and his tongue, too, to judge from the way he carefully avoided looking at her.

'I am not,' she said, tugging free the moment he relaxed his grip on her elbow to open the door, 'getting back into that vile carriage again.'

He made a jerky movement, as though stifling his first instinct to simply pick her up and toss her in. So tempted did he seem to be to revert to that method of dealing with her that he placed his hands behind his back, as though he needed to get them well out of range.

'Then what, precisely,' he said rather sarcastically, 'do you plan to do? Where do you think you can go? And how will you manage when you get there? Unless…do you happen to have family, or connections, in Coventry?'

He brightened up a bit as he asked that last question, as though hoping she would be able to tell him that, yes, she had relations she could rely on to take her in, at first light, no questions asked. And even though she'd always believed that honesty was the best policy, no matter the provocation, she was sorely tempted to invent a distant cousin. Goodness, but he was a bad influence upon her. When she considered how rashly he'd made her act so far…

'No, I know absolutely nobody in Coventry,' she confessed. Because even if she did invent a cousin, she couldn't produce one.

Sure enough, his face fell. Which really, really annoyed her. Did he think he could wash his hands of her that easily after dragging her halfway across the country? 'I should hope,' she said, attempting to look down her nose at him, even though he was an inch or so taller than her, 'that you are gentleman enough to admit that it is your duty to make amends for the injury you have done me. Would you have the goodness,' she said, adding an extra layer of chilliness to her tone, 'to convey me to some respectable inn, where I can get something to eat?' Because if she didn't have something soon she might very well go the way of the Watling women and wilt into the nearest pair of masculine arms. Which would belong to Worsley. And, while she was sure he would have no difficulty in catching her, having already had experience of how strong they were, she had no intention of letting him regain the upper hand just as she was, for the first time since she'd met him, making him take heed. 'And then provide me with the means to return to the Blue Boar to retrieve my luggage and continue on my journey.' Because she saw no reason why she should be out of pocket when he was the one who had forced her to take this detour.

'No,' he said, folding his arms across his chest. 'No, I don't think I better had. Take you to a respectable inn, I mean. Because I don't think they'd let you in, looking the way you do. You have no coat, no bonnet and no luggage. Let alone a comb,' he continued, running his eyes rather critically over her head, reminding her that she must look as if she'd been dragged through a hedge backwards.

Bother him for being right! For thinking of all the practicalities that she ought to have considered! She pulled the horse blanket closer round herself.

'But whose fault,' she reminded herself, as she reminded him, 'is that?'

'Partly mine...'

'Partly?'

'Mostly,' he conceded, grudgingly. 'But how was I to know you weren't eloping with Gregory, when I found the two of you were alone together in that room and he was kissing your hand?'

'You might have asked, instead of jumping to conclusions.'

'Well, I'm asking now,' he said without the slightest hint of apology in his tone. On the contrary, he sounded grumpy and resentful. 'What explanation can you give for being in that inn, with no maid or other companion in sight to lend you respectability? Unless...'

He sort of froze, an appalled expression on his face. Just as though he'd suddenly pictured some anxious maid, or irate brother, laying evidence against him. She was tempted to let him stew in conjecture. But before he could arrive at a vision of officers of the law catching up with him and clapping him in irons for abduction, she decided to lay the fictitious and entirely unnecessary maid to rest.

'I don't have a maid. Why should I? Lots of perfectly respectable women travel alone.'

'Such as?'

'Such as governesses.'

'Ah. Is that what you are? That explains it.'

'Explains what?' She bristled, waiting for him to say something disparaging, because she'd certainly detected something derogatory in the way he'd made that last remark. Perhaps he intended to tell her that he'd known the gown she was wearing wasn't the height

of fashion and never had been. It had also never been
particularly flattering and, now that she'd spent a night
travelling in it, when it had only ever been intended for
going to dinner on a hot summer's evening, it probably
resembled a sack roughly tied up in the middle.

'Your demeanour,' he surprised her by saying. 'The
habit you have of looking at me as though I was one
of your pupils. And not the brightest one in the class,
either.'

Oh. Well, even though it wasn't exactly a compliment, it was very far from being the insult she'd been
expecting.

'But I am not so stupid,' he continued, 'that I cannot see it is high time we moved away from here.' He
eyed the Watling residence with revulsion. 'And since
I don't think you would be well received in a respectable inn, I shall take you to one that isn't.'

'What?' Just as she'd been on the verge of mellowing towards him, he shocked her again. 'How dare you!
I—'

'I meant no insult,' he said, looking distinctly peeved.
'I just meant that you would feel less uncomfortable
somewhere that usually caters for a…for the lower orders. Where they won't care if you look…a bit dishevelled.'

He was so obviously being very careful selecting
his words that she felt she ought to consider them. And
while she was considering, he continued, 'I can promise you will be perfectly safe with me.'

Well, she couldn't let that outrageous statement pass
without comment.

'Safe? With you? When you've done nothing but dis-
rupt my plans and drag me halfway across the country

in entirely the wrong direction?' She was on the verge of saying a great deal more, when she suddenly saw the sense in what he'd said. She would receive short shrift in many respectable establishments.

And the lower orders didn't place as much stock in what people wore.

And she was hungry and had very little money in her reticule.

He was, in short, her best chance of getting back to the Blue Boar, where she could be reunited with her luggage.

'I suppose I don't have much choice,' she admitted. 'But you do mean to take me back to the Blue Boar eventually, I hope?'

'Yes,' he said, looking distinctly relieved. 'If you will just get back into my carriage, right now, without raising any further objections, I promise that I will make full restitution for all the inconvenience I have caused you.' He placed his right hand on his heart. 'This I vow, on the lives of all the cattle currently in my stables.'

She supposed she had to take his word on it. She was at a disadvantage, knowing nobody in Coventry, and not having enough money to escape from it.

But she was still too angry with him to admit that. Because he'd think she might be ready to let him off the hook, which she wasn't.

So it was with a disdainful sniff, and her chin up, that she turned to the carriage. And when Lord Worsley opened the door for her, she climbed in without deigning to utter one single word.

Chapter Four

Worsley climbed swiftly back up to the perch and urged the horses into motion. The sooner they got away from here the better. He had no intention of bringing the family name into disrepute by tangling with the local law.

He'd been bitterly disappointed in Gregory for doing that, but at least all the lad had done was run off with a woman who *wanted* to run off with him. Miss Phillips had, rightly, accused him of disrupting her life and dragging her halfway across the country in completely the wrong direction. He wouldn't have blamed her if she'd slapped his face, just now, when he had, with his customary lack of finesse, demanded to know what she'd been doing in the room with Gregory and why he'd been kissing her hand. She'd looked as if she'd been sorely tempted to slap him. Instead she'd drawn her dignity about her like a mantle and demanded he undid the damage he'd done her. She hadn't wasted a moment in useless recriminations, the way his sisters were wont to do when he'd committed some blunder. And none of the things he'd ever done to upset them could hold a candle to the injury he'd inflicted on poor Miss Phillips.

Poor Miss Phillips? She was nothing of the sort. She had never broken down and wept, or complained about what a brute he was being. She'd just drawn herself up and looked down her nose at him. She had far more self-control than his sisters. Nor did she seem to want to draw attention to herself, the way they always had.

Which was just as well, in the circumstances. If he was going to brush through this escapade without word of what he'd done falling into the ears of people who lived to spread malicious gossip, then he'd chosen exactly the right woman to abduct. Not that he'd chosen to abduct any woman. But anyway, the point was, she was the kind of woman who could see the sense of making a strategic withdrawal from a potentially dangerous situation. The kind of woman who even wore clothing designed to make men look right past her. Well, she would if she was a governess, wouldn't she? That gown she wore, now, it was exactly the sort of thing the many governesses employed to tame his sisters had worn.

Not at all the sort of thing a woman intent on seducing a green boy would wear, come to think of it. So why on earth had he taken one look at her and decided she had?

Because he'd felt such a strong jolt of attraction, when he'd seen her standing over Gregory, looking down at him like a queen accepting homage from a supplicant, that was why.

And because he was already so angry at her, or rather at the woman who was responsible for Gregory losing his head so completely, he hadn't behaved rationally. He'd seen an attractive woman alone with

Gregory and had jumped to the conclusion that she was *the* woman.

Ironically, if she really *had* been the woman Gregory was eloping with, then Worsley wouldn't have been half so opposed to the match, no matter who her parents happened to be. She had a certain sort of…dignity about her. Which would have made her acceptable, as the future Countess of Worsley. Even if she was older than his ward…

Although none of that excused his behaviour. Still, he'd vowed to make amends and she'd taken him at his word. Eventually. Probably because she was as keen to get away from the Watling house as he was. He'd just have to hope she didn't change her tune once she saw the Bird in Hand.

The stable yard there was orderly and the cattle he'd hired from there passable, which was all he'd cared about when he'd driven up there last night. But when he drew back into that yard, in the full light of day, he couldn't help dreading what Miss Phillips would make of such a humble establishment.

When he opened the carriage door and offered her his arm to help her down, she glanced past him, giving the place a swift perusal. Then she stepped down, pushed a hank of rather knotted hair from her forehead and rested her hand on his arm. She stalked, head held high, with him to the long, low building on the far side of the yard, making him wonder why he'd ever thought she might not be able to cope with the kind of customers they were likely to find inside.

The man in the greasy apron who was standing behind the bar looked them up and down when they went in, then wiped his face clean of expression.

'How may I,' he asked, 'be of service?'

'We want some breakfast,' Worsley replied, while Miss Phillips looked round the single room which was all the place could provide.

'Well,' said the landlord, looking at Miss Phillips doubtfully, 'I can do that. And I can provide Your Lordship with a tankard of my best bitter to wash it down. But what to give the lady to drink I don't know. We don't have no cause for stocking tea, or anything suited to the quality, hereabouts.'

Worsley wasn't all that surprised that the man assumed Miss Phillips was a lady, in spite of the state of her hair, and the fact that she still had a horse blanket wrapped round her shoulders. There could not be many women who could look so...queenly in such garb. In fact, none of the ones he knew would have been seen dead in such disreputable attire. They never went outside without spending hours tricking themselves out in the latest fashions, which cost more money than most people earned in a year.

'What,' said Miss Phillips, while he was still pondering her unique ability to make a horse blanket look as suitable as an opera cloak, 'do the other ladies who come here drink?'

'Well, that's just it, we don't have no ladies in here. Just farmers wives and the like, mebbe on market day...'

'And what do you serve them?'

'Well, some of them do enjoy a glass of cider...'

'That sounds lovely, thank you,' she said, before

making for the one table that was free of abandoned tankards and dirty dishes.

The landlord wiped his hands on his apron, which wouldn't have improved their condition, then went away, presumably to get their breakfast. And their drinks.

Worsley went to sit down at the relatively clean table opposite Miss Phillips.

'Thank you for not…kicking up a fuss,' he said. 'I know this place isn't what you must be used to.'

'Do you? How remarkable, when you know next to nothing about me.'

Ah. So it was like that, was it? She was going to save her best manners for everyone else, while reserving her bile for him.

But then her face changed. Actually, her whole demeanour changed. It was as if the fight went out of her.

'I am going to have to get used to…well, fitting in with servants, and the like, now I am one, though, aren't I?'

'You mean, you haven't been a governess for very long?'

'I am not a governess yet at all,' she said ruefully. 'You…er…intercepted me on the way to my first post.'

'But you…' He made the mistake of glancing at the dowdy gown he could see where the horse blanket wasn't covering it up.

'Have all the appearance of being a governess already? The dowdy clothes and the scornful looks,' she said, giving him just such a look, 'and so forth?'

'Well—'

'Yes, you have already told me that I made you feel like an unruly pupil.'

'Yes, that was what I meant, not the clothes. Your demeanour. You have the air of a woman used to taking charge, somehow. Even when I stopped to see to the horses and I looked in, expecting to find you in a state of collapse, you sat up and demanded a blanket. You addressed me as if I was an unruly pupil, rather than weeping and imploring me to have mercy, the way most women would.'

'Of what use is weeping and begging for mercy? If a man has reduced a woman to that state, then he is likely to be immune to tears, isn't he? Far better to get up and do something constructive is what I always say.'

'Are you speaking from experience?' He didn't like to think of some man mistreating her. 'Has some man mistreated you?'

'Other than you, you mean?'

He supposed he'd walked right into that one.

'Oh, that was mean of me,' she said. 'I don't know how it is, but you really do bring out the worst in me.'

'In many people, so they tell me,' he replied, thinking of all the people, through his life, who'd told him he was impossible.

'I do tend to become snappish if I miss a meal,' she continued, still looking abashed. 'Or if I've had a disturbed night,' she added, raising a weary hand to her brow.

'Yes, you don't need to remind me that it is my fault you are in this condition.'

The corners of her mouth twitched. 'No, you are not as stupid as your behaviour has led me to believe, are you?'

'I am not in the habit of mistreating women the way I have mistreated you, at all events. But who else—?'

'Oh, nobody, not personally. It is just that I have witnessed many women in distress, due to the behaviour of their male relatives. They used to come to my father covered in bruises, or half-starved because their husbands spent their wages on drink rather than food for them and their children...'

'Your father?'

'He was a vicar. The vicar of Lower Withering. It is near Manchester.'

'Ah. That is precisely the sort of background I ought to have known you hailed from. And the *was*? I take it that means your father is no longer living?'

'No, he died just before Christmas. Hence the mourning,' she said, waving a hand over her black gown.

The landlord returned, at that point, with a tankard in each hand. 'Breakfast will be ready in a trice,' he said, as he set them down on the table.

'Oh, I'm so thirsty,' said Miss Phillips, lifting her tankard, and taking a deep draught. It was a mistake, clearly, for her eyes began watering and she had to put the tankard down swiftly as she coughed and spluttered.

It was only when she began to wipe her streaming eyes with the sleeve of her gown and brought the horse blanket dangerously close to them that he thought of lending her his handkerchief, which was at least clean.

'Here,' he said, holding it out. She took it and wiped her streaming eyes.

'Thank you,' she said, once she'd stopped spluttering. 'I had no idea cider would be so potent. When he said that farmers' wives drank it, I assumed it would be something like, oh, lemonade, perhaps.'

'Shall I see if the place can run to something less... er...troublesome?'

She shook her head, vehemently. 'No. I have no wish to make the poor man uncomfortable when he is clearly doing his best. And it is not unpleasant to taste. And if I had taken just a ladylike sip, it would not have had such an effect upon me. I shall be more careful in future.'

She then took a dainty sip and, though she pulled a face, she didn't cough and splutter this time.

'So...' he mused, having had a chance to put a sequence of possible events together in his head while Miss Phillips was experiencing her first taste of rough cider. 'The new vicar would have installed his own family, would he not, as soon as he took over from your father. Which meant you would have had to find a new home. Is that why you have to go out and work for your living?'

She nodded. 'In the weeks after Papa's death, Timothy and I went over the finances many times, but always came to the same sorry conclusion. Papa had not left enough to ensure we could carry on as we had when he was alive. One of us was going to have to go out to work to support the younger ones...'

'Younger ones?'

'Yes, there are five of us. Three girls and two boys. Timothy is the older of my brothers, but he is still at university. When he spoke of abandoning his studies, to take a job...well, I couldn't let him throw away his whole future, when I...well,' she said with a weary shrug, 'I never really had one, beyond caring for my family. So it made sense for me to be the one to take paid work. And, because of my experience in the village school, and my...er...forceful personality, he thought the best thing I could do was hire myself out as a governess.'

Why had she never had a future beyond caring for her family? He supposed, given what she'd said about the family finances, she might not have had anything in the way of a dowry to bring to a marriage, which was the normal ambition of most respectable young women. But he'd learned, through having so many sisters of his own, that it was a risky business, asking a female about her marital ambitions. He downed about half of his pint in one and returned to the topic in hand. 'So, when I met you, in the Blue Boar, you were on your way to your first job.'

'Yes. And Timothy had arranged for me to stay overnight, because I'd already spent much of the day settling the girls into their new school.'

'No wonder you look done in.'

'Hmm,' she said, shifting in her seat. 'Oh, how much I want to say, yet again, that it is all your fault, but I cannot help remembering that you are about to buy me breakfast,' she complained. 'And that I ought not to forget my manners.'

'No matter what the provocation,' he agreed, solemnly.

'But it is so hard, isn't it, to...to bite back what you would so dearly love to say?'

'In my case, no. I always say whatever I want.'

She tipped her head to one side. 'I suppose you can get away with being rude, because of your size.'

'Partly. Though it probably has a lot to do with my rank, as well. People don't usually think it is a good idea to cross swords with a belted earl.'

'Except for governesses, possibly.'

'Mr Watling, too, he didn't mince his words, did he?'

'No, well, it sounded as though he had something against the entire aristocracy, didn't it?'

'Perhaps he had cause. We can be a selfish lot. Take the way I treated you, for example. I should have at least asked if you were hungry or thirsty,' he said ruefully. 'But I was in such a hurry to get you home, before word of your escapade could leak out…but it wasn't even your escapade, was it?'

'No. And I did take note of the fact that you took better care of your horses than you did of me.'

'I'm not in the habit of taking much notice of other people's feelings, or wants…'

'Really? I would never have guessed.'

'I did give you a blanket, though.'

'Only after I'd asked for one.' She drew in a sharp breath. 'Oh, dear, just when I'd decided I was going to be polite, because you are at least, now, making an attempt to get me back to where I wish to be…'

'Only it is damn difficult, when I'm so irritating,' he said for her, since she was wriggling on her seat with the effort of keeping her words in check.

'I… I never said that.'

'No, but I could see you wanted to. And plenty of other people have said it, since as far back as I can remember.'

'Not,' she said, looking shocked, 'when you were a child, surely?'

'Oh, then most of all. I was a very great disappointment to my father, particularly. Not bookish, you see.'

When she looked puzzled, he added, 'I was the only son my mother managed to produce, so the weight of all his hopes rested upon me. He wanted me to be a great statesman, like he was. But I was, as you have already deduced, a bit of a dunce.'

He still had the occasional nightmare about his boyhood. He would be sitting, alone, in his chilly classroom at the top of the house, listening to other people moving about freely outside. Laughing and chatting to one another with an ease he'd never been able to master, even on the occasions his tutor wheeled him out for inspection by his parents and their guests. Only in his dream there was never a door. No means of escaping the endless Greek and Latin, and algebra...

'Truth is, I only feel at ease on horseback.' And he never just opened his budget like this. Not to people he'd known for years, let alone a sharp-tongued woman he'd only just met. 'The lord knows why I'm telling you all this.'

'Perhaps it is for the same reason I confided in you about my own circumstances just now. We are both so tired and out of sorts that it's hard to maintain our usual barriers against the rest of the world. And then again, we are in this very strange situation together. It creates a kind of...intimacy, for want of a better word.' Her eyes darted away from his face. 'And then again,' she went on hurriedly, 'I don't suppose our paths will ever cross, again, once we part company at the Blue Boar. It makes it feel...safe to say whatever we want, knowing there will be no consequences.' She finished on a shrug.

'You could be right. But...' he peered into his half-empty tankard '...perhaps it has something to do with the strength of the local brew on an empty stomach.'

'Well, if that is the case, then here comes the remedy,' she observed as the landlord came in with a tray bearing platters of steak, eggs, fresh bread, cheese and fruit. After that, neither of them made any attempt to resume conversation, apart from the occasional request to pass the bread, or to ask if the other had finished with the cheese.

But it didn't feel awkward between them somehow. Not until Miss Phillips bit into a peach and the juice ran down her chin.

'It is just as well you lent me this,' she said, flourishing his handkerchief, before using it to mop up the peach juice. And then blushing bright red.

'Yes,' he said, 'otherwise I'd have to...' He swallowed back what he'd been about to say. He couldn't offer to lick the juice away, before tasting her lips, which he'd been thinking, ever since she began eating, looked as succulent as ripe fruit. Or admit that the sight of that juice dribbling down her chin had produced a surge of lust so strong that he didn't care that she was unkempt and far from clean, and smelled rather strongly of horse. He just wanted to kiss her.

But he couldn't. Couldn't even let her suspect such a thing. Not when she was completely reliant on him. And he'd promised to make amends for abducting her. It would be the act of a scoundrel to...to take advantage of her, when she trusted him.

Fortunately, before he could make an attempt to finish what he'd said, Pawson appeared in the door to the yard.

'New team ready to harness up whenever you're ready,' he said.

Miss Phillips looked up with a guilty start.

Had she guessed what he'd been thinking? Had he

given himself away somehow? She'd blushed, hadn't she, so...

'But have you,' she said to Pawson, 'had time to get anything to eat?'

'Don't you worry about me, miss,' said Pawson. 'I took supper on the road last night and the landlord here, he brought me out a hunk of bread and some cheese while I was seeing to the horses.'

'Indeed?' Miss Phillips turned away from Pawson to give Worsley a narrow-eyed stare. 'So, I was the only one to go hungry last night?'

'No, I didn't eat anything either.' Although that had been his choice, hadn't it? 'Shall we set off? If you've finished?'

'Oh, yes, I have finished,' she said, getting to her feet. 'And the sooner we leave, the sooner I can get back to my real life,' she said, turning and stalking from the room.

Worsley sighed. The brief truce between them was clearly over.

Chapter Five

It felt to Dorothy as though it was taking a lot longer
to get back to the Blue Boar than it had taken to travel
the other way down the same road the night before.
But then, last night, he'd been determined to get rid of
her, or at least Pansy. And there was more traffic on
the roads, which probably meant he had to drive with
more care. And the yards where they stopped to change
the horses were far busier.

Also, he made a point, at every stop, of coming to
ask her if there was anything she needed. Which made
it all far less uncomfortable. Except that now she had
no sense of injustice to nurse. He'd made a mistake and
was doing his best to put it right, so he could put her
out of his life for good. So he'd never have to see her
again. And she'd never have to see him, either.

All she'd have left of this night's adventure would
be a stained linen handkerchief and memories. Of a
man who was more at ease with horses than people,
which wasn't surprising given the horrid way his parents had made him feel. He wasn't a dunce. Far from
it. He was just… She sighed. Far too handsome for his

own good. And far too used to getting his own way. By whatever means necessary, to judge from the way he'd hoisted her over his shoulder when she wouldn't meekly do as she was told.

He would be glad to see the back of her, no doubt.

Although, when they eventually reached the Blue Boar and he came to open the carriage door, he did not openly display his relief that their adventure was almost at an end. And, strangely, she did not feel any either. Because after this, she was going to have to knuckle down to the wearisome lot of a governess. And who in their right minds would look forward to that?

'I will make sure you have a seat on whatever stage it was you intended to take yesterday,' he said. 'And pay for your room here tonight, so you won't be out of pocket because of my…er…behaviour. That is, I am assuming you won't want to try travelling any further today?'

Well, she supposed she had to give him credit for eventually asking if she was happy to go along with what he'd already planned for her.

'No. That is, I would like to get a decent night's sleep in a bed that isn't bouncing along the road, having a wash and changing into a fresh gown. I have no wish to arrive at my first post in a dress I have been wearing for several days.' Especially not in this heat.

'Allow me,' he said, holding out his arm so she could rest her hand on his sleeve. She did so with a sense of… something extraordinary coming to an end. An adventure that hadn't been the slightest bit comfortable, yet one that she thought she probably look back on with amusement. Perhaps even fondness. Well, it wasn't every day that a girl from her background spent a night with a handsome earl, was it?

When they reached the inn door, it was to find the landlord standing there, his arms folded across his ample belly. And he was eyeing them with blatant hostility.

'If you think I'm going to let you and your doxy in here,' he spat, 'you've got another think coming.'

Doxy?

'I am no such thing,' she gasped in outrage. 'As well you know. I am a…a governess!' Or at least, she would be in another day or so.

'You *were* a governess, I grant, yesterday,' said the landlord. 'But that was afore this cove—' he jerked his head at Lord Worsley '—came in here and carted you off to the lord knows where and kept you all night. So *now* you ain't nothing but his doxy and I don't harbour such in my ken.'

'Now, look here,' Lord Worsley began.

'No, *you* look here,' said the landlord. 'I keep a respectable house, I do. And you ain't respectable.'

Worsley shook her hand off his sleeve as he took a step forward, his fists clenching and a distinctly martial glint in his eyes. The landlord, far from looking the slightest bit intimidated, squared up to him.

'Oh, no, please don't cause a scene,' she begged Lord Worsley. 'The whole point of you coming here in the first place was to prevent a scandal, wasn't it?'

He stood still, breathing heavily.

'Thank you for the reminder,' he said after a few moments when she wasn't sure if he was going to punch the landlord anyway, just to relieve his feelings. 'I shall be only too glad to remove to another establishment,' he said to the landlord, 'once you have returned this *lady's* property.'

'Sorry,' said the landlord, looking not the slightest bit sorry. 'But I can't do that, if it was her trunk you was referring to?'

'What do you mean?' Dorothy, who was recovering from the insult a bit, was now starting to get cross. 'I left my trunk in my room. So why can you not return it?'

'Well, because that young couple made off with it when I turned them out, didn't they?'

'No! Everything I had was in that trunk!' Nothing was of any great value, not to anyone else. But it was all she had.

'You...turned them out?' Lord Worsley's voice had dropped to a kind of growl. The kind of growl a lion might make before pouncing on its prey.

'Yes.' The landlord's face lit with a malicious grin. 'Well, when you pointed out that they was eloping and that at least one of them was a minor, and that you'd ruin me if I was to aid and abet them, what else could I do?' He spread his hands wide, in a parody of a gesture of apology. 'As I said afore, I run a respectable establishment. I don't harbour eloping babes, nor rakes and their doxies, neither.'

'This has nothing to do with keeping a respectable inn,' said Dorothy, coming to the end of her tether. 'You are just taking a petty revenge on Lord Worsley because he made a few empty threats last night.' Was it only last night? She felt as if she'd spent days and days going from one bad situation to increasingly worse ones. 'And you are making me pay for it, too, when you know full well that none of this was my fault.

What kind of man are you? No, don't bother to answer that. I already know.' She lifted her chin. 'Come along,' she said to Lord Worsley, who'd fallen strangely silent. 'There is no point in staying here bandying words with this fat fool. The service here is slack, too. I never did get the supper I'd paid for.'

Although it was a puny insult, in comparison with the one he'd flung at her, she did have the pleasure of having the last word on the topic, as she turned on her heel and stalked back to the coach.

Lord Worsley caught up with her before she reached it and opened the door for her. When she climbed in, he did not immediately go to the front, climb up and drive off. Instead, he stood with one hand holding the door open and the other braced on the frame.

And his face was grim.

'I've ruined you,' he said.

'No, you haven't. You mustn't let what that spiteful man said affect you. You know as well as I do that the whole episode was entirely innocent.'

Lord Worsley shook his head. 'No. Once a man has spent a night with a woman…' He ran his fingers through his hair, making it stick up in random tufts. 'I was thinking about it on the way here…about leaving off pursuing Gregory, that is. If I could have returned the Watling chit to her parents before anyone knew of her flight, she might still have… Only I didn't. And now that she's been in Gregory's care overnight, then, dammit, no matter what I think of her, or what their future might be like, he has no choice but to marry her. And I for one will make sure he does.'

'Well, yes, I see that, but—'

'And it's the same for us. Now that you've spent the

night with me, I have to marry you, to make it right. That landlord is already calling you... Your name is ruined. You've lost your reputation.'

'No, I haven't—'

'Yes, you have! Look, if I were to cut you adrift, what do you suppose would become of you? Do you really believe that your employer will still be willing to give you work, once word of this night's episode gets out? And as you said, you don't want to turn up in a dirty gown, with no luggage. You are going to have to provide some sort of explanation for that, and pardon me, but you don't strike me as being the kind of female who can tell lies with any degree of success.'

'Well, no, that's true...'

'And how much worse will it be to tell the truth? You heard what the landlord called you. It's what everyone will say, even though it isn't true.'

'Oh, no,' said Dorothy, feeling her heart sink. 'They wouldn't.' But it was only a token protest. She knew how much people delighted in spreading malicious gossip. The parish of Lower Withering had been a seething mass of it.

'Believe me, they will. You are going to have to accept the fact that, if you don't accept the protection of my name, you are going to face grave difficulties.'

She bit down on her lower lip because she had no intention of conceding that he was correct. 'I... I...' She couldn't think of anything to say.

He sighed. 'Look, I know that marrying me is probably the last thing you want, after the abominable way I've treated you ever since we met. But just...think about it, will you? And you can give me your answer when we get there.'

'Get where? Do you know of another inn here-abouts?'

His face twisted in revulsion. 'I am not going to take you to another inn. I have no intention of answering any more questions about…why you don't have any luggage, or a coat, or…' He swallowed as he ran his eyes over the state of what had once been her second-best gown. 'I shall, instead, take you to my sister. She has a place not much more than a couple of hours drive from here. And she will be able to provide you with night attire and so forth.'

She supposed she ought to put up more of a pro-test. But a sister did sound like the perfect person to turn to. Because she *could* lend her night attire and a toothbrush, and if she felt half as much for her brother as Dorothy did for either of hers, then she would be just as keen to keep this entire episode quiet as either Worsley or herself.

And the truth was she'd never wanted to be a govern-ess. She'd agreed to apply for a post because she hadn't wanted Timothy to sacrifice his career for the sake of the younger ones. And because she could see herself presiding over a couple of children, in one family, after learning how to control a whole group of village chil-dren. But she'd never been entirely sure she would have been able to take orders from employers, especially if she thought their orders were foolish, or went against her principles. She'd been so used to being in charge, of acting upon her own judgement.

He leaned in, then, and seized her hands. 'You need not be afraid of me,' he said, earnestly. 'My behav-iour last night is not…typical. I would never, normally, abuse my strength in the manner in which…' His face went red. 'I would not be a demanding, let alone a violent husband, you have my word.'

'I am not afraid of you,' she said scornfully. She supposed a truly feminine woman would have been, considering the bald facts. Yet at no time had she felt frightened. Not of him, at least. Of the consequences of his actions, perhaps. She had been afraid her new job might be in jeopardy and now she was worried about the fate of her trunk. But of him…no.

'You have nerves of steel,' he said.

'Yes,' she said ruefully. 'Or at least…' No nerves at all. No sensibility. No delicacy…

'Then that is settled,' he said, looking not the slightest bit triumphant.

But then why would he? He'd set out to prevent his ward from making a disastrous marriage. Not only had he failed in doing that, but now he was going to have to marry someone he hardly knew.

'No, wait,' she began. But it was too late. He'd shut the carriage door.

And once more, Dorothy sat still, thinking, instead of leaping out and doing something to stop him from making what she suspected was another big mistake.

Because her hands were tingling, where he'd been holding them. And because, years ago, before she'd decided there was not a man alive who could overlook her many faults, she'd dreamed of getting married and having her own children.

Oh, she'd been a mother, of sorts, to her brothers and sisters ever since their real mother had died, but it wasn't the same.

And it had been one of the worst things about finding that post as a governess. It had meant giving up any hope of ever having a child of her own.

Though it had been only a faint hope at best. She hadn't ever been able to see herself getting married, not with all the responsibilities she'd had, with the younger children and the running of the vicarage. Besides which, nobody in Lower Withering, or any other place, had ever looked twice at her. She wasn't pretty. She was often as snappish as she'd been with Lord Worsley, tonight, which made some people say she was a regular termagant. Timothy had always comforted her by saying that she just didn't suffer fools gladly, that was all. That those who knew her well appreciated her practical nature and the warm heart and generous spirit upon which they could all rely. But eligible men never wanted to get to know her well enough to find that warm heart, did they? All they saw was the termagant.

Even though this was not the ideal way to get a husband, it wasn't as if she'd ever been likely to get one in the normal way of things, was it? The eligible men in her social circle before had all thought her too direct, too manly, or just too tall.

But none of those things bothered Lord Worsley. He was just as blunt as she was. And taller. And…

And, oh, dear, the carriage was moving. It was too late now to offer to talk about finding another solution. Not that there could be a better one, for her.

But before they reached his sister's house, she'd think of something. She'd have to. She couldn't let him marry her, when it must be the very last thing he wanted to do.

Chapter Six

Worsley climbed wearily back up to the perch and sat down heavily. He shook his head when Pawson made as if to hand him the reins. For the first time in his life, he wasn't going to derive any pleasure at all from tooling his own cattle. Not considering the fate that awaited him when they arrived at their destination.

'To Lady Waddesdon's, will it be, my lord?' said Pawson, who must have been listening to be able to make such a declaration. Well, he could hardly have helped overhearing what had passed between him and that poor woman, could he?

Worsley nodded, too choked up to speak. Tilly was going to love this. It would absolutely make her day, if not her year, to be the first person to meet the woman he was going to have to make his Countess. Especially given the circumstances under which he'd met the woman in question. But Tilly was the one sister of his who would be more likely, after seeing Miss Phillips in her current state, to show sympathy rather than disdain. Tilly, after all, had tumbled from one scrape to another until Waddesdon had married her and taken her in charge. If it wasn't falling out of a tree or into a pond it was getting caught kissing unsuitable youths. No, Tilly would not be able to say a word against Miss Phillips.

What she'd say to *him*, though… He almost shuddered. When he thought of all the women she'd pointed out as suitable candidates and the peremptory way he'd rebuffed the ones who'd put themselves forward…

Oh, lord, she'd claim this was some kind of divine retribution.

As Pawson drove the carriage out of the inn yard, Worsley wondered if this was what aristocrats in France had felt like as they sat, helpless, in their tumbrils, with the peasants—in the form of that fat, vengeful innkeeper—jeering as they went past. Partly wishing the horses would go slower than the steady walking pace the driver had decided upon to put off the hour of their doom, and partly wishing the man would hurry up and get them off the streets and away from the jeering peasants.

At least he could be thankful, once again, that the woman he'd abducted wasn't the kind of person who wanted to draw attention to herself, or he would have created a scene on the threshold of the Blue Boar, which would have drawn crowds and caused talk to reach far and wide. And it wouldn't just have been him at the centre of gossip. Or Miss Phillips. But Gregory, too, because people would want to find out what had brought him to the Blue Boar and how he'd come to have Miss Phillips at his side. It would all have come out, if not for her wise and timely words. Yes, he had a lot to be thankful to her for.

But, hell and damnation! He'd never planned on getting leg shackled. Women always wanted to change a fellow. The ones he'd had relations with had never been happy with anything about him except the amount of money they could extract from him. They either wept whenever he told them the truth about what he thought they looked like in the latest fashion, even though they'd asked him for his opinion in the first place, accusing him of being unkind. Or they stormed and raged when he forgot an assignation, because, for example, one of his mares was about to foal, complaining that he treated them with less respect than he did his horses. Which he supposed was true. He understood horses and enjoyed being with them.

People, though…they were so complicated. And incomprehensible. They said one thing when they meant something else. And they always *wanted* things from him. Particularly females. Particularly his sisters. They wanted him to show his face at events he had no taste for. They wanted him to speak in the Lords over issues he had no interest in. And most of all, they were always nagging him to marry and set up his nursery.

What good would he be in a nursery? Yes, he knew it was part of his duty to provide an heir to take over. But then he had Gregory. He frowned. He'd *thought* he had Gregory. He'd thought he'd been training him up to step into his shoes when the time came. But he no longer felt so certain of that. This elopement business had shown him that Gregory thought with his heart rather than his head. Would he really be able to care, properly, for all his holdings and his tenants, if he kept on following that trait?

He heaved a sigh. He thought he'd be able to avoid the whole messy business of marrying and fathering babies. It was of no use his sisters saying that he could think of any babies he fathered the way he'd regard a stable full of prize foals. Babies were nothing like foals. Foals could stand up within moments of being born, while human babies were such frail little things. He'd be afraid of dropping them, or snapping their floppy little bodies. And when his sisters had added that if he wasn't all that interested, he could safely leave all that side of things to the mother, and nursery maids, he'd wanted to ask what was the point of having children if you never had anything to do with them?

And what about the effect of childbearing on a woman's health? And her temper? How could his sisters have forgotten all the miscarriages their mother had over the years in the attempt to produce a second son?

Still, it was all academic now. He was going to have to make amends for the way he'd treated Miss Phillips and offering marriage was the only way he could see of doing so. Though how he was going to be able to undo the dreadful opinion she must have of him he had no idea.

He'd already assured her that he could behave like a gentleman. But somehow he'd have to prove to her that he wasn't the kind of brute who went about the country routinely tossing women over his shoulder and abducting them, like some kind of...marauding Viking or something.

He'd warned Miss Phillips that it was going to take a couple of hours to reach Tilly's place, but his mind was so full that before he knew it they were bowling up the carriage drive.

'Shall I go straight round to the stables?' Pawson

asked as they approached the turn off which would take them to the back of the house.

'No,' he said without hesitation. 'I will take Miss Phillips in by the front door, as befits her station as my...' His throat closed up before he could utter the fateful word, *betrothed*. 'I won't have her think I am ashamed of her.' He was the one who ought to be ashamed of himself.

Pawson grunted, in a way that sounded as if he thought it might be a mistake, but it wasn't his place to say so. It never ceased to amaze him how the man could inject so much expression into one sound.

And then they drew to a halt and there was nothing for it but to climb down, help Miss Phillips out of the coach and leave behind a way of life he'd hoped to enjoy for many years to come.

Dorothy should have known, given the fact that Worsley was a lord, that his sister would be married to one as well. That they would live in a stately mansion such as this, set in acres upon acres of beautiful parkland.

But she hadn't. She hadn't been able to think about anything but...well, *him*. All the way here. And what excuse she could manufacture for not marrying him, when, the more she thought about it, the more appealing the prospect seemed.

Still, it looked as though she was about to get her just deserts for thinking she could get away with marrying so far above her station in life. He was going to make her walk up those front steps, draped in a horse blanket and with her hair all anyhow, and try to get her

past a doorkeeper whose job it was to protect his employer from encroaching interlopers.

Again.

The coach drew to a halt and she felt the weight
shift as Lord Worsley climbed down. She ran her hands
over her hair in the vain hope that she might be able to
restore it to some semblance of order before meeting
his sister. For who knew how a woman who lived in a
mansion such as this would react when Lord Worsley
foisted some scruffy, unknown woman on her? Badly,
she suspected.

Her heart was banging against her ribs when Lord
Worsley opened the door and extended his hand to help
her alight. She found herself gripping it rather more
tightly than was probably correct. But, well, it was
just that he was *there*. And so big and so strong. No,
no, she didn't care for that sort of thing. She'd never
cared about such aspects of a man. Nor had she ever
been tempted to lean on one. So it must be because he
was the only person she knew in, well, wherever this
was. Oh, lord, she didn't even know his sister's name,
never mind the first thing about her temperament. She
might be lovely. It was just…the fear of the unknown
that was making her want to grasp Lord Worsley's arm
rather than just rest her hand upon his sleeve as he led
her inexorably up the front steps, before rapping on the
door with the butt of his whip.

Funny, to think that she was more nervous of the
woman she was about to meet than she'd ever been of
this man, even when he'd been at his worst. She ought
to be shrinking from him and anticipating flinging
herself gratefully into the sanctuary this female was
going to provide. She shook her head at herself. People

were always telling her she was an unnatural sort of female. The churchwarden and his wife, for instance. She
suspected they would have approved of her far more if
she'd fainted occasionally, or sat down and wept and
begged for help, rather than just rolling up her sleeves
and getting on with things.

Oh, if only she *could* faint. Right now. So she
wouldn't have to endure the humiliation of…having
his family, and their servants, learning what had happened and what solution he'd come up with, while she
looked like…like well, she didn't know exactly what
she looked like. But it was most definitely not the prim,
correctly behaved, capable, occasionally intimidating
woman who'd set out from Lower Withering the day
before.

But there was to be no escape. She could hear footsteps proceeding at a stately pace across the hall, then
the door was opening.

'My lord,' said the butler who looked exactly the
way she'd expect one who worked in such a splendid
mansion to look. 'We were not expecting…that is…
Her Ladyship is at dinner.'

'Good,' said Lord Worsley. 'We are famished. We'll
join my sister at table, if you'd be so good as to set a
couple of extra places.'

The butler's eyes swivelled in her direction and
stuck. He cleared his throat.

'And whom shall I say is accompanying you?'

'My betrothed,' said Lord Worsley in a rather ag-
gressive tone, before making the most of the butler's
start of surprise to push past him into the house. Dragging her with him.

'As you can see,' said Lord Worsley, half turning

round to shut the door behind them, 'we are in need of some assistance.'

'Indeed, my lord,' said the butler, who'd finally managed to school his features into an expression indicating it was not his place to comment if the brother of his employer took it into his head to bring a woman who looked as if she'd been dragged through a hedge backwards, and smelled as though she'd been through even worse, to dinner.

Her face flamed with a combination of knowing she looked a sight and wondering what his sister would make of her, as they followed the butler through the hall, up a flight of stairs, and into the grandest room she'd ever seen. All chandeliers and shiny furniture, along with a pair of very well-dressed people, sitting at a table strewn with all manner of delicious-smelling food, on delicate, matching china. At which point, when it was most inconvenient, she did, genuinely, feel faint. And in spite of wishing she could have made a better impression on these people, she simply tottered to the nearest chair, which she managed to reach only just before her knees gave way.

'Goodness,' cried the woman, who looked remarkably like a miniature, feminised version of Lord Worsley. 'Who on earth is this?'

'And why, Worsley,' came the dry voice of the man, who looked much older than Lord Worsley's sister, 'have you brought her here?'

'Don't pay any attention to Waddesdon,' said the lady, bustling over to Dorothy on a cloud of attar of roses. 'It is plain to see you have suffered some sort of catastrophe and Toby brought you here so I could help you. Isn't that it?'

'N…not *exactly*,' Dorothy began.

'I beg your pardon, naturally, if I appeared rude, or unfeeling,' said the slender, older man, rising to his feet. 'Perhaps, instead, I should be offering you a glass of brandy.'

'No,' snapped Lord Worsley. 'No more alcohol. She can't hold it.'

The man, who had been recovering from his initial shock at the sight of her, and who had been trying to be sympathetic, now looked anything but.

'Is that,' said the fragrant woman, 'what has happened? If so, you really ought not to drink so much, and then you wouldn't fall into…whatever kind of scrape this is.'

'She doesn't drink, Tilly,' snapped Lord Worsley, coming to stand beside her chair. 'And the catastrophe that befell her was me. I am the catastrophe here, the… the villain of the piece if you like. She has done nothing wrong and I won't have you treat her as though she has.'

'Of course, if you say so,' said the fragrant lady. 'But I wasn't judging her at all. I was just trying to be helpful.'

'Well, don't,' said Lord Worsley.

'If you don't want my wife's help,' said the man, 'then why have you brought this…female here?'

'Because, thanks to me, she has no job, no luggage and no reputation. So I'm going to marry her.'

Dorothy, who'd been recovering from the moment she sat down, decided that it was time to speak up. Especially now that Lord Worsley's family had looked exactly the way she'd expected them to look when he'd announced his intention to marry her. Appalled.

'No, you are not,' she said, causing the woman, whose name seemed to be Tilly, to gasp.

'Oh, yes, I am,' said Lord Worsley, running a finger round his collar as though it was too tight. 'You must see that it is the only way I can make restitution.'

'Nonsense,' she snapped. 'There is no need for you to make such a sacrifice. As long as your sister will give me a bed for the night and…and…'

'Yes? And then what? We've already established that your reputation is shot to pieces after the way I picked you up and tossed you into my coach.'

'You picked this woman up?' Tilly's eyes widened. 'Bodily tossed her into your coach? And now you are going to make restitution by marrying her? Oh, that is too funny,' she said. And promptly burst out laughing.

'Excuse my sister,' Lord Worsley said to her. 'If anyone around here has had too much to drink, it is clearly her.'

'Not a bit of it,' retorted Tilly, dabbing at her streaming eyes with the napkin she held in her hand. 'But you must admit, this is just too delicious an irony. When I think of all the women who have cast out lures, and the ones we have brought to your attention, and then you go and abduct an unwilling one…' She doubled over with laughter once more.

'I didn't do it on purpose,' he said, which sent her off into fresh peals of laughter.

'H…how on earth,' Tilly asked, through her giggles, 'can you abduct someone b…by mistake?'

'I thought she was eloping with Gregory.'

'Eloping with Gregory? Well,' said her husband, with heavy sarcasm, 'that makes perfect sense, then.'

'Yes, it does,' he retorted. 'Because he sent me a

mawkishly revolting missive, explaining why he felt he had no choice but to rescue Pansy Watling from persecution, and, since I was brute enough to have told him she should never darken my doorstep, that he would be obliged to carry her off to Gretna Green.'

'That boy,' said Tilly, shaking her head, 'is an idiot. I have always said so. And why you had to make him your heir I have never been able to fathom.'

'Worsley did not *make* the boy his heir,' said her husband, with a shake of his head. 'He simply *is* the heir, by right of birth. He is the only surviving male child of the last Earl's younger brother...'

'Yes, yes, I know all that,' said Tilly with an impatient wave of her hand. 'But he wouldn't be if only Toby got married and had his own son. Which,' she said, rounding on him, 'is what we have been trying to get you to do for an age. But now you *will* be marrying, won't you?' she said, her eyes sliding to where Dorothy sat hunched in her chair. 'So good riddance to Gregory.'

'No, excuse me,' said Dorothy, forcing herself to sit up straight, 'but I will not be marrying Lord Worsley.'

'Oh, please do, Miss Watling. No. He said you weren't the girl running off with Gregory after all. So what is your name?'

'This is Miss Phillips,' put in Lord Worsley, before she could commit the social solecism of introducing herself.

'And I am Lord Waddesdon,' said the slender man, strolling away from the table so that he could make his bow. 'But, forgive me for being very stupid, but I don't quite understand why you must abduct anyone, Worsley.' He turned a cold stare in Lord Worsley's direction.

'I thought,' said Lord Worsley, his jaw clenching, 'that it would save the Watling girl's reputation if I could get her back to Coventry before anyone noticed she was missing. That if her parents made sure she was out and about, first thing this morning, then even if anyone had got wind of the elopement, they'd be convinced it was all a hum.'

'Very noble of you, I'm sure,' said Waddesdon in that sarcastic way Dorothy was beginning to think was his habitual style.

'And it's very noble of you to offer to marry this lady instead, now that you have compromised her,' added Tilly, with genuine warmth.

'Yes, and don't think I'm not grateful for the offer,' said Dorothy. 'But surely you need not go to the lengths of marrying me?'

'I don't see what else I can do,' he said, in a tone that brought home to her that if there had been any other way for him to make restitution, he would already have suggested it. It was not a very flattering thought. 'Nor do I see why you are arguing about it, now. After all, you were the one who said that as the whole thing was entirely my fault then it was my duty to make amends for the all the indignities that have been heaped on you.'

'Oh, please do marry him,' put in Tilly. 'You could well be the making of him. Why, look at the way he is practically grovelling to you, already, when he always swore he would rather have all his teeth drawn than propose to a woman.'

'I did no such thing,' he snapped.

But he clearly felt it. 'I can see,' said Dorothy, 'that you don't really wish to marry me, or anyone. So it would not be right to take advantage of your offer…'

Which was not the way she'd meant to say it. She shouldn't be letting anyone guess how much she wanted to accept...

'Oh, take advantage, Miss Watling, or Phillips, or whoever you are,' said Tilly, before frowning. 'Although, how did my idiot brother mistake you for the Watling girl? I have seen her, you know.' She made a moue of distaste. 'A tiny, wispy little creature with a lot of frizzy yellow hair. Pushing, vulgar sort of girl, I thought her.'

'Miss Phillips is the daughter of a vicar,' Lord Worsley began.

'Oh, far more suitable already,' said Tilly. 'Miss Watling's father,' she explained to Lord Waddesdon, 'is in trade of some sort.'

'And she was on her way to a new post as a governess,' Lord Worsley continued doggedly in spite of his sister's constant interruptions.

'And Gregory flung you into my brother's path, did he, to save his poor pathetic Pansy? Typical of the sort of selfish behaviour I would expect from him.'

'That's about the size of it,' growled Lord Worsley, wondering what on earth Miss Phillips must be thinking of his family. First Gregory had thrown her in his path like some sort of sacrificial lamb, so that he could make good his escape. And now Tilly was treating the whole thing like a joke, while Waddesdon was looking down his nose at her, the way he always did to everyone, but which was particularly unfortunate after the insults and injuries she'd already sustained on his account.

'When I accused Miss Phillips of getting her talons

into him, he did nothing to disabuse me of my mistake. He just stood there, arms folded, while I picked her up and carried her away. How could he have behaved in such a scaly fashion? Has he no idea how a gentleman ought to behave? And to make matters worse, when we went back to the Blue Boar to retrieve her belongings, he'd made off with them. Her trunk, that is. When I catch up with the scoundrel...' He clenched his fists. He would like to horsewhip him. Although it was too late for that. Years too late. Somewhere along the line he'd failed to instil proper values into the lad who should have been his successor.

It was all his fault. The whole mess.

So of course it was up to him to put right what he could, no matter how reluctant he was to inflict himself on this poor woman any further.

'Oh,' said Miss Phillips, suddenly raising her left arm, from which dangled her reticule. 'I... I have the key to my trunk in here. I remember now, I dropped it in right after unlocking it, to make Pansy a drink of chamomile tea, so that I didn't mislay it. So...well, no wonder they didn't like to leave it behind. That innkeeper had the look of a, well, a bit of a rogue. So perhaps they thought it would be safer with them and they could return it, later, when...'

'When they found out where you'd gone? Did they know the address of your new employers?'

'Well, no, but they did see you carry me off, so I expect they assumed they'd be able to find me through you. And, honestly, I don't think Gregory is as bad as you are making out. You had not seen the state of poor Pansy, or you would completely understand why he was willing to sacrifice a complete stranger in order to protect her. She was prostrate with nerves when I arrived in the inn. I had taken her up to my room and given her a soothing draught to get her to sleep and had just gone down to tell him that she had dozed off. And to be fair, he *did* make an attempt to tell you that you had grasped the wrong end of the stick.'

'Not much of an attempt,' he grunted, wondering why she was so determined to stick up for the lad who'd thrown her to the wolves. Although he was glad to hear there were extenuating circumstances. And it was decent of her to point them out. Especially when most women would have been tallying up the wrongs done them and demanding recompense.

'No, well, he clearly knows you very well, doesn't he? And saw that there would be little point.'

'Touché,' cried Tilly, who seemed to be enjoying this as much as if she was watching a play.

'I wish you would keep out of this,' he said.

'Then why did you come to me?'

'Because Miss Phillips, thanks to me, has nothing but the clothes she stands up in.'

'She's sitting down.'

He'd known that Tilly would enjoy his discomfiture and that he'd have to give her a certain amount of leeway as she revelled in it, so he unclenched his fists and said, in what he hoped was a measured tone, 'Standing or sitting, the point is, because of me, she is in dire straits. I brought her here so that you could give her a bed for the night. And lend her all she needs until you can take her about and help her purchase her own things. I had hoped,' he said witheringly, 'that I might also rely on your family loyalty to quell any gossip that may arise from my sudden, unexpected marriage.'

'Oh, you can absolutely rely on me to spend as much of your money as I can on turning her out in the style befitting your new Countess,' she said with a mischievous smile.

'No, no, no, no,' said Miss Phillips, shaking her head and looking alarmed. 'I won't have you spending money on me. I am completely capable of earning my own living. I only need...'

'But you *won't* be able to earn your own living after this. Not in a respectable manner,' he reminded her. 'Which is entirely my fault.'

'And you need not worry about spending his money, either,' put in Tilly. 'He has so much that he hardly knows what to do with it. Why, when I think of the fortune he positively threw at his last little ladybird, I was aghast until Waddesdon pointed out that it would hardly make a dent in—'

'That's enough, Tilly,' he snapped. 'Good God, what kind of woman are you, to even mention that kind of woman to my intended bride?'

'I beg your pardon, Miss Phillips,' she said, looking abashed. 'Forgot myself. Do say you forgive me, Miss Phillips. You know that I was only trying to tempt you into accepting my brother's offer. Only, I expect...he put you off, didn't he, mauling you about like that? I dare say you were terrified. Oh.' Her whole demeanour changed. Instead of looking as if she found the situation to be a huge joke, she suddenly looked rather upset. 'Oh, dear. Oh, poor Miss Phillips, I never considered that. And if that is the case, then—'

'If that is the case,' said Lord Waddesdon, 'then you may rest assured that I shall offer you sanctuary. Neither my wife...' he looked at her sternly '...nor I

would blame you in the slightest for being unwilling
to ally yourself to a man who, it appears, has behaved
like a complete brute, in your regard. Even unto trying to persuade you that you now have no choice but
to marry him. That is not so. If you really hold him in
revulsion, for which I would not blame you, then I can
shield you from any scandal that may arise from his
reprehensible conduct.'

'No!' Miss Phillips had wrapped her arms round
her waist in a gesture that even he, as insensitive as he
was to other people's feelings, had no difficulty in in-
terpreting as a defensive gesture. 'I mean, thank you,
but you are wrong. I have never, not for one moment,
been afraid of your brother. And,' she said, turning to
Waddesdon, 'I have no intention of accepting charity,
either, from a virtual stranger. I would rather…work
as a washerwoman!'

'But you do have to provide, somehow, for your
younger brothers and sisters, don't you,' Worsley reminded her. 'Couldn't you just think of marriage to me
as another kind of employment? One for which you'd
certainly get better wages than you would have done
as a governess, never mind a washerwoman.'

She knotted her fingers together in her lap. 'But neither of us really want this marriage, do we? I mean,
you said you'd rather have your teeth drawn and I…'
She gulped. 'Surely, if we put our heads together, we
could come up with…a better solution?'

He had one of those rare flashes of insight, which his
father had described, in scathing terms, as a proof he
possessed a kind of low cunning. 'Well,' he said, strok-
ing his chin as if he was seriously considering the offer
he was about to make, 'I could simply buy you off, I

suppose. Pay you enough money to provide for yourself and your family. I'm wealthy enough. But you'd hate that even more, wouldn't you? Accepting my charity?'

Miss Phillips looked him up and down. 'You really are so wealthy that taking on a wife will make no difference to your own comfort?'

Not in a physical sense, no.

'He could afford to marry a dozen wives,' put in Tilly, helpfully. 'If it wasn't for the fact he swore he'd never marry at all.'

'And for the inconvenience of going to prison for bigamy,' he pointed out, drily.

But Miss Phillips had slumped down again and was shaking her head. 'No, no, it wouldn't be right. You don't *want* to get married.'

'Well, I didn't. Because I thought I had Gregory to take over when I cocked up my toes,' he said. 'Only now, dashed if I wouldn't rather raise my own son to inherit my title and land.'

She blushed. Darted him an assessing look. Blushed a bit deeper.

'But you need not fear,' he put in hastily, 'that I would start making demands at once.' Though he'd like to. Ever since the landlord of the Blue Boar had accused him of dragging her off to his lair and having his wicked way with her all night, he'd started wishing he'd done just that instead of driving all over the country on a wild goose chase.

No, it had started before that. In the Bird in Hand, when she'd eaten that peach and the juice had run down her chin, and he'd experienced a brief, but strong urge to lean in and lick it away before tasting her lips, which looked as succulent as the ripe fruit. Even though she was unkempt, and far from clean, and smelled rather strongly of horse. The swift surge of…well, lust, had appalled him. But if she was his wife, he'd have the right to lick her…no, kiss her, whenever he wished. Once she got used to the idea of him.

'I know you are going to need a bit of time to get used to the idea, since your heart was set on standing on your own two feet. Time for us both to get to know one another, in fact.'

She tilted her head to one side. 'If I did agree to marry you, then, would you let me have an allowance? Which I could spend exactly as I pleased? Or would you be one of those men who insisted I send all the bills to you and raked me over the coals if I bought things you didn't approve of?'

He grunted. He might have known it would all come down to money. In fact, now he came to think of it, she'd only started wavering in her determination to stay single once Tilly had pointed out how wealthy he was.

Still, he supposed if she'd been going to earn her own living, he could see why she'd want to keep control of her own finances. She had already struck him as being a very independent kind of woman.

'If that is what it takes, then, yes. I will make you an allowance which you can spend as you please. The moment the ink is dry on the marriage lines, I will speak to my man of business—'

'You will speak to your man of business *before* I take any vows,' she rapped back.

Perhaps it wasn't a matter of being independent. Perhaps she was simply as avaricious as every other woman he'd ever met. Hell, he didn't know any more.

The only thing he did know was that he wanted this nightmare of a day to be over.

'Fine,' he said wearily. 'I will make the necessary arrangements. Only, not right now. Right now, I want my dinner and I expect you do, too.'

As if on cue, the butler came in and gave one of those gentle coughs they always seemed to feel necessary to announce their presence.

'I have taken the liberty,' he said, apologetically, 'of preparing a room for Lord Worsley's betrothed. Mrs Cousins has had a bath set out, and procured some fresh clothing.'

'A bath,' said Miss Phillips. 'Oh, yes, I do want a bath. In fact—' she got to her feet '—I really shouldn't have sat on this beautiful chair, in the state I'm in, only...'

Tilly went to her and took her arm. 'I will come up with you and help you settle in,' she said.

And hustled her out of the room.

Well, at least he'd done one thing right. Tilly might be a bit hen-witted, but she had a warm heart. She'd look after Miss Phillips. He could rest easy on that score. For now.

Chapter Seven

Dorothy was about halfway up a flight of stairs when she started shaking.

Tilly put her arm round her waist at once. 'Oh, dear! I should have fed you first. Only it was getting so uncomfortable down there that I was sure…'

'It isn't hunger.' Although she was very hungry. 'I think that it has just struck me that if I marry Lord Worsley, then I shall be a countess.' And she had no idea how to be one.

'I know, isn't it too deliciously funny.' Tilly giggled. 'Only think of Toby abducting a governess, of all things. Why, when I think of the misery we inflicted on ours, many of whom ran screaming from the house… well, let me assure you, you wouldn't have enjoyed being a governess at all.'

'T… Toby?'

'Lord, did I call him Toby? How extraordinary. It has been years since anyone has called him anything but Worsley. He's been the Earl of Worsley ever since he was just a boy, you see. Now, our family name is Spenlow,' she prattled on, as though determined to fill the time they were climbing the stairs with the sound of her voice. 'And he really should have told you all that kind of thing himself. Honestly, I despair of him sometimes. He is *hopeless* at all this sort of thing.' She waved her hand between them in a way that Dorothy interpreted as meaning the social niceties. 'And I do hope you will call me Tilly, since we are about to become sisters-in-law, rather than sticking to Lady Waddesdon, which sounds like the name one would call a dowager duchess, don't you think? Do you have a first name?'

'Yes,' said Dorothy, slightly stunned by Tilly's friendliness. 'It is Dora. I mean, Dorothy, really. Only my family and close friends call me Dora...'

'I shall call you Dora, then. I detest formality, as you have probably already guessed.' She went on chattering all the way to the room in which they found not only the promised bath, steaming on the hearth, but also a maid setting out a substantial supper from a tray.

'Oh, thank you, Peters,' said Tilly to another maid, who was setting out some brushes and a comb on a dressing table. 'And look,' she cried, pointing to the foot of the bed. 'She has even brought one of my nightgowns for you to borrow.'

The maid called Peters dipped a curtsy. 'If you leave your gown over the chair, miss,' she said, waving in the direction of a screen, next to which there was, indeed, a spindly little thing covered in gilt which either of her brothers would have reduced to matchwood in seconds, 'I will have it cleaned and ready for you in the morning.' She pursed her lips. 'If it is beyond rescuing, I believe the gardener's wife would not object to lending you her Sunday best. She is of your height. I do not believe anything of my lady's would fit,' she added, when Tilly looked as though she was about to make an objection.

'Good point,' said Tilly. 'Miss Phillips is much taller than me. Anything of mine would never reach her ankles, never mind doing up round the waist,' she said, smoothing her hand over her trim little figure. And making Dorothy feel like a lumpy, frumpy giantess. 'There is a woman in the village who is frightfully clever with her needle. We shall send for her tomorrow, to make you something fit to wear for your wedding.'

Heavens, yes. She might not ever have dressed in the latest fashion, but even she would hate to get married in something borrowed from a gardener's wife, or indeed what she had on now, even if Peters did somehow manage to get all the stains out. She really did need new clothes if she wasn't going to spend the first few weeks of her married life being mistaken for a governess.

'Well, if you think you can spare me, I will go back downstairs before I miss anything.' She gave Dorothy a rather impish grin before darting out.

Once left to herself, Dorothy ate every scrap of food from the tray, before stripping off and plunging, with sheer relief, into the bath of by now tepid water. Nothing had ever felt as good as sponging off the dirt of two days and emerging fresh and sweet smelling once more.

Wrapped in a towel, she then went to the bed, where there was what Tilly described as a nightgown and wrapper, but which looked to Dorothy like two completely inadequate scraps of lace interspersed with narrow strips of silk. She picked one of them up. Surely, people didn't wear such insubstantial garments to bed, did they? Even the panels of silk were almost as revealing as the lace, being so fine that light shone right through. And how on earth was she to get this on without ripping something? Apart from the fact that everything had about as much strength as a cobweb, Tilly was, as the maid had pointed out, much smaller than Dorothy. In every dimension.

But if she didn't at least try, she'd have to sleep in her shift. Her rather sweat-stained shift. And if that maid came in before Dorothy woke in the morning, and saw her in it, she'd assume she'd turned up her nose at what was undoubtedly a very generous loan, preferring to sleep in something dirty.

Dorothy held the nightgown against her body. And that was when she noticed that all the little bows, which she'd assumed were for decoration, were actually a series of ribbon ties. Which meant she could adjust the fit around the bosom and hips. The in between sections didn't cover very much of her, but she would be under the sheets anyway, so who was to see her arms and the lower part of her legs? And it was a warm night. Even if she did feel a draught, she could always pull the curtains round the bed. So she'd hardly notice she wasn't tucked up snugly in her more comfortable, all-encompassing flannel nightgown.

Well, that was what she told herself as she got ready for bed. But she soon discovered that silk felt nothing like flannel against her skin. It sort of slithered warmly across her stomach and thighs, making her feel very aware of those areas. And the lack of that slithering, over her upper arms, made those areas feel extremely naked by comparison. She felt strangely aware of her body in a way she never had before. And not like herself at all.

She didn't think she'd felt like herself since the moment Lord Worsley had picked her up and slung her across his shoulders. He had turned her, literally, upside down. Now he was going to marry her. And, worse, she was going to let him. Because, as he'd pointed out, marrying him would deal not only with any damage he might have caused by his impetuous actions today, it would solve *all* her immediate problems.

He'd promised her an allowance that she could spend however she wished. Which would definitely be larger than the wages she would have earned as a governess. So she'd be able to make sure that the girls, and Paul, had the extras that their schools did not include in the basic cost of their education. And Timothy would be able to finish his degree without worrying about any of them. They would still be scattered across the country, at their various schools, but they would all be secure, which was more than they'd been after Papa had left them practically destitute.

At the time, she'd assumed she'd be able to carry on looking after the younger ones, in a house they could rent…but, no. After all the lectures he'd given about doing her duty, it turned out that he hadn't done his. He hadn't made sure there would be enough money for them to stay together. It had only been thanks to the generosity of various family members that they'd been able to come up with the governess scheme, which had been far from what she, or indeed any of them, had wanted.

But now, if perhaps she could get on Lord Worsley's good side, he might, one day, allow her sisters and brothers to spend their school holidays with her, instead of with the various relatives who'd so grudgingly agreed to take them in.

No, no, she mustn't get her hopes up too much. For one thing, he might not have a good side. And for another, he wasn't likely to agree to having more of her family cluttering up his house when he clearly wasn't really ready to abandon his bachelor lifestyle at all. He'd shown it in every line of his body. The way he'd stood as far from her as possible. The disdain on his face when he'd had to hand her a handkerchief to clean herself up, when she'd dribbled down herself.

And she hadn't helped matters, had she, by arguing with him at every turn? Pointing out his faults?

If only she was the kind of woman who knew how to get round a man. But she wasn't. She was what was known as a managing female and there was no use in trying to pretend otherwise. She'd held the reins of government over her father's household and acted as mother to her younger brothers and sisters ever since she been about ten years old, when their mother had died. It was what had made Timothy say she would be good at being a governess. She stood no nonsense from anyone.

Heavens, Lord Worsley probably already thought she was a shrew, given the way she'd acted tonight. She'd gone beyond *standing no nonsense* to being downright rude. He was probably imagining a lifetime of being thoroughly hen-pecked.

The faint, shimmering image of a sweet little baby, nestling in her arms, wavered and faded away. It might have been the deciding factor, the one thing which had tipped the scales in favour of her accepting his marriage proposal, but there was a long way to go before they could think about that sort of thing. He'd warned her, hadn't he, that he wouldn't be *demanding* and that they'd need time to grow accustomed to the marriage state. She knew full well what that meant.

He couldn't face the thought of bedding her.

Still, it was no use wallowing in what-might-have-beens, or if onlys. Dora was essentially a practical person. And in her experience, all daydreaming ever did was make her more aware of what other people had and she didn't. Much better to think about, well, her duties. And how to perform them well.

And her first duty...oh, dear, but there were so many things she needed to do, given the turn things had taken. So many, she'd better write a list, or she'd never remember them all. Apart from ordering a gown fit for a wedding, there were other, far more practical things she needed. Like a toothbrush and a bonnet, and gloves... She yawned. Fresh stockings and a couple of petticoats, and, actually, better make that a couple of gowns, for who knew how long it might take Lord Worsley to retrieve her trunk? She wouldn't be extravagant, though. Even if he was easily able to afford to outfit her. She didn't want to take advantage... well, not more than she was doing by marrying him. And she could make it up to him by being the very best wife she could be.

At the reminder she was about to become his wife, her mind strayed to a vision of her walking up the aisle to Lord Worsley. Lord Worsley as he'd been the moment Dora first clapped eyes on him, filling the doorway, his head brushing the lintel so that he'd had to duck to come into the room. Then it went to the feel of his shoulders under her waist. Then flitted to the way he'd kept clenching and unclenching his fists while he'd been standing next to her chair downstairs. Then back to the moment he'd held out his hand, the large, linen handkerchief dangling from those strong fingers.

She was going to have to take his hand, metaphorically speaking, in a day or so.

She swallowed, then turned over and buried her face in her pillow, inhaling the clean scent of soap and starch. Poor man. He'd never wanted to marry and now, thanks to his impulsive behaviour, behaviour which stemmed from his completely understandable desire to protect his rather foolish ward, he was going to be saddled with an ungainly, frumpy, shrew. When a man of his rank, and wealth, who also resembled her notion of a Norse god with all that blond hair, and blue eyes, and muscles like steel, could have married anyone to whom he took a fancy.

From what she'd observed of the nature of men, she wouldn't be a bit surprised to learn that directly after she'd left the room, he'd taken to the nearest bottle, and started trying to drown his sorrows.

And on that depressing thought, she finally fell asleep.

What with thinking about Lord Worsley's hands, not long before drifting off, and warm silk slithering over her skin, while feeling hot and half-naked, she ended up having some very disturbing dreams involving those big, strong, yet gentle hands. Dreams that made her feel ridiculously hot and bothered.

And extremely guilty.

Chapter Eight

The next morning, Dora woke to find one maid drawing the curtains and another just coming into the room carrying a tray. As light flooded the room, Dora perceived, for the first time, how very beautifully it was decorated. She'd been too tired the night before to think of more than the steps required to get into bed. A bed which was the most comfortable in which she'd ever slept, once she got used to the lack of covering over her arms and shoulders. The upper classes clearly had a thing about silk, she mused, glancing round at the wallpaper which looked as though it was silk and matched the covering on the chairs dotted about. And if this was how they decorated what was clearly only a guest room, whatever must the family rooms be like?

But she couldn't ponder that issue for long, because the maid with the tray was approaching the bed now and there was a most tantalising smell emanating from it. To be precise, from the small silver pot.

Chocolate.

Dora's mouth began to water. Nobody had ever brought her a pot of hot chocolate in bed before. It was almost worth being thrown over a man's shoulder, and tossed into a carriage, and carted all over the country wrapped in a smelly blanket.

But the chocolate wasn't all. There was a toast rack, containing the most delicate slices of crisp toast, a dish with a generous pat of butter and a little silver dish full of jam.

That was only the start of a couple of days during which she kept on feeling as if she ought to pinch herself to make sure she wasn't dreaming. By now she should have been starting to work for a family she'd never met, in a place she'd never even heard of before the churchwarden's wife had said that if she really wanted to find a job then she should take it, since it was the best she was likely to get without any previous experience, or indeed references.

Instead of which Tilly brought a succession of tradespeople to her room, bearing all sorts of commodities. And she succumbed to the temptation to buy not only the practical things, like toothbrushes and stockings, but lengths of fabric she would never have dreamed of making up into gowns before, which was down to Tilly.

'You will, naturally, do some shopping in London when you are married, but when I take you to my modistes, you won't want them to think you are a dowd, will you?'

'I don't think I particularly care,' she began.

But Tilly was adamant. 'You are about to appear in society as the Countess of Worsley. People are bound to speculate about your sudden advent into Toby's life. But you can at least make them think twice about saying he appears to have taken a misstep, can't you? By making sure you look as though you truly belong at his side.'

Dora didn't think she'd ever feel as if she truly belonged at his side. She wasn't the wife he would have chosen, even if he'd been looking for a wife, which he certainly hadn't been. What was more, she had nothing to recommend her. She wasn't pretty, or feminine, or even from the same social sphere as him. She probably ought to make an effort not to look as dowdy as she usually did so that at least he would not have cause to be ashamed of her. And she had vowed to be the best wife she could be, hadn't she?

With that vow in mind, she ended up buying fabrics and colours she would never, ever have even considered before.

'Now, I hope you won't be offended,' said the local dressmaker, holding out a frivolous confection of mostly amber silk, 'but this here gown was ordered by another client and I have good reason to know she won't be returning for a final fitting. I could have it ready for you to wear by this evening. I would not normally suggest that any friend of my lady's would take something that was ordered by another client, but you did say the need was urgent...'

Dora tried not to wince. Oh, not because the gown had been created for another lady, but because the amber silk overdress was teamed with an underdress of lemon satin. Surely, it would look...gaudy?

But Tilly nodded that she should try it on, so that the dressmaker could make any necessary adjustments. And when she stood before the mirror, critically studying her reflection, she was glad she hadn't spoken her mind.

'Oh,' cried Tilly, clapping her hands. 'That combination of colours is perfect for you. At least, once you have a shawl to drape over your elbows and evening gloves…'

'Yes,' said Dora, regarding the rather girlish little puffed sleeves. 'I do need to cover my arms.'

'Cover them? Gracious, no,' Tilly replied. 'You need to *em*phasise them. They are so shapely and smooth. I would kill to have arms like that, what with the fashion being for short sleeves. Mine look like chicken skin,' she ended on a pout.

Dora had never thought much about her arms, or the consistency of their skin, since they normally stayed safely covered up by layers of cotton, or twill. So it was rather heartening to hear that they were a feature of which she need not be ashamed.

Later that first day, once the flood of merchants had reduced to a trickle, Dora asked for a paper and pen.

She needed to write to the family who had been expecting her to arrive yesterday, explaining…no, apologising to them for her absence.

She needed to write to her younger brother Paul, and her sisters, too, to let them know that instead of going to work as a governess, she was going to become a countess. The letter to the younger ones wouldn't be too hard to write. She could make what had happened sound like one of the adventure stories they loved to read, with a hero sweeping her off her feet the moment he'd clapped eyes on her. The letter to Timothy would be harder, since he would deserve something much closer to the truth, after all the effort he'd put in to finding her the job in the first place. Perhaps she could emphasise the fact that Lord Worsley had mistaken her for someone else, while trying to save his younger relation from taking a disastrous step. Yes, for Timothy would understand a man taking drastic steps on behalf of his younger, dependant relations, since that is exactly what he'd urged her to do. He would also understand a man attempting to put right what he'd done wrong, by offering to marry her.

She hoped.

Dinner that evening would be informal, Tilly had told her, since she only had the gown she'd borrowed from the gardener's wife to wear. Waddesdon was polite to her, but reserved. Tilly didn't seem to find his attitude unusual and kept up a flow of inconsequential chatter during the course of which she managed to obtain his agreement to frank all the letters Dora had written that day and any more she might care to write in future.

The next day passed in a similar fashion to the first, except that the village dressmaker was able to deliver a couple of finished gowns. Tilly insisted that Dora wear the amber silk, since they expected Lord Worsley to return in time for dinner and she wanted him to see how much they'd achieved in two days.

'And you must let my woman cut and dress your hair,' she added.

By this time, Dora had decided it was pointless to argue. Tilly was having so much fun, trying to turn her into the kind of woman who would look as though she had the right to marry an earl. And so she sat meekly down, while the woman set about her with scissors and tongs.

'There,' said Tilly, with a sigh. 'You are finished.'

Dora blinked into the mirror the hairdresser held up to her.

Well, she certainly didn't look like a governess any more. A governess would never wear clusters of little ringlets all round her face, nor coil the rest of it into such a fantastical arrangement on the crown of her head. Especially not a governess who was already far taller than most men.

But Tilly was beaming at her maid and, as a guest in this house, Dora didn't feel as if she could do anything but express her gratitude.

And then it was time to dress for dinner. Would she be seeing Lord Worsley again? She hadn't heard that he'd returned yet.

She swallowed, suddenly wondering if he would bother coming back. Might he just leave her here?

The maid who brought in her breakfast helped her to get ready while Tilly dashed off to her own room.

'Would you mind just checking in the mirror before you go down, miss?' asked the maid nervously. 'This is the first time I've dressed such a grand lady as yourself and I wouldn't want you to think…that is… I just hope I've done all to your satisfaction.' She dropped a curtsy.

With a sigh, Dora turned to the mirror, which she'd been avoiding ever since the shock of seeing what the hairdresser had done to her hair.

Well, she decided after a swift glance at herself, thanks to Tilly's efforts she did, now, look a bit more like the kind of woman Lord Worsley might have considered marrying. What with the new hairstyle and the expensive and stylish outfit she looked… She tilted her head and tried to be objective. She looked elegant and fashionable.

Which made her want to laugh. She was a vicar's daughter, for heaven's sake. Not a fashionable lady. Even if she did have smooth skin. It was the clothes, that was all.

'Thank you, Maud,' she said to the maid. 'You have done well.'

How did that saying go? About fine feathers making fine birds? She might look like a fashionable person, but inside she was the same as she'd always been. And she very much doubted if anything could change her.

She went down to the drawing room with her head held high and her shoulders back. If Lord Worsley had not returned, she was not going to let anyone know she cared. And if he had, she would *not* yield to the temptation to apologise for ruining his life. His was not the only life at stake in the business. If he hadn't wanted to marry her, he shouldn't have insisted.

She need not have agreed to marry him, though...

But then marrying him meant she would be able to provide so much better for her brothers and sisters than she would ever have been able to dream of if she'd stuck to her resolution about becoming a governess.

Although that wasn't the only reason she'd yielded, was it? She'd always had reservations about taking a job as a governess. And then there was the hope she now had, albeit a faint one, that agreeing to marry Lord Worsley meant that, one day, she might have a baby of her own to hold...

'Ah, Miss Phillips,' said Tilly, bustling over to her the moment she stepped into the room. 'You do look lovely. Tell her how lovely she looks, Waddesdon,' she said to her husband.

'You do, of course,' he said with a slight bow. 'But I would much rather repeat my offer to provide you with sanctuary, should you have changed your mind about marrying Lord Worsley. And who could blame you, after the abominable treatment you have received at his hands?' His nostrils flared in distaste. 'My wife is inclined to find the incident amusing. But I cannot take such an outrageous act with levity. If all men were to go around abducting females in his high-handed manner...'

'Oh, shush, dear,' said Tilly. 'You will put Miss Phillips out of countenance.'

'No, please,' put in Dora. 'Marrying him is for the best.' For herself. He wasn't going to gain anything from the union. She almost felt as if she was taking advantage of him. But she couldn't back out now. There were her brothers and sisters to consider.

'Do not worry about me. I am not made of such poor stuff that a little adventure like that could overset me. At no time did Lord Worsley make me afraid, not truly afraid, or not of him, anyway. I could see that he was driven to do what he did out of concern for his ward. And since I have younger brothers and sisters I can totally understand that feeling of being willing to go to any lengths to protect them.'

'See?' Tilly turned to her husband with a triumphant expression. 'She is a perfect match for him. It is fate, that is what it is.'

The conversation promptly ceased then, because the butler flung open the door and announced Lord Worsley. He'd come back!

Her sensation of relief didn't last long because he looked utterly magnificent in his evening attire. She'd already known that there was an awful lot of him, and that all of it was extremely muscular, but tonight, for some reason, the way he ran his eyes over her made her aware of how very male he was. And how very lacking as a female she was. She might be draped in silk and satin, and have a new hairstyle, but underneath it all she was the same person she'd always been. Too tall, too opiniated, too…*man*nish in her ways.

And yet she was about to become this man's wife. Their lives would be intertwined, for ever. And she knew next to nothing about him. Was he a Tory or a Whig? Was he devout, or did he merely conform to the outward appearance of religion? Was he kind? Did he gamble? Was he a libertine? Tilly had mentioned expensive mistresses, which made her suspect he might be. Although from what she heard, men of his rank were more inclined to indulge in that particular vice than the lower orders. Although that was probably only because the lower orders couldn't afford it.

He had stopped Tilly from speaking about those kinds of relationships, though, so perhaps he did possess some sensitivity.

Or was she, now she'd agreed to marry this handsome stranger, clutching at straws?

Chapter Nine

She looked magnificent.

Tilly had found her a gown that brought out her stunning figure, with one of those cross-over bodices that drew a man's eye to her cleavage. Which in turn made him recall what those full breasts had felt like against his back, which he was free to do now that he knew she didn't belong to another man.

He tore his eyes away before he could embarrass her, or at least he hoped so, and noticed Waddesdon looking down his thin, aristocratic nose at him. He lifted his chin and looked straight back at him with the advantage of his added inches. They locked gazes for a moment or so and for once Worsley had no trouble understanding what the man was thinking. Or what he wished he could say and indeed would have said if there hadn't been ladies present.

Tilly brought the silent hostilities to a close by coming over, reaching up and planting a kiss on his cheek.

'Well, what do you think?' She waved a hand in the direction of Miss Phillips, who was standing stock still, head up, shoulders back and cheeks flushed. 'Haven't I wrought a miracle?'

'No,' he snapped. She'd simply brought out Miss Phillips's best features, that was all. Decked her out in clothes that suited her, rather than ones designed to conceal her figure.

'Toby, really,' said Tilly, 'that is a most ungallant thing to say.'

Miss Phillips clearly thought so, too, because her chin had gone up a notch and her eyes were shimmering with some emotion that could have been either anger or hurt. See? This was why he'd never wanted to marry. He would always blunder about, wounding a sensitive female.

Waddesdon closed his eyes and shook his head.

'We have spent the entire time you've been away,' Tilly complained, 'scouring the locality for clothes and having her hair cut, so that your bride can look beautiful for your wedding—'

'She was already beautiful before you rigged her out in that get-up,' he snapped, shocking his voluble sister into silence. 'I suppose I can see that it is more stylish…'

'Yes—apparently,' said Miss Phillips frostily, adjusting the shawl which was dangling precariously from her crooked elbows, 'horse blankets are not *in* this year.'

Waddesdon made a noise that sounded suspiciously like a smothered chuckle. Tilly rounded on him and took a breath, but before anyone could really get going, the butler came to the rescue by announcing that dinner was served.

He went to Miss Phillips and held out his arm. 'Allow me to escort you in to dinner,' he said.

A look flashed across her face. It made him wonder if she was thinking of telling him she was perfectly capable of walking to another room without the help of any man, thank you very much, particularly not one as odious as him. But then her eyes flicked to where Tilly was laying her own hand upon her husband's sleeve and after a brief struggle with herself, the only outward sign of which involved a tightening of the lips, she followed suit.

She might have taken his arm, but she didn't deign to look at him during the short walk to the dining room. She even managed to ignore him while he saw her seated, before taking his place beside her.

It wasn't surprising, really. She hadn't had long enough to get over the way he'd snatched her up and thrown her into his carriage like a sack of coal, brutally overturning all her plans. And she'd spent the whole time with Tilly, who never stopped talking. And to cap it all he'd annoyed her by not paying her fulsome compliments on the effect she'd taken such pains to create.

It said something about the strength of her character that she was at this table at all, rather than lying, prostrate somewhere, alternately weeping and making use of a vinaigrette.

Her face was flushed, though, and she was alternately fiddling with her cutlery, or plucking at the shawl which was forever sliding from her arms. Which made him suspect she was nervous of him, as well as cross with him.

He signalled to one of Waddesdon's footmen to fill his wine glass. He wouldn't blame her for feeling either of those things. Though she could scarcely be any angrier with him than he was with himself. What sort of man would think it acceptable behaviour to abuse his superior strength, by picking up a woman and depositing her where she'd had no intention of going? It was of no use arguing that he'd thought he was acting in her best interests. That he'd intended to save her from disgrace and ruin, and return her to her parents by whatever means necessary. For she hadn't been the one who'd needed saving.

Nor could he dare hope that she would ever reach the point of forgiving him. Or, if she did, which she might try to do since she was a vicar's daughter, that she would return the regard he was already starting to feel for her.

Regard? He shook his head at himself. Why not call his feelings exactly what they were? Admit that many of them were far from respectable. But no matter how often he vowed to do better and demonstrate to Miss Phillips that he was a gentleman, not a savage, the moment he'd seen her tonight, he'd…

He set down his wine glass, surprised to find it empty. And that the footmen had set several removes on the table.

He had to pull himself together.

'May I help you,' he said, turning to Miss Phillips, 'to some chicken?'

'Thank you,' she replied, without lifting her head to look at him.

As he placed slices of meat on her plate, he couldn't help noticing that she didn't smell of horse tonight, but of soap and clean linen. Not that it had made any difference when she had smelled of horse. The only difference was that instead of wanting to lick peach juice from her chin, he wanted to place these slices of chicken directly into her mouth so that she could lick the juices from his fingers.

Good God above, he had to suppress these inappropriate thoughts. Or at least, not let her suspect he was imagining doing so many intimate things to her, or she'd run for the hills. He might well be relieved to discover that he found the woman he was obliged to marry so alluring. But it would be different for her. A man could easily contemplate bedding a woman he found physically attractive. But a gently reared woman could not simply tumble into bed with any man, even if she did like the way he looked. Not that she'd given any sign that she did like anything about him. Well, why would she? He was a stranger. A stranger who had, moreover, treated her shabbily.

It was more than likely that she would be dreading the approaching nuptials. Nevertheless, he had to discuss a few matters of business with her. And then put her mind at rest about his intentions about what would follow. Even though he found her attractive and could easily consider making their marriage a full, normal one, in due course, he was not going to demand what clergymen termed his conjugal rights straight away.

For the last two days, while he'd been dashing about all over the place making the necessary arrangements, he'd been alternately cursing himself for a brute and wondering how on earth he could ever atone. In the end he'd decided that he'd just have to treat her the way he'd treat a highly spirited and unbroken mare. Not make any sudden moves. Not give her any reason to be even more nervous of him than she already was. He'd do the equivalent of putting her in a lush pasture, where she could graze in peace until she'd grown used to her new surroundings. He only hoped that, as with a horse, he'd be able to judge the moment when he could approach her with bit and bridle, as it were.

And if that moment never came?

Well, he'd never intended to marry anyway. They'd have to come to some agreement as to how to conduct their lives along parallel, but separate, lines. The prospect was unappealing, but at least reminding himself that it might come to that, if he didn't get things right with her to start with, helped him to sustain a reasonable and polite attitude throughout the meal. Which was all anyone could do, in such a situation, with so many servants flitting about the place.

Tilly and her husband led the way and he followed along several courses of completely banal topics, although Miss Phillips never managed to contribute more than a few subdued commonplaces. She hardly ate a thing, either. And when Tilly asked if she had finished and would like to withdraw, she set her cutlery down with an air of profound relief.

The moment the ladies had left the room, Waddesdon's polite facade dissolved.

'I must say, Worsley,' he began, menacingly.

'You cannot possibly say anything I haven't already thought myself.'

'Hmmph. Well, before we join the ladies, let me tell you—'

'Don't want to hear it,' said Worsley, getting to his feet. Waddesdon might be senior to him by a few years, but he was damned if he was going to meekly allow the man to ring a peal over him as though he were a scrubby schoolboy. 'Anything that is worth saying should be said to Miss Phillips,' he said, making for the door. Leaving Waddesdon with no alternative but to follow him.

Miss Phillips was standing by the piano, behind Tilly, who was sifting through the sheet music just as though this were merely one of her typical evenings at home.

'I hope,' he said, 'you are not going to make Miss Phillips turn the pages for you. I need to talk to her.'

'And you shall,' said Tilly sweetly. 'But I fail to see why we cannot be civilised—'

Miss Phillips's brows shot up, as though the last thing she expected from him was an attempt to be civilised.

'Miss Phillips needs to know exactly how things stand,' he argued. 'I have no intention of keeping her waiting while you string out the drama of the situation. Won't you,' he said to Miss Phillips, 'sit with me, so that we may discuss…things?'

Her chin went up. She looked as though she was thinking about insisting on playing the piano for a good half hour just to keep him kicking his heels. But then she appeared to relent and contented herself with glowering at him as she made her way to the chair nearest to where he was standing.

'I have procured the licence,' he said, the moment she was sitting down, 'and spoken to the vicar of St Andrew's, who has agreed to marry us tomorrow. After my man of business has been to call on you.'

'Tomorrow?' Tilly slapped the sheet music down on top of the piano. 'But the dressmaker hasn't finished her wedding gown, let alone—'

'It hardly matters what Miss Phillips wears,' he said, eyeing the gown she was wearing right now and wondering why she couldn't simply wear that. She looked lovely in it. Waddesdon winced, then went over to a sofa at the far end of the room, sat down and folded his arms across his chest as though determined to hold his peace.

'But time,' Worsley continued, 'is of the essence. The sooner we get the deed done, and post the notice in the *Gazette*, the sooner we can look everyone in the eye.'

He couldn't, in all conscience, leave her prey to speculation and gossip, should anyone learn of her presence in his sister's house, one moment longer than absolutely necessary.

'And then you will present her to society? Oh,' cried Tilly, clapping her hands, 'I could introduce her about. I would love to. Would you like that, Miss Phillips?'

'Um…' she began, as though choosing a tactful way to tell his sister that it was the last thing she wanted. Which showed sense. She had never been to London before. And it wasn't easy for any young bride to find her feet in what could be a cut-throat world. Let alone a bride who knew next to nothing about her husband. Apart from bad things. He had swooped down and carried her off like some Viking marauder, after all. It said a great deal about her character that she hadn't slapped, or scratched, his face. Instead, she'd behaved, on the whole, with impressive dignity. In time, she would be an impressive countess, he had no doubt—if she wanted to take to the role. But he wasn't going to put any pressure on her to do anything she did not want to do. Apart from marrying him, that was.

'Far too soon for that,' he said. 'Miss Phillips will need time, and space, to get used to the change in her

circumstances before we pitchfork her into society.'
Time to learn that he was not the brute she must think
him, for one thing.

'I have a tongue in my head, you know,' she snapped.
'I might have an opinion of my own, if either of you
would take the trouble to ask me for it.'

She flushed, then, and hung her head. 'I beg your
pardon, that was rude of me. I know that both of you
are only trying to do your best for me.'

Yes, but they were still treading all over her. Her response put him in mind of a small, frightened terrier,
nipping at a bigger dog that posed a threat. It confirmed
his theory that she was frightened and lashing out the
only way she knew how. With words. At least, he would
rather think that of her than assume she had a naturally
shrewish disposition. A part of him was hoping that if
he gave her the benefit of the doubt, she might extend
the same courtesy to him. The truth was that so far,
neither of them had seen the other at their best. But he
had glimpsed several hopeful signs in her...

But anyway, he'd much rather be married to a
woman who spoke up for herself than one who resorted
to tears and tantrums to get her own way. To his way
of thinking, that was more honest and straightforward.

In time, when he'd proved that she had nothing to
fear from him, she would, hopefully calm down.

And if she didn't, then he had nobody to blame but
himself for ending up with a shrewish wife.

'Think nothing of it,' said Tilly. 'You have had the
most trying time and neither of us is renowned for our
tact.' Tilly scurried over to Miss Phillips and put one
arm round her shoulders, while he stood, looking down

at the crown of her head, wondering what sort of character she really had.

'Very well then, Miss Phillips,' he said. 'I shall tell you what I propose and then you can let me have your opinion of it. A full broadside if you like. I can take it.'

Miss Phillips slowly lifted her head and looked up at him. A wry smile tugged at her mouth. 'I shall try not to sink your suggestions out of mere temper,' she said.

'Good girl,' he replied.

Waddesdon placed one hand over his eyes as he shook his head, though the man need not have bothered. As soon as the words left his mouth he could tell they had been the wrong ones from the way Miss Phillips's tentative smile vanished and her eyes narrowed.

'What I suggest,' he began, since in his experience if he attempted to apologise for offending her, he'd be floundering about all night without getting anywhere, 'is that we commence our married life down at Maybush House, in Essex, so we won't be far from London should you wish to go there to do some shopping. I am aware that you have not had much time to purchase what you must need. And it won't look odd, either, since most of the polite world will be leaving Town soon to go to the country for the summer. Or somewhere like Brighton.'

'Goodness, Worsley, that's really rather clever of you,' put in Tilly.

'Thank you, but it is not your opinion that matters at the moment, but that of Miss Phillips.'

'I...' Miss Phillips began, hesitantly, glancing from him to Tilly. 'I think it is a good idea to go into the country to begin with. Later, I should love you to be the one to introduce me to society,' she said to Tilly.

'But it will definitely be easier for me to become accustomed to…er…being married out of the public eye.'

'Essex it is, then,' he said. 'I should point out that it is not one of my larger properties. I only suggested it for the convenient location and because it should afford you plenty of privacy.'

She suddenly sat a little straighter. 'Not one of your—you mean, you have more than one house?'

'I do,' he said gravely. 'Besides Maybush House, there is my town house in London, my country seat in Sussex, my racing stables in Suffolk and a couple of places in the far north, although they are let out at the moment.'

'You cannot possibly use all those houses?' she said, looking at him with a frown.

'No, but I visit them all from time to time.'

'Yes, but who lives in them when you are not visiting?'

'Just a few members of staff, to keep the places habitable for when I do visit.'

A strange look came over her face. It was not precisely hunger. Not precisely excitement. But it made something inside him twist in disappointment. Because the only time she ever appeared to show any enthusiasm for their match was when the topic of his wealth, or his property, came up.

Well, wasn't that the way of the world? Most people of his class only married for financial gain, or increased social status. He ought to be glad that there was something about him that made her think of him with less revulsion. Something that made the prospect of marrying him more appealing.

It was the height of folly to wish that it was something about him, as a man, that could put that look on her face, rather than what he possessed.

Chapter Ten

Worsley's man of business waited on her first thing the next morning. When he told her how much money his employer meant to give her, Dora was glad she was sitting down. Especially when he explained that, no, it wasn't an annual allowance, but a quarterly one.

Her heart began hammering in her chest. It was like a fairy tale. One where wishes came true.

Never mind paying for extras at school. Dora could probably buy a school outright with the amount of money she was soon to have at her disposal. No, no, she didn't want to buy a school. But there would certainly be enough to put aside to provide dowries for her sisters, so that they wouldn't have to go out to work, unless they wanted to. She could even take them out of school altogether and hire a governess... No, perhaps not. Because there was Paul to consider and he'd need a tutor...but then, she could afford to hire a tutor, as well, couldn't she? Especially as there would be no need to hire a house for them to live in. Lord Worsley had empty ones, scattered all over the place. Might she be able to make one of them a home, a proper home, for all of them? Was there a chance that she could reunite them all again?

Her mind was a veritable whirlpool of gratitude and disbelief at her good fortune, and hope, and guilt for getting so much out of him when she had so little to give in return, as she prepared for the ceremony. She was still in a bit of a daze when she stepped into the carriage that was to carry her to the village church nearby.

She was going to walk down the aisle on the arm of a lord, to marry another one, after which she would be a countess!

Oh, how she wished her family could see her now.

If only it was her father walking her down the aisle and not the rather disapproving Lord Waddesdon.

Although her father would probably not approve either. He'd told her she was to put any thoughts of marriage aside until the younger girls were settled. *You are the oldest. It is your duty to put their needs first*, his voice seemed to echo with each step she took.

I am putting their needs first, she answered him. She'd be able to do much more for them, as a countess, than she'd ever have been able to do as a governess.

But, oh, dear, how could she help wondering what it might have been like to walk down the aisle, on the arm of a father who…who wanted *her* to be happy? To a groom whose face would light up when she reached his side? And to be marrying a man she couldn't live without, rather than because she'd seen that he was the best option for her brothers and sisters?

What about her? When would she be the first in someone's life?

Stop it, Dora! It wasn't as if she was giving up anything she'd really wanted, was it? Would she really have preferred going to work as a governess, for a set of people she didn't know, who could all be totally horrid? Hardly seeing her brothers and sisters again, because governesses didn't have the luxury of holidays, or the funds to travel the length and breadth of the land whenever they felt like it.

And honestly, marrying a man who looked as though he'd stepped out of the pages of a story book, with his golden blond hair and his broad chest, and those shoulders the width of a mantelpiece, as well as the bluest eyes she'd ever seen, and whose character had led him to go to the enormous lengths of sacrificing his bachelor status, just to save her from any repercussions from his temporary bout of insanity, was not going to be such a hardship, was it? That timely reminder meant that by the time she reached the altar, she had managed to muster a tremulous smile and only needed to dab just one tear from her eye, with the tip of one of the new gloves Tilly had bought her.

Her heart was hammering hard, though. And once she darted a glance up at his face and saw how tense, stern and uncomfortable he was looking, her stomach contracted, too, making her feel a touch unwell.

The vicar didn't help matters. He looked as though he was itching to be elsewhere and read the words as though he might get a prize for getting through it in record time. And what with Lord Waddesdon's air of reserve, her groom's grim face and her own guilty conscience, she grew increasingly uncomfortable.

But at last the service ended, and the vicar pronounced them man and wife. Tilly just managed to give her a brief hug before Worsley took her arm with a proprietorial air, before striding down the aisle and out to where his carriage was waiting.

He'd warned her that he planned to leave straight after the ceremony, and take her to Essex so she wasn't surprised when he handed her into the carriage—a carriage with which she was all too familiar—before mounting up on to a horse that had been tethered behind.

She was surprised, however, by the transformation to the interior. Last time she'd been in it, no effort had been made to see to her comfort. But this time, instead of a smelly horse blanket, tossed to her as an afterthought, there were soft lap rugs and a picnic hamper strapped to the seat opposite hers, and even posies of flowers fastened into the brackets for the lamps and the window straps, filling the air with a sweet fragrance.

She couldn't help smiling. For it was as if he was showing her that he intended to do everything differently, this time. That he was acknowledging each of his errors and doing practical things to make up for them.

Who would have guessed that he had such a thoughtful side? Although, she'd already perceived that beneath his high-handed, rather brusque manners he held some very commendable principles. Or he wouldn't have gone to the lengths of marrying her, in order to right the wrong he'd done her. Yes, he was a man who preferred *doing* to talking. Unless…had all this been Tilly's doing? Her attempt to make everything seem… romantic?

That would be far more likely than that he'd thought

of it all himself. Because he hadn't wanted a wife at all, had he?

She'd better not read too much into the flowers and the food. There was no point in getting her hopes up only to have them dashed. She would, instead, be thankful that he wasn't sulking, or... She glanced out of the carriage window. Or perhaps he was. That would explain why he was riding his horse, out there, rather than...

But at least he wasn't flinging bitter words at her about ruining his life, was he? He might well be putting a bit of distance between them, rather than travelling in the carriage with her, to make sure he wouldn't be tempted. He'd said, hadn't he, that they would both need time to get used to the idea of being married.

Perhaps he'd get used to it quicker if she kept out of his way, too. He'd probably appreciate it if she kept very much in the background, so that he'd hardly notice he had a wife at all.

The scenery she could make out through the window went blurry then, but not for long. For Dora was a firm believer in finding something to be thankful for. She wouldn't have survived her younger years if she hadn't reminded herself, over and over again, that it didn't matter so much that she couldn't go for walks when she chose, or any of the other things that other girls her age enjoyed, for there were families nearby who were far worse off than she was. She always had enough to eat and a roof over her head that didn't leak. Though her father might be strict, he wasn't addicted to drink, or anything like that. So, even if her husband didn't particularly like the idea of being married to her, at least she wasn't going to have to be a governess. And she might be able to gather her family about her again.

It didn't feel like very much later when they stopped to see to the horses, and Worsley opened the carriage door and put his head inside.

'How are you faring in here? I wonder if I should have chosen an open carriage to convey you to Essex since the weather is so hot. You must be stifled in here. Only I thought that you would prefer a bit of privacy. You have always struck me as being the kind of woman who dislikes drawing attention to herself and the people round Tilly's place would have all gawped at you as you drove through…'

Goodness. She'd never heard him string so many words together before. And all of them conveying his concern for her welfare. Time to start showing him that she wasn't going to be a troublesome, complaining, demanding wife.

'It is a bit stuffy, but I had the sense to pull down a window a bit, see?' She indicated the near side door, the panel of which she'd lowered several miles before. 'Just enough to admit a bit of a breeze, without too much dust.'

'Yes, the road is very dry. Hard going. I hope you are not being jolted too much.'

'I am a good traveller. Fortunately.'

The moment she said that last word she regretted it. It brought back memories of the indignities she'd suffered on her first trip in this coach. It reminded him of the same thing, to judge from the way he shut his mouth firmly and withdrew a couple of inches.

'I, ah—this may be a good time to open the picnic I

had Tilly's cook pack for you. You should find something in it you will enjoy.' Taking a breath, as though steeling himself to do something very daring, he leaned into the coach again and flicked open the buckle holding the picnic hamper closed.

The first thing she saw was a dish of peaches.

'Oh. You remembered,' she said, darting him a shy smile.

He looked at the peaches, then at her mouth—and sort of froze.

Dorothy suddenly remembered the juice which had run down her chin and the way he'd handed her a handkerchief before swiftly withdrawing his hand. It looked as though he was remembering the same incident, because he was doing it again. Withdrawing, clearing his throat and looking constrained again, whereas a moment before he'd been almost…friendly.

Bother. He'd been trying to treat her as though she was truly a lady, deserving of such consideration, but all it had taken was one glance at a peach to remind him that she had no rank and no table manners. No wonder he was taking her to a house out in the country, well away from anyone who might matter. No wonder he'd shut her in a closed carriage so that nobody could see the woman he'd been obliged to marry.

For the rest of the journey, her spirits were a bit low. She'd got carried away by the flowers and the picnic hamper, that was what she'd done. In spite of warning herself not to do any such thing she had taken them as signs that he was mellowing to the prospect of having her as a wife. No, it had begun earlier than that. She'd started to entertain hopeful thoughts the night before, immediately after he'd said she was beautiful. No man had ever considered her beautiful before and even the irritable way he'd said it hadn't been able to prevent the compliment going to her head.

But he'd probably only been trying to mitigate his unfortunate remarks about the gown she'd been wearing. Which had, truthfully, been too girlish for a woman like her, with its silly little puffed sleeves. And too fine for a vicar's daughter, even if she was on the verge of becoming a countess. You just couldn't make a silk purse out of a sow's ear and that was the truth.

Well, she sniffed, and straightened up from the slouching position into which her heavy thoughts had pressed her, she wouldn't get carried away on flights of fancy like that again. She wouldn't assume anything, from any of his behaviour, or any chance remark he might make. She would be practical and sensible. And remind herself that she was the sort of woman who became a governess, not a wife. And most definitely not a countess.

The house, when they finally reached it, was not at all what she'd been expecting. Worsley had described it as small, but it was at least four times the size of the vicarage where she'd grown up. It was set at the end of a driveway that was about a half a mile long. It looked as though it was Elizabethan, or possibly Jacobean, because there was more red brick than timber in its construction, and it had barley twist chimneys and those windows made up of lots of tiny diamond-shaped panes of glass.

'Welcome to Maybush House,' said Worsley, open-

ing the door of the carriage, and holding out his hand
to help her down.

The moment she took it she experienced a jolt of
longing that pierced to her core. Oh, dear. It had done
her no good at all to decide to be sensible. Not when he
was so handsome. So compelling as a man. Oh, how she
wished they could have met in different circumstances.
And that she was pretty and dainty, or had even the
remotest idea of how to dress to make herself look…

She tore her eyes from his face, lest he notice the
effect he had on her. Because it would be too humiliating if he discovered that she found him wildly attractive, when she must hold as much appeal for him as a
windfall crawling with wasps. As she turned her head,
she noticed a group of people standing by the studded
oak front door, which stood open.

'Oh, I see your staff are waiting to greet you,' she
said.

'Our staff,' he corrected her. 'And they are waiting
to meet their new mistress.'

He walked her to the door, and introduced her to Mrs
Warren, a rather hatchet-faced woman he described as
the cook-housekeeper.

Having bobbed a curtsy, Mrs Warren briefly introduced the rest of the staff. They consisted of a scullery
maid and a youth she described as the boot boy, and a
trio of wizened men who were 'outdoors'.

'I suppose you want to go to your room,' said Mrs
Warren with a faint, but nevertheless perceptible air of
resentment, 'to freshen up after the journey.'

What Dora felt she ought to say was *'if that is not
too much trouble'*. But if she began by being apologetic,
the woman would gain the upper hand from the outset.

And Dora might only be the Countess by accident, but she was not going to provide anyone with the proof she was not up to the job.

'Thank you,' she therefore said.

'I know my way about,' said Worsley. 'So I will leave you in Mrs Warren's capable hands while I go and see the horses stabled.'

She supposed, since there were only three outdoor staff and at least one of them must be a gardener, and Worsley's coach was drawn by four horses, it made sense for him to...

No, it didn't. He had brought his taciturn groom with him, as well as a coachman. Surely they could...

She bit her lip. She'd made up her mind she wasn't going to be a demanding sort of wife, so she must not start clinging to him the moment they got here simply because the housekeeper was in a bad mood.

'I shall see you,' she therefore said, in as sweet, yet confident a tone as she could muster, 'at dinner then?'

'Dinner will be at six,' put in Mrs Warren before Worsley could so much as nod or shake his head. 'We don't keep town hours at Maybush House.'

'Of course not,' said Dora, as Worsley, having given Mrs Warren a brief nod, went striding off in the wake of the carriage, which was disappearing round the corner of the building.

'I've put you in the room that has always been used by the mistress of Maybush House,' said Mrs Warren over her shoulder as she started up the broad oak staircase which led to the darkly panelled upper floors. 'And His Lordship is in the room next over, according to tradition. If you would prefer something else, you have only to say,' she declared, with a touch of defiance as she flung open a dark, plain oak door and gestured for Dora to inspect the room on the other side of it. 'We have another three rooms on this floor as I could have made fit, if I'd had more notice of your intention to come here.'

Three more rooms? On this floor alone? That was one each, already, for Mary, Martha and even Paul! 'I shall have to look them over,' she said, seeing the prospect of making a real home for them all, right here, coming a step closer.

'Well, I shan't have time to show you anything today,' snapped Mrs Warren. 'I've the dinner to see to yet and only that Julie to help out and if I'm not standing over her every moment…' She paused to draw breath. 'It was all I could do to air and make up these two rooms and send to Frinsham for something fit to serve His Lordship for dinner…'

'I can see that our sudden decision to come down here has put you to a great deal of trouble,' said Dora, finally understanding why Mrs Warren was so cross. 'But this room is lovely,' she added, having briefly glanced round and taken in a rather charming and very old four-poster bed, a selection of sturdy and equally ancient furniture and a view from the window over an expanse of lawn bordered by a belt of venerable trees. 'You can show me round the house properly tomorrow and let me know what you require in the way of extra staff, and so on, while we are staying here.'

'Hmmph,' said Mrs Warren, folding her arms across her waist. 'I shall send the lad up with water for your wash. Dinner at six,' she said, as though to remind Dora not to be late. And then she turned on her heel and bustled away.

Chapter Eleven

Dora had half expected dinner to be little more than a roast chicken and a few over-boiled vegetables, given Mrs Warren's attitude. But when she went downstairs promptly at six, and found her way to the dining room, she saw that, if nothing else, the woman knew how to produce a dinner.

There were several raised pies, a fricassee of rabbit and a ham, as well as a neatly jointed chicken. And an impressive array of side dishes.

'I will stay here tonight, if you have no objection,' said Worsley, as he handed her to her chair. 'The day is too far spent for me to wish to continue.'

Continue? But she'd thought, when he'd said they were to begin their married life in the country, that they would be *together*. Now it sounded as though he'd never had any intention of doing more than…than depositing her well out of the way.

She took a deep breath. She was not going to complain. Not going to demand anything from him.

'Why should I object?' He'd given her his name. And a home. And a generous allowance. She had no right to expect him to give of his time, too. Nor would she ask him for anything he did not wish to give. 'This is your property. Surely, you may do as you please.'

'From now on, I want you to think of this as *your* home. Your word will be law here. You are its absolute mistress, from this moment on. Do you understand?'

'Yes,' she said. Oh, yes, she understood all right. He was depositing her here and, once he'd gone, she might hardly ever see him again.

Oh, how easy it was, if you were wealthy, to get round the inconvenience of taking on an unwanted wife. Why, all you had to do was take her to one of your *smaller* properties, then leave her to get on with her life while you got on with yours.

Although why she should feel resentful she couldn't think. She'd known from the outset that he didn't really want her. Could never want her. And she hadn't married him for…for *that*, anyway.

No, she'd married him because it was the best way, given the circumstances, to continue being able to provide for her younger siblings. Which she would certainly be able to do, in this house. There was plenty of room for them all. She glanced round at the sturdy, age-darkened furniture which had already survived several generations of enterprising children, by the looks of some of the deep, though polished-over gouges.

And what was more, since he'd just insisted that she was to be absolute mistress here, she wouldn't need to ask his permission to remove the girls from their school immediately and bring them to live here.

She'd have to start looking about for a governess, but then she would have had to hire more staff anyway, since Mrs Warren was clearly struggling. But the allowance he was making her was generous enough to pay for all of them.

Worsley picked up a spoon and helped himself from the tureen of buttered carrots as his wife of less than half a day went off into some sort of reverie. A very pleasant one to judge from the smile playing about her lips. He might not be very perceptive, or so Tilly was always telling him, but even he could see that, for the first time since she'd signed the marriage lines, she was starting to brighten up. And that the change in her had started from the moment he'd told her he was going to leave her here, to do as she pleased.

She'd probably be even better pleased if he told her that he had never had any intention of forcing his beastly self on her, even though it was their wedding night and it was his legal right. But it was not the sort of thing one brought up over the dinner table.

He'd find a better time. Though, when, exactly...

Well, she'd know anyway, when he didn't go to her room. So why speak of it and ruin her mood? One of them might as well be happy tonight.

'I will be on my way at first light tomorrow,' he said. 'So I might not see you to bid you farewell if you are not an early riser.'

'Oh?'

What did that mean, 'oh'? She might express some curiosity about where he was going. Well, never mind, he'd tell her. It might help her to think better of him.

'I'm going to head north to see if I can get wind of

Gregory and that…that is to say, his wife, as I hope she is by now.'

Her face changed at once to an expression of concern. 'I hope you won't be too hard on them.'

'After all the trouble they've caused? I…' She looked at him with a sort of melting expression he found impossible to withstand. 'Oh, very well, I will treat them with kid gloves, since *you* request it.'

Her face lit up. 'Thank you.'

Lord, but she had a dazzling smile. It made a chap want to perform some mighty deed, so he could win another just like it.

'And anyway,' he continued, 'the main reason I am going to track them down is so I can recover your trunk. You looked so upset to hear they'd taken it…'

'I was. Oh, thank you. It isn't that there is anything of great value in it, you understand. Except to me. Some mementoes of my mother. Her prayer book, you know, and the pair of evening gloves she was wearing the night she met Papa. It's not even as if I can wear them. Her hands must have been so tiny…' She gazed down at her own, then, ruefully.

He wasn't given to paying a woman pretty compliments, but even he could see that this was exactly the time when he ought to say something to counteract the poor opinion she had of her charms.

Think, man, think!

'I don't care much for tiny, fluttery females,' he said brusquely. 'To my way of thinking, your hands are much more appealing. They look strong and capable.'

She glanced up at him, her lips pursed. 'Well, thank you for saying so.'

'You sound as though you don't think I mean it.'

He leaned back in his chair, one hand on either side of his plate. 'You may as well know now that I *never* say anything I don't mean. Don't see the point.'

'That,' she said thoughtfully, 'is why people say you are rude?'

'That's about the size of it.'

She gave him a half-smile. 'People say I am too outspoken. For a female.'

'I would rather you were. Then you can tell me when I annoy you. As I'm bound to. I'm not good with people. Horses, yes, I understand horses. But people...' He shook his head.

He'd thought they had parted, that night, on good terms. But she didn't come out to bid him farewell the next morning, even though he'd told her how early she'd have to get up if she didn't want to miss him.

Clearly, it was far too soon to hope she might start showing some signs she wanted to behave like a wife. Although, come to think of it, not even Tilly, who claimed to have a great deal of affection for her lord, was likely to get out of bed before eleven, not even when in the country, not for any reason.

He was expecting too much. Too soon.

But at least over the next few weeks he was too busy to miss the wife he'd never intended to marry. Or wonder what she would be doing with all that money she'd been, mentally, spending in her mind already, rather than attempting to make conversation.

It was three weeks, almost to the day, before he next had a moment to wonder if Miss Phillips—no, Lady Worsley he had to think of her as now—would be amenable to receiving a visit from him. He spent a further few days wondering if he should write and warn her of his intention to visit. Or whether that would sound too high-handed. It might be better if he phrased it as a request. Only then he risked receiving a reply he would not like. She might tell him he would not be welcome. And he'd have to abide by her refusal, since he'd told her she was the absolute mistress of Maybush House.

And of course, he wanted her to feel secure, and in control of her destiny. Only...

Hang it all! He was not normally the kind of man who sat about dithering, for days, over what course of action to take. He never thought twice about doing whatever he felt like doing. Only he'd learned a salutary lesson, hadn't he, when he'd gone blundering into Miss Phillips's life and upending it, because he hadn't stopped to think, or to listen to voices raised in opposition to his own.

Yes, but this wasn't the same. He wasn't going to go barging in and taking over. He was just going to go and see her. Make sure she was faring well. He'd been uneasy about the reception that housekeeper had given her. He didn't like to think of her struggling, alone, with a woman who looked as though she was not going to give up her authority easily. He didn't like to think of her feeling she had to put up with the conditions of a place where she'd never be happy.

And he *was* her husband. He'd taken a vow to cherish her. And how the devil was he supposed to do that when he was in Suffolk and she was in Essex?

He slammed his tankard down on the table, uttered a few terse commands to his butler, strode round to the stables, saddled up his horse, and simply rode down to Maybush House before he came up with any more reasons to stay away. It meant that it was approaching midnight when he got there, and the place was in darkness. Everyone had clearly gone to bed and would of course have locked up before doing so.

As he unsaddled his horse and settled him in for the remainder of the night, he wondered what his wife's reaction would be if he started pounding on the front door to demand entrance. The servants would all wake up in a state of alarm. And then, when he admitted that, no, there was no emergency, he'd just come down on a whim...

Muttering to himself under his breath, he made for the back of the house and soon found a window that yielded to a bit of persuasion and scrambled through it. He then removed his boots and groped his way through the house lit only by the occasional moonbeam streaming in through a window, up to the room he'd stayed in before.

The room next to the one where his wife lay sleeping.

Since nobody was expecting him, the bed was not made up. But it only took a moment to unroll the mattress. And there really was no need for a sheet, or blankets, since the night was mild and the house had never suffered from damp that he knew of. In fact, his room was rather stuffy. So, before he stretched out on the bed, he opened one of the casement windows to let in a breeze. Along with it came the soothing night sounds of the countryside—the soft hoot of an owl, the sharp cry of a vixen.

For the first time since he'd married the woman who would much rather have been a governess, Worsley slid to sleep almost at once. He had the impression, as he was closing his eyes, that the cloud of worries which had been buzzing round his ears for the past few weeks, had taken flight.

He awoke with a start, to the sound of splintering glass and the crash of something landing on the dressing table under the open window, then rolling across the floor.

He sat up, bemused for a moment as to where he was and why it was light when a moment ago it had been as dark as it only ever became in the countryside. As he swung his legs out of the bed, he recalled his moonlit canter down to Essex, and his, at the time, perfectly rational decision to break in rather than announce his arrival. Which meant that the cricket ball which had just come to rest next to his riding boots was unlikely to have been lobbed through his window on purpose to annoy him.

He bent down and picked it up. The only way he was going to find out what the deuce was going on would be to go and find out. And it was of no use poking his head through the window and looking down that way. There were little bits of glass all over that side of the room, which had showered like blossom from the ancient, leaded Tudor window by the looks of it, when the cricket ball had struck it on its way in.

He strode as far as the door before it occurred to him that he ought to put on a shirt, at the very least. His wife was going to be surprised enough to see him as it was, without offending her by striding about the place in his natural state. There was that housekeeper, too. The prospect of coming face to face with her made him take a moment to thrust his legs into his riding breeches, for good measure.

He made short work of the staircase, though he was barefoot, and reached the front hall in less than the shake of a lamb's tail. The door stood open, admitting a fresh, early morning breeze, which blew right through the house, since the back door, too, was open. He went to that back door, since that was the direction from which the cricket ball had come. And there, on the back lawn, he saw the culprits. A trio of children, who were huddled together, arguing, the way children did when they had just done something naughty.

'Who,' he said, leaving the shade of the rear porch and approaching them, 'is responsible for this?'

He tossed the cricket ball up and caught it as he walked across the lawn, so that they'd know exactly what he meant.

The group split apart into three separate units. Two girls in matching pinafores and a gangly schoolboy.

'If it comes to that,' said the boy, taking a stance in front of the girls and looking him up and down with suspicion, 'who are you? And what are you doing in my sister's house?'

'More to the point, you cheeky young scamp, who are you and what are you doing on my property?'

Before the boy could make any excuses, Worsley heard a flurry of footsteps from behind him.

'Oh, Worsley,' came a breathy voice. The voice of his wife. He turned as she came scurrying out of the house and noticed her face was all tense with worry. He also noticed that she was wearing the same gown in which he'd first seen her, the one that made her look like a governess. Good God, was she carrying on with her profession, using his house as her base?

'I am sorry,' she said, coming up to him and laying one hand on his forearm. 'But you did say that I might do whatever I wished with this house. That I could treat it as my home...'

Yes, he had said that. But for some reason, he was finding it hard to say anything. All he could think of was that this was the first time she'd touched him of her own volition. And that it felt... He breathed out, heavily. It would have felt better if she'd been doing it out of affection, or attraction, or some other positive motive, rather than to placate him.

'These are my sisters and one of my brothers,' she said. 'Come and make yourselves known to my husband,' she continued, turning to the children and beckoning. As they came closer he could see they all had the same eyes as her, though set in different-shaped faces.

'Mary is sixteen, Paul, my brother, is fifteen, and Martha is almost twelve.' The sulky boy made a bow and the girls dipped graceful curtsies. 'Now, then,' she said to them, 'apologise for...whatever it is that you have done to result in him having your ball. Oh, dear, have they smashed a window? I told them not to play too close to the house...'

'No, they did not smash a window.' Not technically. 'The ball sailed right through the open window of my bedroom and woke me up, however.'

'Oh, dear!' Her hands flew to her mouth. 'I hope you are not hurt.' She made as though to run her hands over him, to check for injuries. And then stopped, her hands about an inch from his chest. Leaving him wishing he hadn't put his shirt on after all, or that she hadn't realised that she was behaving with such lack of propriety.

'We are sorry, Dora,' said the taller of the two girls. Mary, he reminded himself. 'We didn't think we'd hit the house. We set up stumps right over there by the cedar tree,' she said, pointing at the far side of the lawn.

Dora. He liked that name. It suited her, somehow. And he couldn't keep thinking of her as Miss Phillips, not now he'd married her. Especially since he couldn't get into the habit of thinking of her as Lady Worsley. In his mind, that was his mother.

'But why,' said Dora in exasperation, 'did you have to aim this way? If you had only bowled from the other end...'

'Their ball would have ended up in the garden,' he put in at that point, scanning the gravel path that bordered the formal lawn and separated it from the gardens.

'Or the pond,' said the boy. *Paul.* 'We have already spent a lot of time wading about retrieving balls from that pond,' he said resentfully. 'And come out all covered in green slime. And then we get into trouble for ruining our clothes.'

Ah, yes. He had forgotten about the pond. So, too, must the gardeners if it was full of green slime.

He looked at a makeshift wicket, almost directly under the cedar tree, and raised his brows. 'Did you actually manage to get a ball through my bedroom window, from all the way over there?'

'Not me, sir,' said the boy. 'It was Mary.'

He looked at the taller girl, who was, indeed, the one holding the bat. She lifted her chin, in a gesture so like Dora's that it emphasised the family resemblance.

'I suppose you are going to say that you don't believe me,' she said. 'That I am trying to cover for my brother, or some such nonsense. As if girls can't hit a cricket ball just as well as a boy...'

'I wasn't going to say anything of the sort,' he replied, amused by the way she had gone on the attack before so much as hearing what he had to say on the matter. Which was beginning to look like another family trait. 'I was simply going to suggest that if you must play cricket so close to the house, you would do better to use tennis balls, which won't do any damage.'

'We haven't got any,' said Mary.

'Then,' he said, 'I shall order a crate full to be sent down from London.'

'Oh, why,' said Dora, a look of chagrin crossing her face, 'didn't I think of that?'

The girls both smiled at him, but the boy, who seemed to be determined not to like him, or trust him, shook his head. 'Tennis balls will be even worse. They will go much further and then we'll spend hours searching for them.'

'I had better see about getting you a dog, then. Some form of retriever...'

The boy's face lit up. 'A dog? I've always wanted a dog.'

It never ceased to amaze him how easy it was to turn a lad's scowls into a smile. He'd only ever had to buy Gregory a dog, or later a hunter, or a new pistol, to get him out of the dismals.

His wife, however, did not look the slightest bit mollified.

'If you must bribe the children with dogs,' said Dora, tartly, 'you would do better to promise them a terrier.'

He was not trying to bribe the children. He was just…being a big brother to them. They were his family now, by marriage. So it was his job to provide for them. In fact, he wanted to. Just as he'd wanted to do something to cheer up his young cousin, who'd been so forlorn when he'd first arrived, orphaned, at Brinkley Court, expecting that once they'd met, Worsley would foist him off on to one of his sisters.

'Dora, please say we may have dog,' said the smaller of the girls, who'd been hanging back, eyeing him warily before now.

Which made him see what he'd done. Even though he'd decided he was going to do better with her, this time, he'd marched in and taken over. Again. Worse, he'd interfered in what she must surely consider her own business, without stopping to ask her what she wanted.

Before he could begin to frame a suitable apology, she sighed and rubbed at her forehead in a gesture that spoke of weariness. 'If Worsley is kind enough to get you a dog, or dogs, because I really do think we could do with a terrier to deal with the rats…'

'Rats?' There were rats in this property? He'd abandoned her in a place that was riddled with vermin? Could he do nothing right with this woman?

'There are rats in the wainscoting,' said Dora. 'At least I think it is rats. We can all hear them scampering about at night.'

It was a wonder she hadn't written to him, complaining that his promises were hollow, that he was a callous brute—which she might have known from the way they'd met—that she wished she'd never met him…

'Yes, but what conditions,' said the boy, eyeing both

adults warily, 'are you going to lay down for us having a dog each?'

'Nobody said anything about you *each* having a dog of your own,' said Dora. '*One* retriever, and *one* terrier, is more than enough. And I was going to stipulate that you train them and look after them yourselves.'

'We will, we will,' cried all three at once.

'No, you won't,' she said, with exasperation, which still had an underlying trace of fondness. 'Or at least, you might while you are here, but what about when you go back to school? They will be my responsibility then.'

'But you said we need not go back to school,' put in the taller girl, Mary. 'That you would get us a governess, if we wanted. And we would much rather stay here with you than go back to Bowden's Academy.'

'I will think about it,' she said. 'Now, run along indoors and wash your hands, because breakfast is going to be ready very soon. And give me that bat,' she said, holding out an imperious hand to Mary, just as though she suspected the girl of thinking of going on a rampage with it indoors.

The children wasted no more time arguing. With the prospect of a dog and release from school in the offing, they were clearly taking no chances on making her take back what she'd half promised them by annoying her.

Once they had all gone trotting obediently indoors, he and Dora stood for a moment, eyeing each other. And it took only that moment to become aware that he was not properly attired. That he was wearing scarcely anything at all.

'I…er…beg your pardon for coming out here unsuitably dressed,' he said.

Her face flushed. 'At least you stopped to pull on

your breeches. For which I am very grateful. On behalf of my sisters, that is,' she said, eyeing him up and down in what looked like a speculative manner. He couldn't help curling his bare toes into the grass. And as he did so, her face flushed an even deeper shade of pink.

Interesting…

Chapter Twelve

'I am also very grateful,' Dora said, clutching the bat to her chest like a shield, 'to you for not ripping up at them. It could not have been very pleasant, the way they woke you, and before having breakfast many men would…' She trailed off, looking as though she had plenty of experience of the temper of men first thing in the morning. It made him feel a bit uncomfortable to wonder what sort of experience his bride had known at the whim of other men.

'That is, my father…' she continued. 'Well, we often had to tiptoe round the house first thing in the morning.'

He felt a weight shift from his shoulders.

'I *was* angry,' he admitted, 'to start with, it is true. But when I saw them all clustered there, the picture of guilt, with the cricket bat in evidence, I couldn't help remembering how I felt as a boy, in possession of a bat and ball, and only a small space in which to play.' And nobody to play with, anyway.

'I wouldn't call this lawn small,' she scoffed. 'I would have thought they had plenty of room for a bit of cricket practice before breakfast.'

He eyed the distance from the cedar tree to his bedroom window. 'Well, that was another thing. I couldn't help being impressed that anyone had managed to hit the house from that distance.'

'A girl, you mean?'

'No, anyone. The precision it took to get it through the only open window, too…'

'They didn't do it on purpose,' she said hotly, as though in their defence.

'No… I don't suppose anyone could,' he replied absently, tossing the ball up and down. 'It would be something of a feat…'

She looked over her shoulder. Then the other one. Then stepped closer. 'Do you want,' she said, at a volume scarcely above a whisper, 'to try it? While nobody is about?'

He looked at her lips. God, yes. He'd been wanting to kiss her from almost the first moment he met her. And then, when she'd bitten into that peach…

'The children's rooms are all on the far side of the house and Mrs Warren will be too busy with breakfast to notice what we are doing.'

His heart began to pound. He moved in closer.

'Are you sure about this? You don't mind?'

She smiled up at him in a rather conspiratorial manner.

'Of course not. In my experience, no male could stand seeing a girl perform a sporting feat without immediately burning to prove they could have done it as well. Or better.'

Sporting feat? A girl? What was she…?

'Unless,' she said, looking a bit uncomfortable, 'you think it would be a bit…childish?' Her face flushed.

'No, never mind, forget I said anything, it is just that sometimes, you know, just sometimes, I get tired of always having to be sensible. Occasionally I'd like to go off and play cricket rather than doing the accounts or drawing up menus. Foolish of me, I know,' she said, looking downcast.

Cricket. She was talking about playing cricket.

Well, they might have started out at cross purposes, but now that he'd grasped the fact that she was suggesting they attempt to get a cricket ball through a bedroom window, from the same spot as Mary, he could see *exactly* why she'd suggested it. Who would have thought she would have such a…playful side to her nature? Not that he minded. Not one bit. In fact, it was a dashed good thing. He couldn't stand women who took themselves too seriously.

What was even better, though, was the fact that she'd owned up to her wish to do something so playful, even though she risked him thinking her childish. It showed a certain amount of trust. It showed she didn't think he was the kind of man who'd mock her. Even though she might easily have been afraid he was a bully, or an ogre, given their past interactions.

Well, now was the time to cement that opinion of him, by indulging her in her whim. Besides, hadn't a part of him just been wishing he'd had someone to play cricket with, when he'd been a boy? And, though he wasn't a boy any longer, and cricket wasn't really the sport he truly wanted to play with her…

'If you were a man,' he said, 'you wouldn't think it childish at all. In fact, we'd already be wagering on which one of us would be able to hit that window from the cedar tree.'

Her face lit up. 'I knew it! I knew you wanted to have a go. Come on,' she said, hitching up her skirts and making for the wicket. He followed, admiring the sway of her hips as her long legs made short work of crossing the lawn.

'Would you prefer to bowl, or bat?' he asked when they reached the cedar tree.

'I think,' she said, eyeing his shoulders and arms, 'that you have a far better chance of getting a ball through a window than me.' She held out the bat. 'I will bowl.'

'Very well,' he said, a grin tugging at his lips. And couldn't resist adding, 'Do you know, I would never have suspected, the night I flung you, spitting with fury, into my coach, that you had a sense of mischief.'

'If I didn't, I would have made you listen to me long before we reached Coventry,' she said and then went rigid.

'Do you mean to tell me that you spent the whole time laughing at how foolishly I'd behaved?'

'Um, no, not the *whole* time. I mean,' she went on, looking flustered, 'I couldn't help finding it rather amusing. I mean, you mistook me for the kind of woman some man became so infatuated with that he ran away with her. Me! And I believe I was wearing this gown at the time,' she added, gesturing to the shapeless and rather worn gown that he had thought he'd recognised.

'But I could easily see why some man might run off with you,' he protested, disliking the way she seemed to put herself down all the time. 'And it has nothing to do with what you were wearing. Any man who only looks at what a woman wears is…well, it doesn't matter what you wear…'

'Yes, you said that about my wedding gown,' she said, with a bit of a grimace.

'And I think I pointed out that I admired you from the first…'

She snorted. 'You thought I was a designing hussy!'

'No, well…' Yes, he had, or he wouldn't have tossed her into his coach. 'That is…'

'No, please, stop talking. With every word you are floundering further and further away from the truth. Which is that I am a maypole. Men look at me and immediately start…well, never mind,' she concluded, darkly. 'However, my saving grace is that I have a keen sense of the ridiculous. According to my brothers, that is the one thing that saves me from being unbearable to live with, the fact that I can usually manage to see the funny side of things.'

'I am sure you are not unbearable to live with.'

'You say that because, so far, you haven't attempted to do so,' she retorted. Then took a deep breath. 'Look, just give me that ball,' she said, holding out her hand imperiously.

He did so, ruefully reflecting that although he'd thought he'd taken a step forward in her estimation, he'd now definitely taken two steps back.

'Are you ready?' She tossed the ball up and down and caught it a couple of times.

He took a few experimental swings with the bat, to get the feel of it. 'I am,' he said, taking up his stance.

She turned round, took a few paces away from him, and then delivered the ball in what to him seemed like a most peculiar fashion, taking a little run up and then bowling over arm. Her aim was not great, but when he took a step to the side to take a swing, he discovered that the ball was travelling much faster than he would have expected a woman to have been able to bowl it.

It connected with the bat with a resounding crack. Went sailing straight towards the house and hit the window of the bedroom next to his with a second re-sounding crack.

The window, which was shut, only withstood the force of impact, to a certain extent. The leads bowed. And, just as the cricket ball hit the soft earth under-neath the dining room window, with a thump, several of the tiny diamond panes of glass disappeared.

Dora clapped her hand to her mouth. 'We've broken another window,' she said in horror. 'Whatever will Mrs Warren say?'

'It is of no matter what she says,' he said noncha-lantly. 'I was already going to have to call someone in to repair the window in my room. And the one in the pantry. It isn't going to take him that much longer to fix that one as well, is it?'

'No, but if the children discover we go about break-ing windows with aplomb, however am I going to per-suade them they ought not to do it?' She snatched the cricket bat from him crossly. 'That is what comes of larking about,' she said. 'Speaking of which, it is high time I went in to supervise breakfast.'

'I shall go in and dress, and join you all,' he said, once more aware how dishevelled he must appear. He hadn't even shaved. He ran his hand over his chin, to feel how bad his whiskers must look.

'A word of warning,' she said, eyeing the movement

of his hand. 'Or rather, a plea, not to take too long over your toilet. We...ah...try to attend meals punctually.'

He frowned. 'Mrs Warren still being strict about mealtimes, is she? I had no idea she was such a tartar. I did not mean to leave you to deal with staff that won't serve you as you should be served.'

'Er...no, it isn't that. I have had some...er...issues, but...there really isn't time to go into them now...'

It was just as well he'd come down when he had. By the sound of it, she'd had to deal with rats, belligerent staff and a mountain of household management that kept her indoors when she'd much rather be outside enjoying herself. There was a lot for him to put right.

'After breakfast, then, we must have a long talk,' he said grimly. And then, because he was going to have to make a series of apologies and explanations, and he didn't fancy doing so in front of those children, he added, 'in private.'

'As you wish,' she said, in the kind of tone that implied it was not what she wished at all. 'We could perhaps take a stroll through the formal gardens,' she said, waving one hand in the direction of what was now something of a wilderness. 'The day promises to be a fine one and I can guarantee we won't be disturbed by anyone, out there, not if we go directly after breakfast.'

Especially not, by the overgrown state of what she'd referred to as the formal gardens, by gardeners.

A talk. A long talk, in private. Dora wasn't sure she liked the sound of that. Oh, from a purely practical point of view she supposed there were some things they did need to discuss. They'd never really talked about their future—well, there hadn't been time to talk about anything. And even if he had made time, what could they possibly have said? She, for one, had no idea what she thought about any of it.

However, now he'd had time to think, he'd clearly made a few decisions. That must be why he'd come down here. To tell her what they were.

And from the grim cast to his features, he wasn't expecting her to like them.

Well, at least she already agreed with him on one thing. It would be best to keep the children well away from the formal gardens. If she became upset, or angry, or he did, she didn't want them seeing them coming to cuffs. She wanted their memories of Maybush House to be happy ones, filled with laughter and games. Not ones of their big sister having a stand-up row with the husband she'd tried to make them believe had swept her off her feet in a fit of…gallantry. A husband, moreover, who was already showing signs he was prepared to be generous to them.

So, after breakfast, she encouraged them to go and play in the woods. It didn't take much. The mere hint that she wouldn't disapprove caused them all to give a cheer and go charging out of the room like missiles fired from a cannon.

Worsley watched their eruption from the room with an expression of amusement. Which was encouraging. But then the more she learned about him, the more she tended to think he was a decent sort of man. He'd had every right to be grumpy, given the way he'd been woken this morning. And the conditions in which he'd had to sleep the night before… She'd peeped in through his door, to see how bad the damage was, and been shocked to see not only glass all over the floor under the window, but also evidence that he'd slept on a bare mattress. He hadn't bawled at the children, but on the contrary had even ended up trying to see if he could equal Mary's feat. With the result that her room, too, now had a damaged window and glass on the floor.

Then he'd meekly borne her lecture about being punctual for breakfast, had turned up on time, immaculately dressed and shaved, and had been an affable, if somewhat subdued, presence at the head of the table.

'Shall we make a start?' He stood up, his expression sombre, as he offered her his arm.

Oh, dear. He must really not be looking forward to their discussion. Well, neither was she. But if he could behave like a gentleman, then she could behave like a lady. Except when she was raking him down, or egging him on to smash windows...

'Of course,' she said, getting to her feet, and though she placed her hand on his sleeve she couldn't meet his eye. Whatever must he think of her?

As they passed through the open back door, she couldn't help glancing up at the clear blue sky. It was going to be another lovely summer's day. Just a breeze to keep things from getting unpleasant, later on, a breeze which was just playful enough to tug a strand of hair from her hastily pinned-up bun. She tucked it behind her ear, wishing she'd insisted on going upstairs to fetch a bonnet. Only that would have looked as though she was trying to put him off. Wouldn't it? Or would it have looked as though she knew how a countess ought to behave?

She sighed. Normally, she would have enjoyed nothing more than taking a stroll through the gardens at this time of day, trying to puzzle out where the borders had once been and work out which plants were growing where they were by design and which were happy accidents. But today there was that dark cloud hanging over her. That 'talk' he'd insisted on having. Which was making his face, when she glanced up at it from time to time, look so stern.

Perhaps she could prevent their talk from descending into open conflict if she were to attempt to...er... butter him up a bit.

No, that wouldn't work. For one thing she had no idea how to do it, having never once attempted to do any such thing in her entire life. For another, he'd probably see straight through her. He didn't seem to be a particularly stupid man and she was no good at acting.

It looked as though her only option would be to apologise. Not that she was in the habit of doing that, very often, either. Although she was sorry about the conditions he'd had to sleep in last night.

'I am so sorry about your room,' she began, with the benefit of being completely sincere. 'I had no idea that you intended to pay us a visit, or of course I would have had it made ready for you. Even, when you came in, I could have...although I have to say I did not hear you arrive. It must have been in the dead of night. Oh, it never occurred to me before, but is there something wrong?' That would account for everything. His sudden arrival, as well as his grim face when he'd said they needed to talk in private. 'Is that why you flew down here without warning? Do you have bad news, or...?'

'No, there is nothing wrong. I just felt that it was past time that I came down to see how you were settling in. I rode down on a whim. Stupid thing to do, really,' he said, rubbing one hand across the back of his neck, as though the sun was burning it. 'As soon as I got here I saw that my arrival was going to set everyone on edge, rousing you all from your slumber. That is why I...er... broke in through a pantry window. Which will need to be repaired, as I already mentioned. Can't leave you prey to burglars, or what have you.'

So that was what he'd meant about having the pantry window repaired. It had sounded odd, when he'd said it, but she'd put it out of her mind until now, since there had been more important things to deal with. But then it struck her that within a few hours of his arrival, they'd contrived to break three windows between them. She had to press her lips tightly together to prevent a grin from forming. 'No, quite.'

'And, look here,' he said, 'I am sorry about the rats. Should have had the place checked out before bringing you down here.'

'Well, it wasn't as if you had much time, was it? And it is probably only mice, after all. But Mary and Martha have such vivid imaginations that they would have it that if it isn't rats scampering about at night then it is the ghost of a Catholic priest, who took shelter in a secret room and who couldn't find his way out.'

'There is no priest hole in this house,' he said, 'not to my knowledge.'

'Please do not tell my siblings that. They will be devastated.'

'Like ghosts, do they?'

'They like stories.' Which had come in jolly handy when she'd been telling them about her adventure at the Blue Boar. '*Robinson Crusoe* is their favourite, at the moment, but they all have very lively imaginations and enjoy nothing more than making up stories of their own. But the point is, I was hoping that next time it rains they would be able to amuse themselves inside searching for hidden doors in all that linenfold panelling.'

He cleared his throat. 'While we are speaking of the children, it occurred to me, when I told them they could have a dog, that I ought, perhaps, to have consulted you first. I always had dogs about the place, growing up, and they were of great…' He paused and took a deep breath. 'But that is neither here nor there. The thing is, until you spoke of it as a bribe, I never considered that I might be…but then I saw that you might interpret my belief that it is my duty to ensure the children have all the things they want as an attempt to undermine your authority with them. I have a tendency to act first and think after,' he said, with a pensive frown.

Well, she had no problem believing that. Only look at the way he'd picked her up and tossed her into his carriage, when Gregory had refused to meekly return to London.

'It comes,' he continued, 'I expect, of having so many people around me who accept me giving them orders, without expecting any sort of explanation.'

Goodness. No wonder he looked a touch uncomfortable. It couldn't be easy for a man like him to attempt to explain himself. Come to think of it, the very fact that he'd questioned his behaviour, to the extent that he'd thought an explanation might be in order, was an enormous point in his favour.

'I totally understand,' she admitted. 'Because I'm just the same. I regard myself as being decisive, but I have to tell you that people on the receiving end of my…er…decisions often resent what they see as my interference. The kindest thing they say is that I am a managing female.' She shrugged her shoulders. 'And anyway, I was just so glad you did not ring a peal over them for damaging the window with that cricket ball, that the matter of the dog was…' She peeped up at him, shyly. 'To be frank, I was half expecting you to have brought me out here to ring a peal over me, too, not to apologise for offering to get them a dog.'

'Two dogs,' he pointed out.

'By reminding me of that fact, do you expect me to be twice as cross, or twice as grateful, I wonder?'

He glanced down at her, the ghost of a smile playing about his lips. Lips which she was more used to seeing pulled down at the corners whenever he looked at her.

'Twice as grateful,' he said, with a solemnity she was almost certain he put on for effect. 'Which brings me to my next point, which concerns those children— your brother and sisters, who took me by surprise and not only because they introduced themselves via the medium of their cricket ball.'

Goodness. He appeared to have a dry sense of humour. Which suggested he had a good nature, deep down. Well, of course he did, or he wouldn't have insisted on marrying her, after accidentally abducting her. He wouldn't have been so set on rescuing Pansy from his ward, in the first place. Nor would he have since gone to such lengths to make sure that no lasting harm had been done to her reputation. Or done it all with such good grace. Mostly.

'I assumed they were all at school somewhere. I'm certain you told me you'd just taken the girls to school, the day you were going to put up at the Blue Boar.'

'Well, yes, but I'd never wanted to send them to school. It was just the best of many difficult options open to us.'

'I... I know so little about you,' he mused, 'even though you are my wife. I need to do better,' he said, lifting his chin in a way that suggested he was determined on a certain course of action. 'Which is why I have come down here. To visit you. Even though I promised that I would allow you to live as you choose. I had not intended to interfere, you understand.'

'You just couldn't help it,' she suggested helpfully.

'No,' he agreed. 'The very first thing I did was make suggestions about how you could improve the way you are looking after your brother and sisters.' He frowned and shook his head. 'Once again, I have ridden roughshod over you...'

'I know just how it is,' she said, ruefully, 'believe me. When I see someone in a muddle and the solution seems perfectly clear, and I cannot think why nobody else has suggested it. Although, in my defence, I must point out that Paul only arrived yesterday. Until he came down, the girls were more content to explore the woods, where, I believe, they have been busy building a fortress with bits of brushwood. It is Paul who is so keen on ball games and who has the strength to bowl in such a way that Mary can score imaginary sixes. And I feel I have to point out,' she said with a touch of resentment, 'that I *would* have thought of tennis balls, eventually.'

'But not, probably, given your reaction when I mentioned them, the dogs.'

'Probably not,' she said, since that was the truth. 'We have never had dogs. They require, it seems to me, an awful lot of looking after and I always had enough on my hands without...'

'In what way? You seem to be implying that you had sole care of your younger siblings. Is that correct?'

'Well, yes, since my mother died. I was the eldest, you see, and almost a young lady. And Papa sort of... retreated into his bible. He was a vicar, you know. Did I tell you? Yes, I did, didn't I?' It was only after he'd heard she came from such a respectable background that he'd first spoken in terms of marriage. She'd wondered if he might have come up with a very different solution if she hadn't been a vicar's daughter. But things were in enough of a tangle without going off into the realms of 'what if'?

'So how, if you do not mind my enquiring, did you come to be going out to work as a governess?'

Now, this, she could answer. In fact, if all he wanted to do was find out about her background, then she could see why he might have been looking a touch apprehensive. They knew so little about each other. But if he was worried that he was going to find something shady in her background, it would be an easy matter to set his mind at rest.

Chapter Thirteen

'Well, I told you, didn't I,' Dora began, 'about how Timothy and I arrived at the decision for me to take work as a governess. So, what else would you like to know?'

'Was there no family member to help you?'

'Oh, well…um…there were various offers of help. One uncle volunteered to take Paul, and one aunt spoke of perhaps taking Martha, as she is *biddable*,' she said with a curl of her lip. 'But everyone suggested I send Mary to school. Where she might learn to behave like a young lady. You may have noticed,' she said, slowly, 'that she is a little…'

'Spirited?'

'Yes, well, that is one way of putting it. But the thing is, whichever way we looked at it, it was going to mean splitting the girls up. So we decided that if I went out to work as a governess, we could afford, between us and the money we had inherited, to send the girls to school together, at least. Uncle David agreed to have Paul during the school holidays, while the girls went to Aunt Honoria. Which meant that we were all…well, surviving, but, oh, when you spoke of a house that stood empty, with enough space to house us all, and the freedom to do whatever I wished, then told me my allowance was going to be so…enormous, well, naturally, I brought them all here.'

'That was what finally persuaded you to marry me,' he said, pausing at a spot where nasturtiums were spilling right across what had once been a path, turning it into a flowered carpet.

'Yes. I hope you do not mind? You did say I might do as I pleased, in this house…'

'Yes, yes, I did,' he said gruffly, setting off once more, causing the flowers to release their peppery scent as her skirts brushed across them. 'But the thing is, I would have preferred it if you could have spoken to me about them. You *should* have been able to speak to me about them. Now that you are my wife, they are my family. They are my responsibility.'

Oh, no they weren't. They were hers. She'd been like a mother to them for so long. How dare he stroll in and…and take over?

Although, he'd already apologised for that tendency, hadn't he? In the interests of harmony, she ought really to bite back her instinctive response.

'I am,' she therefore said, in as polite a tone as she could muster, 'completely capable of organising my own life.'

'Yes, yes, but that isn't the point,' he said irritably.

'What is the point, then?'

He removed his hat and ran his fingers through his hair. 'I only intended to give you time to grow accustomed to your new status. As my wife. Instead,

I have…neglected your needs. That was not my intention.'

'I have not felt the slightest bit neglected, I assure you.'

'But you are having trouble with the staff. You said so. I had to scramble into my clothes all anyhow to get to the breakfast table on time. I thought when we were here before that it was just that we had turned up on short notice, but if the woman is still…'

'Oh, no, *she* isn't the one who insists on punctual mealtimes. That is, I have to tell you, entirely my fault.'

'Well,' he said, in the fashion of a man who has been caught on the back foot and was desperately trying to regain his balance, 'you are the mistress here. You are entitled to insist on whatever you wish…'

'Yes, that is exactly what I have done,' she admitted. 'You see, when you left, and I had time to look about at the state of the place I couldn't help noticing a few… discrepancies. Such as, for example, these gardens.' She waved her free hand round to indicate the wild abandon of roses, and nasturtium, and dandelions. 'Even though you hardly ever come here and told me that it was one of your smaller properties, I couldn't really believe that you would have left me here if you hadn't though it was well staffed and well kept.'

'I would not!'

'Precisely so. So, how to account for the fact that there were only three indoor staff and the same amount out of doors?'

He gave her a piercing look. 'Something tells me that you swiftly discovered what it was?'

She nodded. 'I think so. Without examining the books of your man of business, who sends the wages, quarterly, I cannot be sure, but I believe Mrs Warren has been pocketing the money which should have gone to paying staff who no longer work for you. And before you suggest that I should have fired her on the spot, let me just say that if you think it is an easy matter to find a person who can manage a house of this size, let alone cook the way she does, in the blink of an eye, then let me tell you that it is not so.'

'But if she is stealing from us...'

'Yes, yes, I know. Prosecuting her is one option. But she is not a young woman. And if she is found guilty of the crimes I believe she has committed, she might not merely go to prison. She might be hanged.'

'So you choose to be merciful?'

She didn't like the way he was looking down his nose at her. 'I choose to be practical. While I am living here, and my younger brother and sisters, I need a housekeeper more than I need to be calling in the magistrate. Besides, I don't believe she did it deliberately. She was originally employed as a cook, not a housekeeper, but the role fell to her because it is so hard to find replacement staff for...oh, a variety of reasons. But anyway, she knows that I know what she has been up to and is so scared that I might turn her off, or turn her over to the law, that she cannot do enough for me. Only... I am obliged to keep up a...stern appearance, you see.'

He eyed her again, in a way she found hard to interpret. 'Well, as I said, you are the mistress here. I shall not interfere in the way you choose to run the place.'

'Even if you disapprove?'

'I left you here, without any support. I have no right to criticise you for the way you have decided to deal with the problems I bequeathed you. I only wish that you had not had to deal with them. I should have done... something.'

'Well, as far as I am concerned, you did exactly what I wished.'

'I did?'

'Yes. You sent me my trunk, didn't you?' She'd been so disappointed, the day it had arrived on the back of a carrier's cart, because she'd assumed he'd intended to fetch it personally. But she didn't like to say so, because he'd already started to frown.

'You must have been sick with worry when I tossed you into my carriage. Losing everything, like that...' He shook his head.

'But you got it back,' she put in, in an attempt to head him off from the gloomy direction he seemed determined to travel. 'And sent it to me. So you...you must have caught up with Gregory? How is he? And how is the girl... Pansy, I seem to recall her name is?' The moment she succumbed to her curiosity and asked that question she realised she'd made a mistake. For his brows drew down even further and his mouth twisted with distaste.

'They reached Scotland without any further mishaps and went through a sort of handfasting ceremony,' he said, with disgust.

'Handfasting? Is that even legal?'

'I doubt it. So, as soon as I brought them back to England, I got hold of a special licence and made the pair of them go through a ceremony in front of a bona fide minister of the church. To make sure he hasn't ruined the silly chit.'

He had, in fact, been charging all over the country,

by the sound of it, ever since he'd installed her here. No wonder he hadn't brought her things back in person. He'd had far more important matters to attend to.

'And, where are they now? Has her father forgiven her? Or has he cut her off without a penny, the way he threatened?'

He sighed. 'The last I heard he was still breathing fire and thunder. We decided it would be better if they stayed away from London at Brinkley Court, until the scandal has died down, because, and I have no idea how it happened, word of his elopement got out.'

'Oh, dear.'

'Yes, indeed. Tilly suggested that the news I had married would eclipse that, only, because you haven't shown your face in London...not that it is your fault. It was my decision to bring you down here. Which brings me to another thing.'

'Oh?' This was probably what he'd been wanting to say to her all along. The thing she'd been trying to put him in a better mood before he broached. Only to clumsily set him off talking about the elopement of his ward, which was bound to make him cross as crabs. Especially considering all the trouble he'd had to go to, to smooth the affair over.

'Yes. I don't know how to put this, so I shall just say it, bluntly.' He stopped, turned to her and took both her hands in his. 'You have bravely borne everything, so far, with great forbearance. You have been, in short, a good sport.' He smiled.

Her heart thudded. When he smiled, really smiled at her, gazing into her eyes with his blue, blue ones, it was like...well, she didn't know what it was like. She had nothing with which to compare it. Because no man as handsome as this had ever smiled right into her eyes this way before. And said she was a good sport as though he meant it.

It made her feel a bit giddy. A bit breathless.

'I have not, as yet, been any sort of a husband to you. Even though I took vows, I haven't kept them.'

What? Was he confessing some act of infidelity? Or to tell her he still kept a mistress? All of a sudden the sun didn't feel as warm. And the breeze, which was making the gillyflowers nod their heads, had such a chill to it that it brought her out in goose flesh.

She'd thought she was the kind of woman who could take anything in her stride. But the thought of him taking another woman in his arms, of smiling at her, of kissing her, of feeling affection for her….

'I promised to cherish you,' he said, 'and so far, you have had to deal with one problem after another.'

Cherish her? He was referring to that, particular, marriage vow?

'No, no, it is of no matter,' she assured him, absurdly relieved not to have to face a discussion about what he expected of her when he went to some other woman. 'From what you've been saying, you have been far too busy running around clearing up after Gregory to have time for a wife you never wanted in the first place.'

'You are being far too generous. Far too forgiving.' He raised her hands to his lips and pressed a firm, swift kiss on each. And all at once, it was as if the sun had come out again.

'But look,' he said earnestly, 'from now on it will be different, I promise,' he said, giving her hands a little squeeze. 'I wasn't really thinking like a married man. It all happened so fast, so unexpectedly. But now…' he drew in a deep, shuddering breath '… I intend to begin treating you the way a man should treat his wife. And hope that you will be willing to take up your duties as my Countess.'

He looked deeply into her eyes again, with even more warmth than before.

'Do you agree? Are you willing?'

It wasn't just warmth she could see in his eyes. It was a sort of hope. No, more than that, longing. And it sent up an answering surge of longing through every part of her body.

Gracious heavens! He was talking about making their marriage real. Not just a paper marriage, but one where they…where they…

Her gaze dropped to his mouth. Then took in the width of his shoulders. Felt, again, the pressure of them against her stomach, when he'd picked her up and made her feel, for the first time in her life, feminine and helpless. But he hadn't taken advantage of her. He hadn't made any demands on her. Even now, when, as her husband, he could have marched in and demanded his rights, he was asking her if she was willing.

Her cheeks heated at the images which suddenly flooded her mind. Images which made it impossible to hold his gaze any longer. She lowered her eyes demurely to look at where he was holding her hands in his own, strong, capable ones.

There was only one thing she could say.

'Yes,' she whispered. 'I am willing.'

Chapter Fourteen

Dora was busy, as usual, for the rest of the day, see-ing to the hundred and one tasks required of a woman newly taking over a household that had been virtually empty for years. At least, she supposed she must have been, although she wasn't able to tell anyone, when they all gathered for dinner, exactly what she had done.

Because her mind had kept going back to the look in his eyes when he'd asked her if she was willing.

Which meant he must want to…to do whatever it was that men did with their wives that resulted in ba-bies. She wasn't too clear about the details. But that didn't matter. She was sure he would know what he was doing. And he would show her, tonight.

Then, thinking about what the night would bring made her heart flutter and her stomach fizz, and her limbs grow languorous. And she'd remember the look in his eyes and the response that had flooded her body, and off she'd go again.

Yet strangely, even though she hadn't been able to stop thinking about the way he'd looked at her, when she was finally in the same room as him she found herself unable to look at him for longer than a fleeting moment. She definitely couldn't meet his eye. When he spoke to her, she became flustered and tongue-tied, and felt herself blushing.

Which irritated her no end. She'd always despised women who blushed and simpered at men. Now she'd gone and joined their ranks!

Fortunately, she and he were not dining alone. And the children were so used to her distracted moods that they took no notice. Best of all, they'd recovered from the shyness which had afflicted them on first encountering Worsley at breakfast.

'I say, sir,' Paul began, after heaping his plate from every tureen on the table. 'Are you the same Lord Worsley who owns Bobtail? The horse that won the Newmarket Stakes at the Craven meeting?'

'I am,' said Worsley, shooting Paul a look of slight surprise. Which was nothing to the shock which Dora felt, on hearing Paul apparently so knowledgeable on a subject about which she knew next to nothing.

'Is he,' said Paul, a forkful of peas suspended halfway to his lips, 'the horse you have in the stables? The big chestnut?'

'Oh, no,' replied Lord Worsley with amusement. 'That is my own everyday saddle horse. Bobtail couldn't carry my weight, you know. Besides, he is stabled at my stud just outside Newmarket, where he trains.'

'Won't the fellows at school be green with envy,' said Paul without the slightest sign of disappointment that Worsley hadn't brought a famous racehorse with him, 'when I tell them I know you.'

Dora lowered her own fork, which had also been arrested in mid-air, to her plate. 'Do I take it that this is what you have been learning at the exclusive school that Uncle David got you into? The names of all the horses that have won races this season?'

The tone of her voice was so sharp that they all turned to look at her with varying degrees of wariness.

'It's not as bad as you make it sound, Dora,' said Paul. 'Lots of them have brothers, or cousins, or uncles who own and race horses, so of course they talk about all that sort of thing and whose relative is doing best. And now I can, too,' he concluded, darting a grin in Worsley's direction.

She considered that statement. She could concede that it would probably make it easier for Paul to fit in with the sort of boys who went to the prestigious school where he was a newcomer. However, did she really want him to fit in with the type of people who wasted their substance on wagers? Which was what horse racing was all about, wasn't it?

'I can see what you're thinking, Dora,' said Paul. 'But you don't need to worry. I won't start wagering on the horses. Not even Worsley's.'

'Good,' she said. 'Then I won't need to give you a lecture about the folly of wasting your allowance on such evils.'

'You don't approve of horse racing?' Worsley was looking at her as though she'd just announced she had revolutionary sympathies and didn't blame the French peasants for sending the majority of their aristocracy to the guillotine.

'Father always used to say,' she said, giving each of her siblings in turn, a severe look, 'that race meetings were merely excuses to indulge in all the worst sorts of vice.'

'The kind of men who indulge in the kind of vice he probably meant,' Worsley retorted, 'don't need to go to a race meeting to find what they're looking for.'

'What kind of vice,' Paul asked, with an expression of innocent enquiry which didn't fool her for a minute, 'do you think he meant, Dora?'

'Never you mind,' she said repressively, having only had a scanty notion of what he'd meant herself. 'This is not suitable talk for the dinner table.' She jerked her head at Mary, whose face was puckered in genuine confusion.

A taut silence fell over the table, punctuated only by the scraping of cutlery on china.

Well done, Dora. She'd managed to cast a cloud over what had started out in such a promising fashion. Fortunately, none of her siblings ever remained chastened for very long. And this time it was Mary who recovered first.

'Lord Worsley,' she ventured, timidly. 'You...you haven't forgotten that you were going to get us some tennis balls, have you?'

'No,' he said. 'I made you a promise, didn't I? And a gentleman never reneges on his promises.'

Now what on earth did he mean by that? Oh, not the words so much, but the pointed way he'd looked at her as he'd said them. If he had something to say to her, why didn't he just come out and say it?

Although, if it was some sort of rebuke, she wouldn't thank him for giving it openly with her brother and sisters at the table, would she?

Poor man. Whatever he did tonight, he couldn't win, could he?

Eventually everyone had eaten as much as they

could of Mrs Warren's excellent cooking, so Dora laid her napkin aside and got to her feet.

'I should perhaps just explain,' she said to Worsley as the girls took her cue and also stood up, 'that we… ah…all retire to the parlour for an hour after dinner.'

'Dora makes us do embroidery,' Mary added, with a rueful shake of her head.

'I have let you roam free all day, every day since you have been here,' Dora pointed out. She'd been so shocked to hear of the rigid rules which governed the behaviour of the inmates of the school from which she'd rescued them that she'd thought it would do them good to have a holiday from formal education. 'But it doesn't do you any harm to do *something* constructive, each day, does it?'

'And Dora has Paul read to us while we work,' put in Martha, glancing warily between her and Worsley. 'It's *Robinson Crusoe* at the moment. Would you like to listen to it with us?'

'Oh, yes, do, sir,' chipped in Paul. 'Last night Crusoe found a human footprint on the beach and he's in a real pucker.'

Worsley chuckled. 'If your sister doesn't object to me bringing my port with me…' He raised one eyebrow in Dora's direction.

'By all means,' she replied. The children had clearly taken to him and he was showing no signs of revulsion at spending what most men would probably consider a very tame hour. Best of all, even though she suspected she'd offended him, he wasn't making the children pay for her behaviour.

By the time Worsley had finished his port, and Robinson Crusoe had reacted in a predictable fashion to the discovery of the remains of a cannibal feast, Martha was starting to droop.

Dora laid her work basket aside and got to her feet. 'Time for bed.'

'For the girls,' Paul hastily assured Worsley. 'I get another hour.'

'I could stay up another hour, too, if I chose,' said Mary, with a tilt to her chin. 'Only I share a room with Martha, so it makes sense for us to go up and prepare for bed together. And then I am permitted to read quietly or write in my journal until I fall asleep.'

'They are used to sharing a room,' put in Dora, at the look Worsley directed her. 'And even though they could have each had their own, here, they prefer to be together.'

Paul made a scratching noise on the cover of the book he'd just closed.

'I am not afraid of rats,' said Martha, indignantly.

'Off you go, Paul,' said Dora, making shooing motions with her hands.

'Oh, I thought I would stay here, with Lord Worsley,' he said as the girls made for the door.

'Well,' said Worsley, rising to his feet, 'I was about to go down to the stables...'

Paul shot to his feet as well. 'May I come with you, sir?'

'If your sister has no objection?'

She hadn't. She would much rather know that somebody was supervising Paul, since, left to his own devices, he had a boy's propensity for discovering mischief. But Worsley surely couldn't want to have a boy dogging his footsteps?

'If you do not mind?'

'Not at all. And, once the children are all abed? What is your habit then? Do you return to this room? Do you read? Write letters?'

'Well, to be honest,' said Dora, 'I am usually so tired that I just go to bed myself. I know it is not fashionable to go to bed so early...'

'No matter,' said Worsley, with a politeness that held a hint of something she could not identify. 'I shall bid you goodnight now, then.'

Had that look betokened disappointment, she wondered as she oversaw the brushing of Mary's and Martha's teeth? But why would it have been? Surely, if he meant to consummate the marriage, he would want her to be in her bed, ready and waiting for him.

She knelt to pray with her sisters, but her mind had never been further from spiritual matters. It was too full of *him*. The way he looked at her, the deep, rumbling tone of his voice, the feelings that surged through her whenever he took her hand...

And then suddenly her sisters were saying their *amens* and she had to join in without having any idea at all what either of them had prayed for.

She was trembling when she got to her feet and though she kissed her sisters as usual, she felt no inclination to linger at their bedsides, the way she'd done on previous nights. She needed to get to her own room so that she'd have plenty of time to prepare...

Oh, no, she couldn't though, not yet. She still had to oversee Paul's prayers and make sure he had some sort of a wash when he came back from the stables.

She paused by the landing window from where she could just glimpse the path leading from the stables, if she leaned out. And saw Worsley, loping along with

Paul trotting at his side, just like a faithful hound. Her heart did a funny little skip. She reared back, unwilling to let them see her. She didn't want *either* of them thinking she was watching out for their return.

When Paul came to his room, he was full of his trip to the stables. From the number of times he quoted one of Worsley's maxims, he was evidently well on the way to developing a bit of hero-worship for her husband. Not that she could blame the boy. Worsley might have been specifically designed to instil awe in youths on the verge of manhood, as well as spinsters who'd believed themselves at their last prayers. He was tall and broad, and good-natured, and had eyes the colour of the sky on the best kind of summer day…

'Goodness, it is hot this evening,' she said, going to Paul's bedroom window and flinging it open. She leaned out for a moment or two, to allow the breeze to cool her heated face before turning back to her brother.

'…and Lord Worsley says he will teach me to shoot,' he said with a touch of defiance that drew her attention fully back to him.

'Does he indeed?'

'Well, I asked him if he would and he said he'd like nothing better, which is the same thing.'

'Hmmph,' she said. Then bent to kiss his forehead. 'We will discuss it in the morning.'

She'd kept her tone gruff, but she floated along to her room with a smile on her face. It couldn't have been easy for Worsley to withstand Paul's pleadings. But it sounded as though he had spoken in such a way that he could consult with her before promising her brother anything.

She closed her bedroom door behind her and leaned back against it with a sigh. Had any woman ever been more fortunate? To think that only a few weeks ago, she'd been on the verge of embarking on a life of drudgery to provide the barest essentials for her family. And now look at her. Married. Mistress of the kind of property she'd never even dreamed of living in. And with a husband who not only didn't mind that she brought a ready-made family with her, but was keen to enrich their lives in a way she could never have done, on her own. And tonight…

She heaved one more sigh, before drifting across the room and tugging open the top drawer of one of her chests where she caught sight of the ridiculous confection of silk and lace which Tilly had given her to wear to bed, that first night, when she'd had nothing else. On that occasion she'd been reluctant to put it on. Had wondered why any woman would wish to wear such a scandalously revealing garment.

On this occasion she could understand *exactly* why a woman would want to drape it round as many parts of her body as she could manage to make it cling to.

She picked it up, thanking Tilly for providing it. For tonight, she was extremely reluctant to receive her husband wearing one of the practical, worn and darned nightgowns in which she usually slept. She didn't want him to even *see* what she usually wore to bed.

So she darted to her bed, removed the nightgown that was under the pillow and, after looking round the room for a place to conceal it, simply pushed it under the bed. She washed herself all over with great care and towelled herself dry, by which time her heart was pounding like a drum and her fingers were trembling so much that it was all she could do to tie up the many ribbons of her frivolous nightgown. She sat down rather heavily on her dressing table stool where she usually sat to complete her preparations for bed.

Her eyes, she noted in the mirror, as she picked up her hairbrush, were sparkling and her cheeks were flushed. She leaned closer, her brows lowering. If she saw any other woman looking like that she'd suspect they'd been drinking. But then, she reflected, putting down her brush while she unbraided her hair, knowing that a man was about to come to your room and do all sorts of wicked things to you was rather intoxicating.

She picked up her brush again, then paused. Should she braid her hair the way she normally did, or leave it loose? Well, with her hair flowing round her shoulders, at least she didn't look like a governess any longer. She looked like...a bride.

Even if she was a rather plain bride, who had spent her whole life thinking she would never capture a man's heart, only to have one handed her on a plate...

Although he hadn't, had he? Handed her his heart? Only his hand.

She sighed again, only this time it was not in a dreamy, hopeful way. She was wearing a borrowed nightgown and was eagerly awaiting a groom who'd only married her because his sense of honour demanded he offer for her.

She set the hairbrush down and swivelled away from her disappointing reflection. If only she had something to give her a bit of confidence. Like...well, scent, perhaps. Worsley was probably used to women who doused themselves with something exotic and alluring. They wouldn't smell of the soap they'd just used for their wash, would they?

But before she could travel too far down that depressing road, she heard his heavy tread on the stairs.

With a squeak of alarm, she leapt up off the dressing table chair, and darted across the room to her bed. She flung back the covers, clambered in and pulled them back up. Her heart was beating so hard she had to strain to hear the sounds he was making, moving about in the room next to hers, above its thunder. But she distinctly heard him drop his boots to the floor, followed by the scrape of a chair. Then a few moments of quiet, then the splashing of water into a basin.

He must have taken off his shirt, during that period of silence. She slid further down the bed, her hands still curled round the bedcovers as she imagined him, stripped to the waist, soaping himself up…

She pushed the covers down, because they were making her too hot. Flicked her hair back from her face. Then, almost immediately, tugged it back so that it covered her shoulders and the upper slope of her breast.

What was he doing now? Whatever it was, he was doing it awfully quietly. Because all she could hear was the sounds of the house settling down for the evening—the creak of floorboards, and small cracks from the wainscoting as it cooled in places where the sun had shone in during the day and warmed it up.

And then, inevitably, the scampering of tiny feet, from behind the cooling wainscoting.

And the cry of an owl, drifting in from outside.

But no sound of footsteps approaching her door.

Had he changed his mind about consummating their marriage?

What had made him change his mind?

Had it been her remarks over dinner about gambling? Surely, he wasn't as sensitive to her opinions as all that? He'd never given any indication of being so...easily put off any course of action he felt inclined to pursue.

Or perhaps the simple truth was that he hadn't been able to make himself go through the ordeal of bedding a woman he'd never wanted in the first place?

Yes, that was more like it. It had been one thing to bring himself up to the mark, in the light of day, during a moment or two when she'd made him feel...playful, by encouraging him to indulge in his yearning to emulate, and surpass, a feat performed by a girl. Another thing entirely to go through with it, after a day of considering what it would mean.

She slumped down on to the pillows, her lower lip trembling. For a few hours, there, he'd made her feel desirable. Like a real woman, rather than a...a...sort of household drudge. Only good for making up menus and binding up children's cuts and bruises, and generally justifying her existence by being useful.

She might have known it was too good to be true. A man like Worsley could take his pick of the most beautiful, accomplished women. Of course he wouldn't want to sample anything she had to offer.

Which wasn't all that much, was it?

Well, he'd had no right to raise false hopes in her breast then, had he? If he hadn't really wanted to make this marriage real, he should never have mentioned it, then she need never have spent the whole day in a dither and ended it by donning this ridiculous, flimsy nightgown and leaving her hair down.

Well, she could soon remedy that! She kicked the bedcovers aside, got out of bed and stalked over to the dressing table where she sat down, parted her hair into three sections, and swiftly braided it up.

There. She looked much more like herself. Her sensible self, that was. For she could no longer deny that deep inside there lurked a version of herself who could simper and get tongue-tied, and dream foolish dreams which resulted in her dressing herself up like a...harlot!

Well, she was never going to listen to that part of herself again. She stood up and raised her hands to her throat so that she could rip off the nightgown which had made her feel like a bride...so that she could stamp on it!

But would that really make her feel better? It wasn't the gown's fault. How could it be? It was an inanimate object.

It was Worsley she wanted to rip up at. For making her hope for something impossible and then dashing it all to pieces.

Besides, she did look...different in it. And if he did, by any chance, happen across her then she didn't want him to see her looking like an impoverished governess in a patched and darned flannel nightgown.

And it had cost a lot of money, she suspected. It would be a dreadful waste. And on such a warm, sultry night, she'd be much more comfortable in it than one of the long-sleeved, high-necked ones.

She stomped back to the bed and got back in. And vowed never to base any of her decisions, in future, on what he might think. She didn't care what he thought! And she wasn't going to waste another minute thinking about him. No, she wasn't. She was going to go straight to sleep, so that she'd wake up bright eyed in the morning, looking as though she hadn't a care in the world. She was not going to go down to breakfast looking haggard, as if she'd spent the night lying there, gazing miserably up at the canopy above her bed and wondering if she could have done anything differently. Anything to persuade him that he hadn't made a dreadful mistake in marrying her.

Chapter Fifteen

He didn't understand women.

Yesterday afternoon Dora had said she was willing to make a go of their marriage. Yet by the end of the evening she'd turned down his invitation to spend time alone with him, without the children acting as chaperons, so they could get to know each other better.

At first he'd put that down to modesty. Or nerves. As he'd lain in bed waiting for sleep to catch up with him, he'd compared her to a skittish mare, still unused to bit or bridle, and needing more time to get used to his presence before trust could grow.

But she was all frosty glances and disproving sniffs this morning. So, could he possibly have done something to annoy her? Was that why she'd run to her room and stayed there?

Come to think of it, she had begun to look annoyed with him during dinner. She'd stopped him talking about horses with Paul, or, to be specific, men's inclination to place wagers on them, and given them all a little lecture.

Well, she was a vicar's daughter, after all. Brought

up with what sounded like a very narrow set of moral values. She didn't regard gambling as a perfectly routine pastime. But other than that, she hadn't given any indication that she disapproved of his lifestyle. Or him. She wouldn't have allowed her precious brother to go down to the stables with him if she feared he was going to be a bad influence, would she?

So, surely it couldn't be her opinion of horses, or wagering on them, which was making her cross as crabs this morning. With him, that was. She was being perfectly affable with the children. He was the only one getting the frosty looks.

He filled his mouth with a large chunk of ham so that it would look as if he was too busy chewing to join in a conversation which she appeared to be conducting with the sole aim of excluding him entirely.

That was women for you. His sisters had always been the same. One moment, caressing, and apparently thinking the world of him, the next, slamming from the room when he walked into it with their noses in the air. He didn't know why he'd started to think she might be different.

No, that wasn't true. She had behaved with such pluck, and such good grace, right from the moment he'd accidentally abducted her. She hadn't made a fuss about anything, to date. She'd just had a think about it, considered the practicalities, then played the hand she'd been dealt. Any of his sisters or cousins would have written to him to complain about the conditions at Maybush House and demanded he come down and see to the rats and the lack of staff. And then rung a peal over him when he *had* come down. Dora had just shrugged, accepted the appalling conditions as her lot and, since there were plenty of empty rooms, invited her brother and sisters to join her.

Which made it even more perplexing for her to behave with such uncharacteristically feminine perversity this morning. If he'd annoyed her, or offended her at dinner, why hadn't she taken the opportunity he'd offered her to have it out with him?

Unless…after they'd been to the stables, had Paul said something to her which had put her in this mood?

He took a pull at the tankard of ale Mrs Warren set at his elbow. Oh, hang it! He was never going to find out why she was upset with him unless he asked.

But…did he really want to know why she was annoyed with him? If he asked her outright and she told him, then he'd be obliged to do something about whatever it was. And if it was to do with his horses, which he very much feared, then he'd have to tell her that he wasn't going to give them up, by God he wasn't! And then they would be at daggers drawn. Which he didn't want, not after starting to hope that they were getting past the dreadful way they'd started out.

He watched her, sitting at the foot of the table, nibbling delicately at a piece of toast, with a surge of resentment. This was one of the reasons why he'd never wanted to get married in the first place. He didn't want to have to tiptoe round his own house in case he offended a woman who felt she had rights to expect a certain standard of behaviour. A standard which he would never meet, no matter how hard he tried. A standard which he was going to have to guess at, what was more, if she wouldn't bloody well tell him!

He set down his tankard of ale and glared indiscriminately round at all the occupants of the table. He'd sworn he wouldn't tiptoe round a woman, so by God he wasn't going to do so. He was going to get on with living his life, the way he always had. And if she, and they, wanted to be a part of it, fine. They were welcome! And if not…

He felt an odd sinking sensation in his stomach as he contemplated doing what he normally did, when a woman became difficult. He *could* walk away, of course. It would be the easy thing to do. He could see that she'd be perfectly content to stay here, ruling over her little kingdom. But for once he didn't want to just walk away. And it wasn't, he didn't think, simply because he'd taken vows that he felt reluctant to break. It was because of her. Dora. And the tantalising little glimpses she kept giving him of…of something… more…better…something he didn't even have words to describe. But it was something he wanted with this woman. And even though he couldn't see it clearly, let alone describe it, he knew that if he didn't make any attempt to secure it, then he'd always regret it.

After all, he'd never give up on a high-spirited horse he'd purchased, would he? If it was difficult to train because previous owners had been careless, or cruel, he'd simply try harder to prove the beast could trust him. And by the sound of it, Dora had led a life of utter drudgery before they'd met. Everyone expected her to be the one who made sacrifices, so the others could do as they pleased. She'd even married him to give the others a home when she hadn't really wanted to. So, yes, it might be something of a challenge to persuade her that he wasn't going to mistreat her as well. But then he relished challenges when it came to training horses, didn't he? Why should this be so very different?

Right, then. He'd make the attempt.

He drew a deep breath. 'About this time of year,' he said, having had an inspired idea, or at least he hoped it was, 'I normally hold a house party at Brinkley Court. Tilly or one of my other sisters or cousins usually act as hostess, but now that I am married people will expect my wife to carry out that duty.' He gave Dora a challenging look. Dora affected to have seen something of interest outside and turned to look out of the window. 'I mean to set out tomorrow,' he informed her profile. 'If you come with me, that will give you a few days to meet the staff, get to know the lie of the land and so on, before any of the guests start arriving.'

He had her attention now. She was looking at him as though he'd made her an indecent proposition.

'This is a bit sudden,' she snapped.

'You did tell me, yesterday,' he reminded her, 'that you were willing to start shouldering some of the duties of being my Countess. Changed your mind, have you?' He sat back and glowered at her.

To his surprise, her face flushed scarlet as she lowered her head and clasped her hands together in her lap.

'Er...no, I have not changed my mind. It is just... that the nature of this...er...aspect of being your Countess is a bit...'

'Never tell me that you think you cannot do it. I know that you have never been the hostess of this kind of party before, but you strike me as being the kind of woman who can take anything in your stride.'

'Of course you can, Dora,' said Mary, whose presence he had temporarily forgotten.

'And we will be there to help you, won't we, sir?' Paul looked at him anxiously. 'You will not be leaving us here on our own with Mrs Warren and the rats, and the ghost, will you?'

'No.' He wasn't fool enough to try to separate Dora from her brood.

Actually, he wasn't above using them to get her to fall in with his wishes, either. He had a notion that if he could make Brinkley Court sound enticing enough to them, they'd do all the pleading for him.

'I had assumed you would be coming,' he said, using Dora's ploy of addressing the children, 'since the house party is thrown primarily for the benefit of the extended family. Even the most far-flung and obscure of them like to say they have spent their week at Brinkley Court. And of course, this year, they will want the honour of meeting my Countess, too.' He had the satisfaction of seeing Dora shifting in her chair.

'The mansion,' he continued, 'is big enough to house as many as wish to come, along with the veritable army of servants they bring. Not that you care about them, I don't suppose. What will interest you, I suspect, far more than the house itself, is the park in which it sits. Which is, well, frankly, enormous. There are several areas where you can play cricket without any fear of breaking anything, or losing your ball in a pond. It is from the home farm, nearby, where I had hoped to be able to find you those dogs I promised you. If you are in luck, you might even be able to pick out a pup of your own choosing.' He had never been so ruthless in pursuit of a goal before. But here he was, bribing children with the prospect of puppies and feeling not the slightest twinge of guilt when their eyes all lit up. And he hadn't finished yet. 'There is a lake, too, with an island on which you can build a fortress fit for Robinson

Crusoe, should you wish to. And the attics are full of all sorts of lumber which you can use to kit the place out.'

'Oh, Dora, please say we can go,' they all cried, more or less in unison.

Dora looked at him, her mouth pulled into a taut line, as if she knew exactly what he was doing.

He gave her a half-smile. She might resent his tactics, but their marriage was not going to get anywhere unless she accepted it, met his family and took up the duties she'd told him, only yesterday, she was willing to try.

And he still had one more trick up his sleeve.

'If you really find you are not up to the task,' he said, in as patronising a tone as he could muster, 'then you can cede to one of my sisters, who was bred to the position, when they arrive.'

It was like a red rag to a bull. 'Of course I will be up to the task,' she snapped at him. 'I am not an idiot. It is surely simply a more extensive form of keeping house, which I have been doing since the age of ten.'

'Well, there you are then,' he said. 'We are all agreed. Make whatever preparations you need to make, today, so that we can set out tomorrow.'

Stiff with dignity, Dora rose from her chair, beckoning the children to follow. They trooped out, chatting excitedly about the prospect of staying in a mansion and picking their own puppies, and building a fortress on an island.

It struck him, as he listened to their voices fading as they went up the stairs that the way he'd described the grounds of Brinkley Court had made it sound like a veritable paradise for children. Children who got on with each other, that was. What would his own childhood have been like if he'd had sisters like Mary and Martha, who enjoyed playing ball games and were thrilled to think they might have their own dog, rather than Tilly and Madge, who'd never wanted to get their clothes, or their hands, dirty? Who'd never been permitted very near him, except on formal occasions, anyway?

Well, that was by the by. The point was those children would make the most of everything the park had to offer. Rather like their big sister, they were remarkably self-sufficient. They wouldn't care when they learned they were the only children there. Which they would be, since the rest of his guests would leave their own offspring, and their nurses and governesses, in their own homes.

Which put him in mind of his need to write to his housekeeper to inform her of his sudden decision to bring not only his wife, but also her little brood, to Brinkley Court, far earlier than she would be expecting him. He usually left it to almost the last minute before going down there, since he'd never cared for the place much. All those rooms stuffed with old heirlooms that served no useful purpose. All the portraits of ancestors, gazing with mournful disappointment, or so it had always seemed to him, at the last of their line.

Still, things would be different this time. He couldn't see Dora's brood being overawed by the traditions and the rules laid down for children. In fact, he'd take jolly good care to make sure they weren't. He'd take them to the home farm and encourage them to explore the grounds. And if it rained, and they couldn't play outdoors, hang it if he didn't set them up with a game of cricket in the long gallery. He'd always wanted to do that, as a lad, wistfully imagining a brother who would have enjoyed doing it with him.

And if they were really going to play at Robinson Crusoe, on the island, then he'd have to see about getting them a spyglass.

In fact, he was going to be very busy today, what with one thing and another. Because, before he left, he was going to have to see about getting someone to clear out the rats, if there were rats, and a glazier to come and mend all their damaged windows.

So what was he doing sitting at the deserted breakfast table?

He pushed back his chair as he got to his feet, his spirits lifting. Because not only did he have a full and productive day ahead of him, but he'd be so busy that he wouldn't have time to meet with Dora and get into a quarrel with her, which might provoke her to change her mind about coming to Brinkley Court. Which now seemed absolutely imperative.

Chapter Sixteen

'Dora,' said Paul hesitantly as he came over to where she was kneeling by his trunk, 'don't you *want* to go to Brinkley Court?'

'Not really, no,' she said, taking the pile of shirts he was holding, so that she could fold them and pack them. 'And before you offer to help me deal with all the things I shall have to learn, when acting as hostess there—' which she didn't believe he would, not when Worsley had made it so clear that there were far more exciting ways for a boy to spend his time '—it is not the reason I am reluctant to leave Maybush House.'

'Well, what is the matter, then? I should have thought you'd want to go. It sounds like a lot more fun that it is here.'

'Yes.' Worsley had deliberately fired her brother and sisters up with enthusiasm for the expedition, when she'd shown a bit of reluctance to fall in with his plans. Because he knew, the sneaky so-and-so, that she wouldn't have the heart to refuse them. 'But I'm not the one who will be building dens on an island and playing cricket, and going to pick out puppies, am I?

I will be…' Well, she wasn't too sure what she would be doing, that was part of the problem.

'You won't have to clear up after the puppies, if that is what is bothering you,' said Paul, returning to his chest of drawers and coming back with a jumble of socks and collars. 'We will look after them, I promise. And anyway, we would have had the puppies here, if we'd stayed here, so…it isn't about the puppies at all, is it?'

No, it wasn't. But she couldn't tell Paul, or anyone else come to that, the real reason why she was so out of sorts over the trip to Brinkley Court. It would be too humiliating to admit that she'd so badly misunderstood her husband's request for her to take up her duties as his wife. She'd wanted to slide off her chair and take refuge under the table at breakfast when she'd finally seen that he'd been speaking of practical duties which had *nothing* to do with the bedroom. Which just went to show how differently they viewed each other. Every time she looked at him, at those broad shoulders, or his large, capable-looking hands, her insides went all hot and liquid, and a sort of yearning sigh welled up within her for touches from those hands, caresses from those hands.

But all he wanted from her was her presence as a hostess. For the sake of appearances, probably…

Because even though she'd vowed she could rise to the challenge, she hadn't the slightest idea how a countess ought to behave. How could she be the perfect wife to an earl if she didn't know what she was supposed to do?

'I suppose,' said Paul, coming back with another random assortment of clothing for her to stow into his trunk, 'it is a lot of work, packing everything up again after we've only just *un*packed it.'

'Yes,' she said, seizing on that for an excuse. 'And we were all just settling in here, weren't we?'

'Now you are married to a lord,' said Paul, leaning against his bedpost and folding his arms across his chest, 'you are going to have to get used to moving every few weeks. They are like...well, gypsies, you know. The chaps at school talk about spending summer at a family seat, then the Season in London and Christmas at shooting parties, as well as popping off to race meetings all over the country in between.'

'Oh, dear, really?' Couldn't she just stay here? All the time? If he took her to all those places, people would stare at her. And she hated people staring at her, which they had been doing ever since she'd grown taller than everyone else in the parish.

She bowed her head over the trunk, trying not to show him how much she dreaded the prospect of having society people sniggering at Worsley's maypole of a bride.

'Hmmph,' she managed to say and then got up and dusted down her skirts. 'I will just go and see how Mary and Martha are getting on with their packing, then I'll go and see to my own.'

In spite of what she'd allowed Paul to believe, it wasn't going to be all that difficult, really. All any of them had to do was put back everything they'd unpacked on arriving at Maybush House.

What was difficult was rousing her spirits after the crushing blow Worsley had dealt them at breakfast. Without even meaning to, she had to bear that in mind. He'd probably thought he was paying her a great compliment in wishing to present her to his family and having her acting as his hostess at this annual gathering. And, given the lengths to which he'd gone to ensure her compliance, perhaps it was. He could have just shrugged his shoulders and gone off without her, couldn't he? But, no, he'd behaved as if he really wanted to see if she could fit into his world.

Right, then. She must roll up her sleeves, in a manner of speaking, and rise to the challenge he'd set her. And most of all, stop wallowing in resentment and hurt.

But as anyone knows who has tried it, it's one thing to decide not to feel hurt, and resentful, and another to actually achieve that state of mind. By the time they all met up for dinner that evening, she'd just about managed to stifle the resentment. Because she couldn't blame him for not desiring her the way she desired him, could she? She simply wasn't the kind of woman who'd ever inspired thoughts of the bedroom. That didn't ease the hurt very much, though. Which was annoying, since she'd thought, before meeting him, that she was past the stage of wanting a man to find her beddable.

But she managed to get through the evening without casting too much of a damper on everyone else's excitement. And when she went up to her room, she donned her silk nightgown again, in a spirit of…

No, she just put it on because she'd found it so much cooler and more comfortable the night before. She was *not* going to sit up in bed, listening to him, on the other side of the wall, preparing for bed. She was *not* going to imagine him stripping off his shirt and sponging himself down. Nor did she lie there wondering what he'd look like, with his eyes closed and his hair rumpled against his pillows. And because she'd slept so poorly the night before, and had been so busy all day, she slept fairly well through most of the night and woke up feeling as though she could cope with whatever the day might bring.

While they were finishing breakfast, two carriages drew up outside the front door, causing the children to abandon their plates and go to the window, while simultaneously peppering Worsley with a barrage of questions.

'One carriage is for you and your brother and sisters,' he explained. 'And the other is for all our belongings.'

'Won't you,' said Mary, 'be travelling in the coach with us?'

Dora could have kissed her for asking the question which had sprung to her own mind, but which she'd been reluctant to voice.

'No,' he replied. 'I will be riding Chancer. If I didn't, one of the grooms would have to, because he wouldn't take kindly to being tethered to the back of one of the coaches, I can tell you.'

It was a good excuse, as excuses went, for avoiding spending the day cooped up in a coach with three talkative children and a wife of uncertain temper, she conceded. And the children swallowed it whole.

If she hadn't still been smarting from the lowering discovery that while she lusted after her handsome husband, he hadn't even shown an inclination to so much as kiss her, she would have enjoyed the journey, she reflected, later in the day. At every stop, ostlers and landlords treated them all with a reverence she'd never experienced in her life. Rank, evidently, made all the difference. Another aspect of the journey which she enjoyed was the way Worsley kept on leaning in through the window to provide snippets of information about their progress, or to check if everyone was well. Which led to a fine view of his back, and powerful thighs gripping his chestnut stallion, whenever he cantered away again.

Eventually, however, even the pleasure of seeing landlords bowing and scraping, and admiring the scenery through the carriage windows began to pall. It was getting near to the time the children were used to taking their evening meal when next they drew up at an inn and Dora wasn't surprised when Martha asked her plaintively if they were nearly there yet.

'I don't know, dear,' said Dora, 'but I shall ask.'

She sent them away to find the privy before approaching Worsley, because she didn't want them to overhear her complaining, if she found that there was going to be something to complain about.

'You do realise, I hope,' she said to Worsley, who was bending to examine one of Chancer's front legs, 'that it is just about Martha's bedtime?'

'Is it?' He straightened up and gave the horse a pat on the neck. 'Well, the next leg of the journey will be the last, so she shouldn't be up much past her bedtime. I thought it best, while the days are still so long and we have the light, to get the journey done in one day.'

'Did you?' she responded tartly.

'Yes. Easier on the children, I would have thought,

than exposing them to the dubious quality of inns about which I know very little, outside of the stables.'

That answer promptly burst her rising bubble of irritation over what she'd thought was the way he was driving them all so hard. 'You are correct,' she conceded. Because it *would* be better for them to get the travelling done with, so that they could go up to their beds, tonight, and wake up fresh, already in the location they would be dying to explore, the next morning.

'Did that hurt so very much, to admit that?'

'Yes,' she admitted stiffly. Which made him chuckle.

'There really isn't all that much further to go,' he said, handing Chancer's reins over to a groom, who led the horse over to a trough. 'We will dine here and then, when we reach Brinkley Court, they can all go pretty much straight to their beds.'

There was nothing about that statement to irritate her. She could not fault the motives behind any of the decisions he'd taken. He was trying to look after them all. When, as a bachelor, he'd never had to think of anything but his own pleasure before, she didn't suppose. He was a decent man, she reminded herself as he held out his arm to lead her in to dine. It was just the way he went about things without consulting her that set her back up.

When she told the children, the moment they all gathered round the table in the private room he'd booked for them, that their next stage would bring them to their destination, far from annoying any of them, they all gave a resounding cheer. Paul began to plan what they might all do in the morning, which perked Martha up no end. After only a short while, Dora began to feel like an outsider. For she was the only one of them to harbour even a shred of resentment.

But then the younger ones were used to having others ordering their lives, weren't they? Whereas she'd always been the one making the decisions.

They would always clash, she and Worsley, she reflected glumly as they embarked on the last stage of the journey, unless she could somehow manage to suppress her desire for independence. Or she could persuade him to consult her before planning anything…no, no, that was being unreasonable. She couldn't fault any of his plans. And why should he consult her anyway? Only a man who cared about offending a woman would consult her about something as trivial as travel plans and he didn't strike her as the kind of man who cared very much about anyone's feelings. No, that was unfair, he…

'Oh, Dora, just look,' cried Paul, who'd been leaning out of the window for the past little while, craning to be the first one to get a glimpse of the fabled Brinkley Court. 'It's the gateposts!'

And indeed it was. The coach was slowing down to make the turn through a set of massive stone pillars, topped with a set of silently snarling lions, at which the children all naturally snarled back, noisily. And then she no longer felt like a stranger in their midst, for she, too, was caught up in the wave of curiosity which swept over them all, making them jostle each other for the best view and argue about who was going to be the first one to spot the lake with the island in it.

But although they went over a substantial bridge that spanned a broad stream, into which they were sure it must run, of the lake itself there was no sign.

Their first sight of Brinkley Court itself more than compensated for any disappointment the children might have suffered, though.

'Just look at all those windows,' breathed Mary.

Dora couldn't help looking. There were four tiers of them, all glistening gold in the rays of the low, evening sun, from a Palladian facade that looked about half a mile long.

'Even you couldn't smash one of those ones right at the top,' said Paul, over his shoulder.

'And you won't be trying,' said Dora repressively. 'Remember, Worsley said there was plenty of space to play cricket in the park without endangering his property.'

'I'll say,' said Paul with a grin. 'The house must be a good mile from the road and then there's all those trees on both sides of the drive that look as if they go on for ever.'

'I wonder where the home farm is,' said Martha, fretfully, before stifling a yawn.

'I am sure Worsley will be able to tell you,' said Dora, soothingly, as the carriage swept round into a sort of courtyard with a fountain at the centre, before pulling up under a porch so massive that the roof sheltered the entire coach and all the horses pulling it.

A footman in dark blue livery with silver buttons came running out of the open front door to let down the steps and help her and the children alight. Behind him streamed a veritable torrent of other servants, wearing similar uniforms, who lined up, like soldiers on parade, females to one side and males to the other.

Dora swallowed nervously as she and her sisters gathered up their belongings. Paul, as he'd done at every other stop, had already jumped out and run round to wherever Worsley would be dismounting from his horse.

When the three of them were finally standing on solid ground, faced with the battalion of servants, Mary and Martha both edged closer to her side.

'Thank you, Mrs Parmenter,' she heard Worsley say, from somewhere behind her, 'for this lovely welcome you have arranged for my Countess.'

Lovely? That wasn't the way Dora would have described it. She was actually glad that both her sisters were clinging to her sides because she had never felt less like a countess and more like a complete fraud. Because all the servants, without exception, were smiling at her, in a sort of expectant fashion, as if she was about to do something miraculous. Like...like turn a cartwheel, or juggle knives, or something of the sort.

'You will be having most dealings with Mrs Parmenter, I dare say,' he said, as a stout, middle-aged woman stepped out from the throng, and dipped a respectful curtsy.

'Mrs Parmenter,' said Worsley, 'does a splendid job of keeping this pile in good order.'

Dora glanced over her shoulder, to see that Worsley had not relinquished the reins and that his horse was tossing his head up and down in an agitated manner.

'Stand clear, Paul,' said Worsley abruptly, as Chancer swung suddenly round in a big circle. 'He can smell his stable. Impatient to get his supper, I dare say. I know I should stay and introduce you to the staff myself, but would you mind if I...?'

He looked so torn that Dora stifled her nerves, and her sudden, uncharacteristic desire to beg him to stay.

Hadn't he told her that he thought she could rise to any challenge? Was she going to prove him wrong, at the first hint of difficulty?

'Not at all,' she said, forcing her lips into a smile. 'We will be fine.'

With a look of relief, mingled with what she thought looked like gratitude, he departed, leaving her to face the ordeal of what amounted to a regimental inspection. If only she felt like the general, performing the inspection, rather than a complete impostor.

'This is Margery, your head housemaid,' said Mrs Parmenter, indicating a lanky, dark-haired girl who was standing at the head of the line.

'Pleased to meet you, Margery,' said Dora, as the girl dipped her a curtsy.

Mrs Parmenter indicated, with a small gesture, that now Dora should step to the next in line, which she did, grateful for the tactful signal.

'This is—'

'Dora!' A female voice, shrieking her name from somewhere inside the house, was soon followed by the sound of feet pattering across a hard, echoing floor.

Mrs Parmenter's face closed up, just a moment before the owner of the voice came barrelling into view.

'Oh, how glad I am to see you,' cried Pansy, pushing her way through the servants and flinging her arms round Dora as though they were bosom friends who hadn't seen each other for years.

When the truth was that they'd only met the once and that very briefly, and that people who were truly her friends called her Dora.

And that, only when she'd given them permission to do so.

Chapter Seventeen

None of the servants was smiling any longer. They'd all adopted the wooden expressions of people who were determined not to reveal what they were thinking.

And Mrs Parmenter had folded her hands at her waist and adopted an expression of extreme patience.

'Oh, Dora, how I've longed for you to come,' Pansy said before bursting into tears.

For a moment, Dora just stood there with Mary clinging to one arm, Martha the other and Pansy draped round her neck.

'I think,' she said to Mrs Parmenter over Pansy's head, 'the formal introductions will have to wait. Do you think you could show my sisters to their room?' The moment she said this, the girls clung to her even harder. 'We'll all go,' she said, after only the briefest hesitation. 'Pansy, you can come, too.'

Pansy let go of her neck. 'Thank you.' She sniffed. 'Your room is all ready for you and we can have you settled in no time. And I am sure your sisters don't want to stand here listening while every single last one of the servants recites their names, do they?'

Mrs Parmenter waved an arm to indicate they should all go inside. 'This way, my lady,' she said to Dora.

Pansy shot the housekeeper a triumphant smile as she led the way across a marble-flagged hall to an oak staircase that swept up the left-hand wall.

Paul's eyes lingered on a full suit of armour, which was standing as if on guard at the foot of the staircase, brandishing a pike, before following the rest of the group. He'd just taken a breath to say something, his eyes alight with glee, when Pansy said, 'I am sorry to be such a watering pot, but at least I spared your dear little sisters *that* particular ordeal. The servants here are such a horrid, stuffy bunch.'

Since they were only halfway up the first flight of stairs, and the bunch in question were filing across the hall in the direction of a door which Dora supposed led to the servants' hall, most of them must have heard that remark. Mrs Parmenter certainly had to judge from the way her shoulders rose by about half an inch.

'They are always going on about what they call the *traditions* of the place,' Pansy prattled on, as though she hadn't noticed either that Paul was offended by having been cut out of the conversation, or that the servants were all silently seething. 'Which I soon found out was just an excuse for the staff to look down their noses at people who don't have titles, so they can get away with ignoring your orders. Children, probably, as well. They aren't used to them, you know. They never have them here, since this summer house party is only ever for adults.'

Dora hadn't noticed any of the staff looking down their noses at her. Or the children. On the contrary, they'd been all smiles until Pansy had put in an appearance and fallen on her neck like a long-lost friend. She wondered what Pansy had done to put their noses out of joint. Should she try to find out so that she didn't make the same mistake?

'I am so glad you have finally arrived,' Pansy said as they began to go up a second flight of stairs. 'I shall never forget how kind you were to me that dreadful day in the Blue Boar.'

Oh, well, that explained the way Pansy had fallen on her neck. And she had told Gregory her name was Dora, hadn't she? So she had no right to resent Pansy bandying it about without permission. Besides, it didn't sound as though very many people had been kind to her, of late. Particularly not her father. Dora couldn't imagine how she would have felt if her own father had cut her off without a penny.

Although, in some ways, his improvidence had resulted in something very similar.

'Though I was expecting you to come here days and days ago,' said Pansy. 'I could hardly believe it when Gregory said that nothing would prevent Worsley from going to the July meeting at Newmarket.' She shot Dora a look full of sympathy over her shoulder. 'Not even acquiring a new bride.'

Newmarket? He'd been attending the races?

Typical. He put horses far above her, or her welfare. Why, he hadn't been here five minutes before he abandoned her to all those staff, because his horse wanted to get to its stable.

She drew a deep breath, as she continued climbing a seemingly never-ending series of staircases, telling herself to calm down. Why shouldn't he go to the races, when he had so much invested in the outcome, from what Paul had told her? What right had she to complain? He hadn't married her because he'd *wanted* to. It had all happened by accident. And to be honest, she'd been surprised he'd turned up at Maybush House at all. Nor had she ever dreamed he would then expect her to come here and act as his hostess.

'Though perhaps you were relieved he hasn't been pestering you with his unwanted attentions,' Pansy continued, as they reached the top floor, wrinkling up her nose. 'It was absolutely disgusting, the way Worsley snatched you up and carried you off. Gregory told me all about it.'

'Not now, Pansy,' said Dora firmly, suddenly seeing why the staff might easily have taken her in dislike, as Paul glanced up sharply. She had only given her brother and sisters a brief outline of how she and Worsley had met, leaving out all the bits that might upset them, so that she could make it sound like a thrilling adventure, rather than the kind of thing they were all far too young to hear.

'Oh, no, not in front of the children,' said Pansy, clapping her hands to her mouth. 'How silly of me.'

But now both Mary and Martha were looking concerned.

'His Lordship told me that the girls would prefer to share a room. So I have put them in here,' said Mrs Parmenter, flinging open a door. 'It has a splendid view of the lake, which, he told me, they would particularly enjoy.'

Dora sent the housekeeper a grateful glance as the girls let go of her arms to go rushing to the window and peer out.

'Your room, Master Paul,' the housekeeper continued, 'has a similar view, being just along the corridor, past the schoolroom.'

The arrival at that moment of some footmen, with their trunks, created a bustle which prevented Pansy from saying anything else to annoy or upset anyone.

And while Mary and Martha were discussing who should have which bed and Pansy was directing a maid as to where to stow their things, Dora drew Paul aside.

'Don't let the girls get into a stew,' she said. 'And don't let them ask Pansy anything about the way I met Worsley.'

His brows drew down.

'I have to go to see to the bestowing of my own luggage and find where my room is, and so forth, but I will be back up to say prayers, and I, myself, will answer any questions any of you have.'

He nodded, once, and stood a bit straighter.

'Do you think,' said Dora to Pansy, 'you could show me to my room now? Only I should like to wash and change out of my travel-stained clothes.'

'Of course,' said Pansy with a smile. 'The children will be fine now, won't they? Even though it is way past their bedtime, to judge from how worn they look.' She sighed. 'I don't like leaving them with a mere servant, but at least they have each other.'

The servant in question, Dora couldn't help noticing, stiffened slightly, before going on with the task of unpacking.

'Of course they will be fine,' said Dora, making for the door. 'They are used to being sent off to school, you know—' at least, they'd been sent once '—where they have to do their own unpacking, so having a maid to help them is a rare treat. Which way?' She paused, looking up and down the corridor, obliging Pansy to come out and show her.

The girl kept up a stream of chatter all the way down to the next floor, about the history of the family and the extent of the park surrounding Brinkley Court. How Gregory's grandfather had moved a village and dammed up a valley to create the lake and the stunning scenery they could glimpse from every window they passed, when he'd abandoned the original house and had this new one built.

But finally, Pansy threw open the doors to what turned out to be a suite of rooms.

'The furnishings are all a bit antiquated,' said Pansy, wrinkling her nose. 'I wouldn't be surprised if the rooms have not been redecorated since the house was first built. Though I wouldn't ask if you can, if I were you. It's sure to be forbidden. Everything in the place seems to be of historical significance,' she complained. 'Or has sentimental value because it was done to commemorate some long-dead earl or his wife,' she finished with a pout.

At that moment, a troop of maids bearing trays, cans of hot water and towels came in.

'Oh, how lovely,' said Dora, seizing upon the interruption with relief. If she had to listen to one more minute of Pansy's complaints she was going to be hard put to it to keep a civil tongue in her head. She could see that Pansy was unhappy, but did she have no consideration for anyone else's feelings? 'I have been wanting a wash and a chance to change. Travelling leaves one feeling so grubby, don't you find? But thank you for showing me to my room, Pansy. I expect I will see you in the morning,' she said, hoping the girl would take the hint to leave, 'at breakfast?'

'Yes,' said Pansy resentfully. 'Because we all have to take it in the breakfast room, instead of having it brought up to our beds on a tray, as it would be done in a more well-ordered household. Although, perhaps *you* might be able to make some changes.'

Pansy flounced out of the room, just as Mrs Parmenter appeared in the doorway.

'Naturally, if *you* wished to make any changes to the way the household is run, my lady,' she said, 'you have only to say.'

'Oh, it is far too soon to be making any decisions of that sort,' said Dora, 'since I don't know how the place is run. However, Worsley said you were doing a fine job, so I don't suppose there will be anything much I would want to change.'

The housekeeper gave her a nod and appeared to unstiffen, just a bit. 'Naturally, you will have your own, personal preferences...'

'Yes, but I should think you have a better idea of what things work, in a place this size.'

Mrs Parmenter's expression softened even more. 'Very wise, my lady. There are reasons why certain things are done in certain ways. In the morning, I shall conduct you round the house and introduce you to everyone, the way I wished to do before.' She stopped, pulling her mouth into a grim line. 'That girl, if you don't mind my saying so...'

Fortunately, before the housekeeper could really start airing *her* grievances, yet another maid arrived bearing a tray of tea things, in spite of what Pansy had said about nobody bringing trays up to the bedrooms.

'Ah, tea,' said Dora with real gratitude, as the maid set the tray down upon a table by a window which gave a view over an immaculately kept formal garden.

'I could not help noticing,' said the housekeeper, 'that you did not bring a maid with you. Would you wish for me to arrange one of our staff to assist you in changing tonight?'

'That will not be necessary. I have been in the way of managing for myself, for many years, now.'

'Ah, I see.' Mrs Parmenter tipped her head to one side. 'None of this,' she said, making a gesture that mysteriously managed to encompass the room, the house, the park and indeed marriage to Lord Worsley himself, 'is what you are used to.'

There was no point in denying it. So she gave the housekeeper a rueful smile. 'No. I suspect it will be me who has to change, rather than me making any changes,' she admitted.

'You can trust me to help you…find your feet in your new role,' said Mrs Parmenter staunchly. Which was all well and good, but…well, she'd only been here about an hour and not only had she discovered that she was going to have her hands full dealing with Pansy's trouble-making tongue, but she was also going to have watch out for the housekeeper. Somehow, the woman had managed to make her admit to her feelings of unworthiness when usually people accused *her* of being a managing sort of female.

She must be more tired from the journey, and overawed by the surroundings, than she'd thought.

Worsley stripped to the waist the moment he got back from the stables, tossed his shirt aside and poured himself a basin of water so that he could wash off the dirt of the day.

It hadn't gone too badly, all things considered, he reflected as he splashed his face with water. At least he'd got her here, with a little help from her younger siblings. And now she was here, he could surely discover ways to court her.

Her sense of mischief—he could utilise that. Getting her to play cricket in the long gallery, or getting up treasure hunts in the grounds for the young 'uns, they were bound to be activities which would provide some opportunities to get her to lower her guard.

He'd start tomorrow, he mused, as he began soaping down his torso, by—

He paused, sponge in hand, at the sound of a knock on the door.

'Come in,' he shouted, dipping the sponge back into the basin to start sluicing himself off.

But it wasn't the door to the corridor that opened, but the one separating his room from Dora's.

Nor was it a footman with a message, or a tray bearing a decanter of brandy.

It was his wife. Who was staring at him, wide-eyed, as soapy water trickled down his chest and soaked into the waistband of his breeches.

Chapter Eighteen

'Ah!' He dropped the sponge on to the floor with a wet thunk as Dora froze, her hand on the door latch, her eyes sliding all over his naked, soapy torso.

'I beg your pardon,' he said as she continued to stand stock still, her mouth agape. 'I wasn't expecting...'

'N...nor was I,' she stammered, her knuckles turning white from clutching so hard at the latch. 'I should n...not have intruded,' she said, her eyes darting past him briefly, before she started inching back in the direction of her room.

'Nonsense! I mean, you are not intruding. You are my wife, after all. You have every right to come to my bedroom if you need me.'

Although she clearly didn't need him in the way he wished she did, because she was still fully clothed.

'I didn't realise this *was* your bedroom,' she said apologetically. 'When Mrs Parmenter said we had adjoining suites I thought this would be a sitting room or something of the sort.'

'It used to be,' he said, reaching blindly for a towel as he strove to think of some way of keeping her talking. Of keeping her here. 'But my parents rearranged the furniture so their bedrooms were next to each other. We can have it all put back how it was in my grandparents' days, if you like. Just…just let me find a dressing gown,' he said, backing away to the foot of his bed to grope for it, because he had the strongest conviction that if he took his eyes off her she'd bolt. And even though she'd strayed into his bedroom, he didn't think she'd take kindly to him deliberately invading hers if he had to set out in hot pursuit.

'There,' he said once he'd thrust his arms into the sleeves and tied the sash at his waist. 'I am at your disposal. In what way may I serve you?'

She blinked, as though coming out of a dream. 'No, it doesn't matter. I should not have disturbed you.' She began to inch away again, although she still didn't seem to be able to turn her back on him. 'It is nothing that cannot wait until the morning.'

He strode across the room and took hold of the door, just above the level of her head, so that she couldn't pull it shut behind her even if she did go back to her own room.

'It must be important to you,' he argued. 'This is the first time you have approached me of your own volition since we met.' Which was a huge step for her to take.

'Is it?' She blinked up at him, a frown flitting across her face.

'I know you have had to endure a great deal today. Whatever complaint you have to make,' he said, taking a deep breath and bracing himself, 'I am ready to hear it.'

'Oh, no,' she said, her free hand flying to her throat.

'I haven't come here to make a complaint. On the contrary,' she said, shifting from one foot to the other, 'that is to say, I fear that…that I need to make an apology,' she concluded in a rush.

Well, that was a new start. A woman, apologising?

Truly, she was unique among her sex. Although he had a feeling he'd better hear her apology before he granted her the absolution she sought. Just to make certain he was forgiving her for the precise error that was causing her to feel guilty. He'd been caught out granting his sisters absolution for things they hadn't been aware had annoyed him too many times to make the same mistake with his wife.

'For what,' he therefore said, 'precisely, do you wish to apologise?'

'Um. Well, I hadn't been here five minutes before I got caught up in…that is, I think I may have offended all your staff.'

'Your staff.'

'What?'

'They are your staff, now, not just mine.'

'That only makes it worse,' she said morosely. 'But, you see, just after you went off to the stables, Pansy showed up and, well…' She ran a hand across her forehead. 'I suspected she was on the verge of causing a…a scene, if you know what I mean, if she didn't get her own way, and I did not wish that to be the first memory my sisters and brother had of your home, so I got them all upstairs to bed as soon as I could.'

'Their home, too, now,' he pointed out.

'Yes, and that's another thing,' she said, her eyes

troubled. 'From what I hear, this house party is usually a strictly adult affair.'

'I will make sure they enjoy their time here, I promise.'

'It isn't that which concerns me. I am sure they will enjoy themselves. They are very adaptable and resourceful. But...won't they be in the way? Of your guests? If they aren't expecting children to be rampaging about the place?'

'No. Brinkley Court is huge. And the grounds are extensive.'

'Nevertheless, I am aware that you only encouraged them to come to...to put pressure on me to attend and act as your hostess. You should not have had to do that. I should have been more...' She bowed her head. 'Amenable,' she breathed, on what sounded like a penitent sort of whisper.

Amenable? Worsley found himself wrestling with a sudden very ungentlemanly urge to laugh. While he was still struggling to control himself, Dora added, 'If I were not such a...shrew, you would not have had to involve them at all.'

'Ah, Dora, no, you are not a shrew,' he said, reaching down and gently lifting her chin with one forefinger, so that she was looking him in the face again. 'If anything, I was a brute to put you in a position where you had to make a choice. I knew you would not want to leave them behind so soon after you had all been reunited.'

'You are not a brute,' she said with a flash of annoyance, 'no matter what some people might imply.' A look of chagrin crossed her face.

'You mean Gregory's wife, I take it,' he said. 'I have already got her measure, believe me. I suppose I cannot blame her for resenting me, for preventing her from getting entirely her own way. Particularly now I have had the audacity to get married.'

'I don't see that is any business of hers…'

'Well, it will be if I should happen to have a son of my own. For that son will supplant her darling Gregory from his current position as my heir,' he pointed out drily.

'Oh,' she said, blushing. 'I never thought of that. But perhaps that does explain…'

'What? What does it explain?'

'Well, at the time I just thought she was being tactless, but now I wonder if she was deliberately trying to…er…sow discord between us when she implied that you would much rather attend Newmarket than dangle after your new bride.'

'She said that?'

'Not in so many words.' She fidgeted. 'Perhaps I misunderstood. She'd already annoyed me, so perhaps I was deliberately taking everything she said the wrong way.' She glanced up at him with a sort of question in her eyes. As if she needed him to put her mind at rest on that point.

'It wasn't that I didn't *want* to dangle after my new bride,' he said. 'More that I didn't think she would welcome my attentions.'

'Oh?' She let go of the door latch and leaned her shoulder on the door, her eyes fixed on him as though she couldn't wait to hear more.

'You definitely gave that impression,' he reminded her.

She bowed her head. 'Yes. I behaved like a shrew

when we first met, didn't I? Nor have I done anything since to alter your opinion of me.'

'No, that isn't fair. That is, who could blame you for it if you were…er…angry? Not considering the way I picked you up and carried you off to Coventry. To be honest, I was, later, very impressed that you didn't attempt to scratch my eyes out. Your restraint was very ladylike, I thought.'

She lifted her head to give him a wry look. 'Ladylike. Hmmph.'

'You have done nothing, since that night, to change my mind on that score. On the contrary, a lesser woman would have found some way to wreak her revenge. All you have done is seize the opportunity to see to the welfare of your family.'

'Well, as I have told you, I have been like a sort of mother to them all ever since our real mother died.'

'Yes, and I adore your determination to do your best for them.'

'Well, and so have you. In your own way. For which I thank you.'

'You have no complaints to make about my autocratic ways? For offering to buy them dogs and spyglasses, and bringing them along to an adult party without consulting you?'

'Well, you did annoy me, the way you went about it, I must admit,' she said frankly. 'But then, you see, I tend to behave in a similar fashion. I just organise the people around me in the way I think best, so when I meet a fellow dictator, although he might annoy me, I completely understand why he behaves the way he does.'

'Even the way he picked up a strange woman in an inn and kidnapped her?'

'Oh, completely. Why, if some designing female attempted to trap either Paul or Timothy into what I believed would be a disastrous match, I don't think I would stop at anything, either. Not that I could physically kidnap anyone. I don't have the build for it,' she said, eyeing his shoulders in a wistful manner.

The way she was looking at him made him want to stand taller and flex his muscles. It was also making his heart beat faster.

'Perhaps,' she suggested, 'you could try to discuss things with me, in future, before making any more decisions on my behalf. Or that of my family.' She flushed, then, and wrapped her arms round her middle. 'No, never mind. That was a very impertinent thing to suggest.'

'Impertinent? Not a bit of it. I think it is a very sensible idea. Except…' He frowned, wondering how to put it.

But he didn't need to. She burst out laughing. 'Except for the fact that you wouldn't be able to do it, would you? Any more than I could.'

'I could try…'

She smiled. 'Thank you for saying that. But really, I can't see why you should. It isn't as if you married me on purpose and have any obligation to try to please me.'

'Oh, but that is where you are wrong. We may have been pitchforked together, because of my ill-judged attempt to stop Gregory throwing himself away on that dreadful girl, but now that we are married, I find myself wanting to…'

Just wanting, mostly. She was a magnificent creature. He'd thought so from the first moment he'd
clapped eyes on her. And since then she'd done nothing to change his mind. He'd been appalled, that time
he'd felt the urge to lick the peach juice from her chin,
rather than offering her a handkerchief. But now...she
was his wife...would it be so wrong to tell her?

'Right from the first, I wanted to kiss you, but I'd
already frightened you—'

She tossed her head. 'I have *never* been frightened
of you.'

'I... I can see that...now,' he conceded. 'You are
pluck to the backbone. But don't you see? If I had given
in to the urge to—' He stopped short of admitting he'd
wanted to lick her face. He didn't think that was the
kind of thing that would get him anywhere. It was too
crude a desire with which to sully her delicately brought
up ears. Far too crude. 'To...kiss you, or attempt to
kiss you,' he said instead. 'You would have thought me
some kind of...depraved...monster. I had to prove to
you that I am, at heart, an honourable man. But how to
prove that, after kidnapping and forcing you to marry
me...' He spread his hands wide in a gesture of appeal.

'I thought,' he continued, 'at least I hoped, that if I
gave you time to grow accustomed to the *idea* of me,
that eventually...'

She tipped her head to one side. 'Are you telling me
that is why you stayed away from me after depositing
me at Maybush House? It wasn't because you just preferred to go to Newmarket?'

He swallowed. It felt as if a great deal was hanging
on this conversation. On what he said next. If he told
her the truth, she might flounce off and slam the door

in his face. But if he wasn't completely honest with her, and she later found out, she might never come to trust him.

There was no point in winning this skirmish at the cost of losing the war.

'Dora,' he said, taking her hands in his. 'I am not going to lie to you. I had several horses running at that meeting. If I hadn't just got married, I wouldn't have thought twice about going to see them run. I always go to see my horses run, if I possibly can. And not just because I enjoy the sport. If I don't go, there is always a risk, albeit a very slight risk, that jockeys or grooms might resort to practices of which, although they might increase their chances of winning, I don't approve. Also, I really did think you would benefit from some time to get used to the idea of being a married woman, without having to put up with an actual flesh-and-blood husband getting under your feet.'

'So you maintain that you were being…considerate,' she said, with a wry twist to her mouth.

'I *hoped* I was. But if I had suspected that you wanted me to stay with you, I would have done. Only I didn't think that.'

'And you wanted to see your horses running,' she said tartly.

'I am beginning to see that this is always going to be a topic of contention. For you don't approve of horses—racing horses, that is—do you?'

'What makes you say that?'

'The way you were that night when I began talking about them with Paul. During the day I thought we'd begun to come to an understanding. But after that, you went, well, the only way to describe it is frosty.'

To his surprise, she blushed. 'I don't approve of gambling, that is true. But that wasn't why…oh, dear.' She shook her head. Snatched her hands out of his and retreated another step closer to the threshold of her room. 'I really must…'

He caught her by the elbow to stop her. 'What? If that wasn't why you were cross with me, then what was it? If you don't explain it to me, clearly, how ever do you expect us to make any progress?'

'Oh, dear,' she said again. 'Must I? I suppose I must,' she answered herself. 'Only it is so…lowering,' she said, hanging her head. 'You see—' her voice dropped to a pitch only just above a whisper '—when you talked about me being willing to take up my duties as a wife, I thought you were talking about…' She couldn't say any more, but even with her head hanging, he could tell she had given a brief glance at the bed.

He rapidly reviewed that conversation. And one thing leaped out at him in stunning clarity. 'You said…' His heart began to beat very fast. 'You said you were willing.'

She nodded.

'I had no idea,' he breathed, 'that you meant…*that*. I thought I had a long way to go before I might even attempt to snatch a kiss.'

Part of the reason why he'd brought her here, before any other guests were due, was to see if he could begin to court her.

But then something else occurred to him.

'No wonder you were so frosty with me the next morning. You must have been deeply offended if you thought I'd asked you to…and you'd agreed, and then I didn't come to your bed.'

She gave a sort of sulky shrug.

'I am an idiot,' he said on a groan. His sisters were always telling him so. When it came to women, and especially this one, it appeared they were right.

'No, not at all,' she began. 'I should not have made the assumption that you would want to…consummate the marriage. I had no right to.'

'No right? Dora, I am not such a tyrant that you should feel you have no rights, in this marriage. Haven't I made you see that, yet?'

'No…no, I have never thought you are a tyrant. That is, I am sure you do not mean to…er…that is…well, I know I am not the kind of woman that men…er… desire…'

'Not desire you? Dora, I have been wanting to kiss you since the first moment I clapped eyes on you! Even when I thought you were Gregory's woman.'

She went very still. 'No…no, you didn't. You… called me a jade.'

'Yes, but I also said that I could see exactly why Gregory had lost his head over you.'

She looked thoughtful and then frowned. 'So if you have been wanting to kiss me ever since then, why haven't you?'

She knew why. He'd just told her that he hadn't wanted to frighten her, or give her a disgust of him. That he'd wanted her to grow accustomed to…

Hold on. The tone of her voice just then hadn't been of a woman wanting to understand his motives. They had sounded much more like…a challenge.

Why hadn't he kissed her? When she was willing?

Well, that was something he could soon answer.

He stepped right up to her, slid one arm round her

waist, put his other hand round the back of her head, and finally did what he'd been dying to do since the night he'd tossed her over his shoulder and carried her off in his coach.

Chapter Nineteen

He was kissing her.

Finally, he was kissing her!

Even if she'd had to practically goad him into it. No, no, that wasn't fair, he'd been trying to be considerate. At least…

No, no more doubts. Not now. Not now that he was, ooh…not just kissing her, but running his massive hands all over her as though intrigued by her shape. Her texture. And pulling her closer into his big, powerful body. The body that she'd seen, at last, and which had been every bit as magnificent as she'd imagined. So magnificent, in fact, with the soapy water flowing over those great slabs of muscle, and the last rays of the sun making his golden hair glisten, that her mind had completely seized up. She hadn't been able to recall why she'd come to his room. She hadn't been able to even move. She'd just stood there, consumed by a sort of awe. And a strange, compelling need to run her hands all over all that glistening muscle. Closely followed by a bewilderingly shocking desire to lick those muscles dry. Which was of course, an impossibility, since her tongue was wet as well.

And then he'd covered it all up with a dressing gown, which had released her from whatever spell had struck her dumb, although it hadn't enabled her to say anything to the purpose. Instead, all she'd been able to think of was how impossibly gorgeous he was. How... unattainable. And how awful it must be for a man like that to have had to marry such a...disappointing sort of woman. A woman who had just admitted to the housekeeper that she had no idea how to run such a great house, let alone be a countess worthy of Lord Worsley.

It had made her want to apologise. And so she had, although not for marrying him. She'd still had *some* pride left.

But then he'd come close and leaned on the door so that his heavily sculpted upper arm was on a level with her eyes. As was a tantalising little glimpse of golden hair, where his dressing gown gaped open. And she'd had to attempt to carry on a coherent conversation while wrestling with the urge to reach out and touch that golden hair. To see if it felt as soft as it looked.

And then somehow the talk had veered round to her stupid assumption about which particular duties he'd wanted her to take on, as his wife, and...

'I don't think I have ever wanted a woman as much as I want you,' he suddenly growled into the crook of her neck.

A shaft of pure pleasure shot through her. He wanted her. He really did.

'Nor waited such a long time before doing anything about it,' he said, before nibbling his way up her neck to her ear, making that shaft of pleasure swell and grow, as if it had been a candle flame, and was now a…a ray of sun, making her shiver as though she was running a fever.

Her mind went fuzzy again. Only this time instead of losing the ability to move at all, she lost the ability to control her hands. They went exploring across his silk-clad chest for a few moments before growing impatient, pushing the irritating barrier aside and delving within to revel in the warmth of male flesh, and marvel at the springy, coarse texture of his hair. Like a barley field in the wind, it had looked like flowing silk. It was only when you got amid the crop that you realised how crisp the stalks were. How strong…

'I can't…' he rasped. 'If you keep doing that…' He tore his lips from her neck. 'If you don't want me, the way a wife should want her husband, you will have to say so, soon, because I may not be able to…' He shook his head, as though tossing aside an unpleasant thought.

'I can tell that you are enjoying my kisses,' he continued. 'And the shy way you are exploring my chest makes me think…'

Shy? She'd thought she was being very bold.

'Makes me hope…' he added. 'Dora, are you ready for this?'

She was about to say yes, when he frowned.

'You don't really know what you will be agreeing to, do you? You have had no mother to tell you about… what happens between a husband and wife when they go to bed together.'

Well, no, she hadn't. But she had a sort of notion. 'You know, though, don't you? You have had…that is, Tilly said…'

He caught her hand to his chest, holding it above his heart, so she could feel it thundering under her palm.

'I have taken lovers, yes. Which means that I am able to promise you that I won't be clumsy. Nor will I be impatient.'

Even though she wasn't too sure what, exactly, he meant, she could tell that he was telling her that she need not worry, that he would take good care of her. And because of his experience, she trusted that he would be able to fulfil whatever promise he was making her.

A sudden burst of shyness made it impossible for her to actually say, *yes, yes, take me to bed!* So she reached up and pressed her lips to his. And put her arms about his neck for good measure.

He was swift to understand her unspoken message. With a low growl, he scooped her up into his arms and carried her across to his bed. There, he laid her gently down, never parting his lips from hers, for a moment.

She'd always known he was strong. But she'd never dreamed that a man with hands that could control four galloping horses, or pick her up and toss her into a carriage, could be so…gentle. Yet skilled. He knew just where to touch and how hard to touch, or how soft, to provoke the most amazingly wonderful feelings.

It took her a while to work out, in the midst of kisses that had been driving her to a sort of frenzy, that he was trying to locate fastenings at the back of her gown. Since she'd never had a maid and had to get into and out of her clothing by herself, they were all either hidden under her arms, or under flaps at the front. It felt a bit as though she was restoring some balance when she had to show him that one thing. But once she had, he made short work of removing everything else.

And then…oh, the pleasure increased tenfold. Twentyfold. Oh, who could think about numbers when he was doing such extraordinary things with his mouth. Not just his lips, to kiss her, but his teeth and his tongue.

Oh, heavens! A flush crept up her face as he began to…surely he couldn't…but she'd agreed to trust him and…ah! Oh! Ohhh…

It was a considerable time before she was capable of thinking anything that she could frame with whole words. She had never known her body was capable of experiencing such pleasure. So many times.

It was only when it was all over and she lay, panting, gazing up at what she could make out of the canopy in the secretive dusk of his room, that she realised he had only experienced a release of his own once.

He'd put her pleasure before his own. Though at times he'd been shaking…with…had that been the effort of holding back?

She reached over and took hold of his hand, gripping it hard, her eyes suddenly, unaccountably, filling with tears.

He propped himself up on his elbow and looked down at her, a frown on his face.

'Is aught amiss? Are you crying? Did I hurt you? I believe, the first time, that it can be a touch uncomfortable, and I am…well, not a small man.'

No, he wasn't. He was big in all the places that mattered. Most importantly, his heart.

She had not only stumbled across the one man in

the world who could make her feel…feminine, since she towered over most men and they treated her like a man. But she had also found one who had as strong a sense of family, and duty, as herself.

'No, you didn't hurt me.' Well, she had felt a searing flash of pain at one point, but it was over so quickly that it didn't really count. Not when weighed against all that pleasure he'd brought her. She flushed as she recalled how…vocal she'd been in spite of not saying any words. How she'd moaned and cried out…

'Nobody has ever taken such care of me,' she said. And then yielded to the urge to kiss the knuckles of that amazing hand, one after another. 'I never dreamed that my body was capable of…feeling…' She felt another blush sweep over her cheeks. And then she squirmed at the memory of what he'd made her body feel.

'So why are you wriggling like that? Are you sure you are not uncomfortable?'

'The reason I was wriggling,' she said, feeling that it was pointless to hold anything back when they were lying there naked, having just been as intimate as it was possible for two people to be, 'was that I was thinking about the things you did to me and how they made me feel, and just thinking about them made me feel the same way all over again.'

'Hmmm,' he said, in a rather smug manner. 'You liked the things I did, then? Which particular things?'

'I cannot possibly say them out loud,' she gasped, suddenly realising that it wasn't so easy to describe things in detail, even though they'd just done them.

'Then how am I possibly going to be able to ensure your complete satisfaction the next time?'

'I am sure you will be able to work it out. After all,

you managed it extremely well this time, without any prior knowledge of my body. Except…'

'Yes?' The smug look disappeared. Now he was all frowning concern again.

'Well, you did have a bit of trouble divesting me of my clothes.'

He chuckled. 'Well if you will hide all the fastenings in such odd places.'

They lay there, both smiling, both well pleased with the other. Until a niggling thought began prodding at Dora's mind.

'Um…what happens now?'

He quirked one eyebrow at her.

'I mean, in a practical sense. Nobody has lit the candles yet and soon it will be too dark to see anything.' Even though the moon had now risen and was painting the world silver. 'And our clothes are all over the floor…'

When she made as if to get up and start tidying, he put one arm round her waist. The mere weight of it was enough to have pinned her in place, without him exerting the least bit of his strength. It made her go all warm inside. And get that strange, feminine feeling again.

'Usually, I would get up and return to my bed,' he said solemnly, 'after activity of this kind. But since you have come to my bed…'

'You mean, I am the one who ought to get up and go back to my room?' She quailed at the prospect. She didn't think she could walk across the room, naked, with him lying there watching her. Although, since it was growing darker by the second, he wouldn't be able to see all that much.

But she would still know she was naked. And to start

an undignified search for some item of clothing to put on was an equally unattractive proposition. She might run into a servant, who'd come to her room for some reason. To light her candles, perhaps…

'I could lend you my dressing gown,' he said. 'If you really wish to leave. You are probably still too shy to go wandering about in your birthday suit.'

'Thank you,' she said on a surge of relief.

'But,' he said, leaning the entire top half of his body over hers, 'you are welcome to stay a bit longer, if you like. There are no rules about this sort of thing between us. We can either write them ourselves, as we go along, or just do exactly as we please, when the mood takes us.'

'As…we…please?' With him looming over her like that, filling her vision, he seemed to fill her whole consciousness. She could not recall why it was she'd been thinking of getting up and leaving, now.

'I cannot guarantee, however,' he said, lowering his head and swirling his tongue round the outer edge of her ear, making her shiver and squirm, 'that you will be safe from my demands, if you do decide to stay…'

'What about,' she said, in a voice that came out as a sort of purr, rather than the normally brisk practical tone she used, 'my demands?' And she slid her arms round his neck.

'I shall do my best,' he breathed into her ear, 'to meet them, my lady. I am strong,' he said, running one hand down her flank, 'and healthy, and more than willing.' To prove it, he nudged her hip with the evidence of what she now knew was that willingness. And then took her to heights of pleasure she should have expected, after the first time, but which somehow still managed to surprise her.

She was surprised, too, by how bold she could be, under cover of darkness, and with the encouragement of a very amenable husband.

It was a different matter, however, when daylight returned and she could hear the sounds of a house coming awake.

The moment she began to try sliding out from under the covers without disturbing him, however, he opened his eyes and grinned at her. 'Going somewhere?'

'I have to go back to my room,' she said, peering round his for traces of her clothing. 'The children might come down to find me. And I don't want them to catch me here, like this...'

'Yes, they are bound to be up at the crack of dawn so they can go off exploring as soon as possible. You had better take my dressing gown,' he said, reaching out a hand to the floor at his side of the bed and coming up with the black silk garment he'd been wearing the night before. Before she'd torn it off him so that she could feast her eyes on the great slabs of muscle covering his chest. And run her hands over the same. 'Although if I lend it to you, I shall expect a favour in return.'

He said that in a playful manner, dangling the gown just out of her reach.

'A favour? What sort of favour?'

'More of a request, really, that in future you call me Toby.'

'Will you please lend me your gown... Toby?'

He smiled and, next time she reached for it, he didn't twitch it away.

'And also, next time you come to make your demands on me, woman,' he growled, leaning back on the pillows and placing one hand over his eyes, as though in exhaustion, 'come suitably equipped.'

'What makes you think there will be a next time?' she snapped, as she thrust her arms down the sleeves.

'Because you were insatiable last night,' he said, opening his eyes a bit, to watch her try to wrap the gown, which was far too big for her, round herself and secure it with a sash that went round her waist twice. 'Not that I'm complaining, mind you.' He stretched his arms and gave a yawn. 'Especially not about the part where you came to me, rather than me having to hunt you down and corner you, and persuade you that it would be a jolly good idea to remove all our clothes, and—'

Before he could go into what they'd done when they'd removed their clothes, she got her hands on a pillow, which she used to thwack him with.

She stormed out of his room, to the sound of his gentle laughter. But then suddenly paused, a wry smile coming to her lips. He'd distracted her from her shyness at having to dress and leave, that was what he'd done with all that teasing. Deliberately tried to make her cross, so that she'd forget about the awkwardness.

She would have to find some way to get her own back, she decided. She'd have all day. All day to plot a suitable punishment...

One that involved reducing him to a writhing mass of need...

One that involved making him *beg*.

Chapter Twenty

'Shall we take breakfast in the schoolroom,' he asked as Dora paused on the threshold of her own room, 'with the youngsters?'

His question had the effect of making her look at him over her shoulder in an innocently provocative pose.

'Don't we all need to go down to some sort of dining room? Pansy said…'

'It will be as *you* wish, once you've arranged it with Mrs Parmenter,' he told her. 'But I thought the children would benefit from us all being together, today, without anyone else present, so we can all talk about what they plan to do and I can inform them how they may go about it, and so forth.'

'You are correct, as usual,' she said with a touch of resentment, before sniffing, tossing her head and flouncing all the way into her own room.

He got out of bed and padded barefoot across his room, poking his head round her half-closed door just in time to catch her sitting down on her own bed, with

a smile playing about her lips that made her look like
a woman who has been pleasured half the night.

'I will escort you to the schoolroom once you have
got some clothes on,' he said, making her startle and
put on a frosty expression.

'You had better put some on yourself,' she snapped,
and then blushed as her eyes went on a swift, greedy
exploration of his entire form.

'Good point,' he said solemnly. 'Don't want to shock
the children. All this,' he added, running his hands
through the air about an inch away from his upper
body, 'is for your eyes alone.'

'I should hope so,' she said tartly, then blushed a
shade deeper. 'That is, I mean, I don't need to see all
of you. That is…oh, go away,' she cried, grabbing a
pillow and flinging it at him. Or at least, in his general direction. It fell to the floor well short of where
he was standing.

'While you are here, we are going to have to work
on your technique,' he said, leaning against the door
jamb and folding his arms across his chest. 'How about
spending some time on the south lawn, later on? We
could use the children as an excuse. Tell them we'd
like to encourage them to play cricket, or something
of that nature.'

She scowled at him. 'I am not going to spend my
first day here playing children's games. I have some
serious damage to undo, with regard to the servants,
today, which I planned to do during the tour of the
house Mrs Parmenter promised to take me on. I'd
thought she might be able to make them all known to
me as we come across them, going about their tasks
where they would normally carry them out.'

It wasn't an excuse to avoid spending time with him. He was almost sure of it. And, to be honest, he had to approve of the way she was approaching the task of managing a great house such as this one. It was vital that she get Mrs Parmenter on her side, from the outset.

'Very well,' he said. 'But I am going to be the one who shows you all over the estate and introduces you to our tenants. I have a nice little mare in the stables, just right for a lady—'

'Oh, dear. I am so sorry. But I cannot ride.'

'Not ride?' They wouldn't be able to go galloping off all over the estate, with stops at secluded spots where he could indulge in a little…courtship? But…that had been the whole point of bringing her here. 'How is that possible?'

'Well, horses cost such a lot of money to keep,' she pointed out. 'And, really, there was no call for me to learn anyway, since most of the errands I had to run, I could carry out on foot. And if I ever needed to go further afield than the borders of the parish there was always someone who would give me a lift in their cart, or carriage.'

'You cannot drive, either?'

She shook her head. A touch defiantly, as though he'd embarrassed her by pointing out her deficiencies.

But it gave him an idea.

'Well, never mind. I shall teach you.' It would provide the perfect excuse for whisking her away from staff and children alike, and having her all to himself for hours at a time. 'There is a little dog cart about the place somewhere that my mother used to use to get about the place. You can learn to drive in that.'

'Oh, no, there is no need—'

'There is every need. This estate is massive and I'm sure you won't want to have to ask someone for assistance every time you have a fancy to go down to the lake, or over to the village, or to visit one of the tenants, will you? Won't it be much better to just go to the stables and get one of the grooms to hitch up a pony, and take off wherever and whenever you want?'

She sighed. 'I would prefer to have some independence, you are right,' she said, shaking her head mournfully. 'I hope you aren't going to make a habit of it. Being right so often, I mean.'

But in spite of her mock complaint, it felt as if, from that moment on, he did keep on getting things right. Before many days had passed he found that the children were looking up to him as though he was their all-powerful and beneficent big brother, the servants were going about their business with smiles on their faces, as though they thoroughly approved of his choice of Countess, and as for Dora herself...

He couldn't have found a better wife if he'd gone out searching, rather than stumbling across her by accident. She was hard-working, cheerful, kind and devoted to her family. She was completely without vanity, too, having no idea how beautiful she was. In fact, she grew uncomfortable if he told her so. She much preferred it when he complimented her on her progress with her driving lessons, which was, he suspected, because she could see that his praise was both sincere and truthful.

Why did she have such a hard time accepting compliments on her person? It was as if everyone around her had convinced her that her only worth was as a kind of mother figure, or housekeeper, when there was so much more about her to love.

Not that he'd fallen *in love* with her, in any sentimental, soppy kind of way. No, he just appreciated the fact that she had bushels of integrity, that she was direct in the way she spoke to him, that she was a good sport and, perhaps best of all, an extremely responsive bed partner. Nobody would know it, to see the rather dowdy way she dressed and the stern manner she kept up during the hours of daylight. But when the sun went down, and those prim clothes came off…well, then he was privileged to discover there was an entirely different Dora. A Dora nobody but he had ever even glimpsed.

It was like the feeling he got when one of his prize mares had just rolled in the mud, then come across to him to receive an apple from his hand. A stranger would not have seen the great lines beneath the unprepossessing exterior, or the heart of her, that had made her win races, time and time again, against much flashier-looking opponents.

His only regret was that he hadn't made the effort to get to know her sooner. Although, would she have been as responsive if he'd pushed his suit straight after the wedding he'd insisted they go through before anyone found out he'd abducted her? Probably not. However, it still rankled that their guests would be arriving any day now and she was becoming increasingly busy with the arrangements.

Every time he told her that she could leave it all in the capable hands of Mrs Parmenter, she'd either look at him with a frown, asking why he'd asked her to come, then, if she wasn't needed, or she would point out that most of what she was doing was just watching what Mrs Parmenter did, so that she could learn the business of running a great house from a woman he'd described as capable.

And once the guests arrived, he had the feeling she'd be concentrating on them, rather than on him. Not that she had ever put him first, in her thinking, except when they were in bed together. The children came first. And now there were all those endless lists she kept making, or that Mrs Parmenter brought to her for her to look over. She was writing one now, at her desk in the little sitting room on the far side of her bedroom. She hadn't even noticed him come to see where she was, when he'd been undressed, and waiting for her, for what felt like close on an hour.

The most irksome part of it was that he was pretty certain that if he told her to put down her pen, because there were more important duties she ought to be attending to, that she'd comply at once. Probably even be a bit apologetic. But he didn't want her to think of their bed sport in terms of doing her duty. Besides, he'd felt so sick at his behaviour, in carrying her off by mistake, he'd vowed never to make her feel he wasn't giving her a choice. Which meant that pretty often he had to hold himself back.

He slouched back to his room, went to his bed and flung back the covers. But just as he was about to get in and sit there with his arms folded across his chest, it occurred to him that if any of his lovers had behaved like that, when he'd been too busy with something that interested him more, he would have accused them of sulking. And that the more experienced among them would have resorted to more subtle means of attracting his attention.

A slow smile spread across his face as he recalled a few ways some of them had indicated they wanted him. Ways that he could employ, without having either to beg for Dora's attention, or ordering her compliance with his wishes.

He was only wearing a dressing gown, so it was a simple matter to pull the material of it away from his neck, so that it exposed a good deal of his chest and the tops of his shoulders. He then crossed his bedroom and entered hers, going straight to a vase of roses which stood on her dressing table. He pulled one bloom from the arrangement and paused. He couldn't tuck it into his cleavage, the way one of his lovers had done, since he didn't possess one. He toyed with the idea of knotting it into his sash, but soon foresaw all sorts of problems arising when he wanted to undress. In the end, he just stuck it behind his ear.

Then he crossed her bedroom and paused in the doorway to her sitting room. He leaned back against the door frame and raised his arms, in a pose he'd once seen an actress adopt when trying to beguile him into offering her carte blanche. Then he heaved a sigh.

'I'll be with you in a moment,' said Dora, without so much as lifting her head. 'It's the dratted seating arrangements for dinner on the last night. Everyone in your family seems to be at daggers drawn with at least three other members.'

He said nothing, but raised his leg so that his knee peeped, provocatively he hoped, through the resulting gape in the lower part of his dressing gown.

'Do you think—?' She finally glanced at him over one shoulder and froze.

He ran the sole of his raised foot up and down the shin of his other leg. And batted his eyelashes.

'Wh…what…?' she spluttered, though he couldn't help noticing that her eyes were following the movement of his foot. 'What are you doing?' Her jaw dropped, round about the moment that her eyes snagged on the rose behind his ear.

'Can you not tell?' He tossed his head, in the manner of a woman shaking her curls so they tumbled tantalisingly round her shoulders. Although since his hair had been cut, last time he was in Town, into a windswept, the effect was somewhat spoiled.

'You…' A smile kicked up the corners of her mouth.

'Me?' He ran his hands down his sides. And pouted.

Which finally made her giggle. 'I think,' she said, getting up and tossing her pen aside, 'that I get the message.' She came across to him, reached up and plucked the rose from behind his ear. 'I haven't been paying you enough attention, have I? Poor, neglected Toby.' She ran the rose thoughtfully between her fingers, while running her eyes across his bared chest and shoulder.

The way she was fiddling with the stem of the rose made him break into a sweat.

'I'm not one to complain,' he said, heaving a mournful sigh.

She pursed her lips, then tutted in reproof. 'No, you just sigh at the top of your voice. And…and…' she waved the rose up and down his torso '…and flaunt yourself. I can see,' she said sternly, 'that I shall have to take you in hand.'

'Oh, yes, please,' he said, his already impatient flesh

springing to life with such enthusiasm that she couldn't fail to notice.

Although she pretended not to have done. She reached up and grabbed hold of his right hand, rather than what he'd hoped she'd grab, before towing him back into her bedroom and over to her bed.

How long, he wondered, would it be before she grew daring enough to actually take hold of his…? Oh! Not as long as he'd feared.

He left her sleeping the next morning, as was becoming his habit, after pressing a kiss to her forehead. He still half wished she could come out riding with him before breakfast, but given the choice between that, or wearing her out in bed at night, he'd plump for what they already had.

It was a perfect day for riding. Well, just about any day was a good day for getting astride a horse, or putting a team in harness, the way he looked at it. But there was something particularly fine about this day. His acres had never looked in better skin. His body had never felt so pleasantly exercised. And as for his spirits…

Well, they were excellent, until he caught sight of Gregory lurking on the path between the stables and the house, after he'd left Chancer in Pawson's capable hands.

'I…er…'

It pained him to see his ward stammering and blushing to the roots of his hair. Toby only wished he knew how to put things right between them. But the lad hadn't been able to look him in the eye since the day he'd caught up with him and told him exactly what he thought of him for letting him abduct poor innocent Dora, who'd only been trying to help.

'It…er…seems to me that you have made your peace with your…wife,' said Gregory, ending on a nervous sort of laugh.

'Yes, I have.'

'But, you haven't forgiven me yet, have you? Or you wouldn't be avoiding me and spending so much time with your new…family.'

Gregory gave him a kind of pleading look that wouldn't have been out of place on the face of a spaniel, the wounded eyes begging for forgiveness, without the lad having to actually come out and admit that he'd cheerfully sacrificed the nearest bystander so that he could get what he wanted. It was a look that had made Toby's heart melt on dozens of previous occasions. This time, however, it merely irritated him, reminding him of the many, many times Gregory had employed it to escape punishment for some misdemeanour.

And, now he came to think of it, he'd often made some little remark that caused him to examine his own behaviour, which often as not made him feel as if he'd been partly to blame. It had then led him to try to coax the lad out of the sullens with gifts and treats, instead of advising him to buck up.

He'd spoiled the lad, that's what he'd done. He hadn't wanted him to endure the cold, harsh upbringing which had left him unsure of how to mingle with most people. But he should have provided *some* discipline.

'I would never have chosen to marry Dora,' he said curtly. 'But now…' He stopped, suddenly reluctant to share just how very much he'd come to admire her. His relationship with Dora was *his* business, not anyone else's.

The lad looked relieved. 'I did think you'd been looking distinctly bobbish of late. Which brings me to what I wanted to talk to you about.'

'Which is?'

'Well, me.'

Obviously. Gregory couldn't just be pleased that he'd observed Toby was happier than he'd ever been in his life, because he didn't really care about anyone but himself.

'In what way, specifically?'

'Well…' Gregory adopted an earnest expression, making Toby wonder if any expression he'd ever shown had been genuine. Or was every smile, every soulful droop of the lips, a way of manipulating those around him into doing what he wanted?

Or was he becoming overly cynical in regard to his ward since the advent of Pansy into their lives?

'It seems increasingly likely,' Gregory was saying, 'that you are going to be producing your own heir before much longer.'

That was true. But for the first time in his life the prospect of becoming a father did not induce a feeling of panic. He had no need to fear he'd damage a child, either with his clumsy hands, or his clumsy manners. Dora would soon set him right. What was more, he could see any children that were a mixture of his blood and Dora's turning out a bit like her brother and sisters. And he got on with all of them with no trouble at all, since they had such frank manners.

'And that being the case,' Gregory continued, 'I was wondering, well, what will happen to me, then?'

He knew it. He knew that Gregory wasn't relieved that he'd done no lasting damage to anyone else. He just wanted to know how the success of Toby's marriage would impact upon him.

'I am not about to cut you off without a shilling if that is what you are getting at. And for the moment, you are still my heir.'

'Well, yes, but, don't you think it might be prudent for me to study for some kind of profession, rather than just carrying on living as though all this—' he waved his hand in the air, indicating Brinkley Court and all the properties up and down the country which Toby currently owned '—will one day be mine? Which is what I have done, up to now. Because, frankly, you seemed the very last man who would ever marry.'

And whose fault was it that he had?

Still, at least this little speech showed that Gregory was showing some foresight. Some responsibility.

'Do you have any particular profession in mind? I will, naturally, support and sponsor you to the best of my ability.'

'Thank you. You could have said…that is, a lot of people say that I'm nothing but an idle wastrel. But the thing is, I do understand about farming. Working the land.'

'Yes, you have always shown an interest in the estates and the tenants.' But he'd thought that it was only in hopes of what he would gain, in due course. 'I always knew,' he added, 'that I'd be leaving it all in good hands.' Which was, now he came to think of it, one of the reasons he'd never felt any burning need to actively seek a wife.

'There you are, then,' said Gregory, triumphantly. 'That is what I could do. Look after the land and manage the people on it.'

He was certainly good at managing people. He'd had Toby wrapped round his little finger since not long after he'd been out of short coats.

'So, you want me to give you a farm, somewhere?'

He shook his head. 'I was thinking more in terms of becoming a land agent, or a steward to some great house.'

'Yes. You would do well in that sphere.'

Gregory's face lit up. It shouldn't have affected him, he supposed, but to see him react that way to Toby's approval made him feel, well, warmed inside. He started strolling along the path again and Gregory fell in beside him.

'It is a pity you cannot simply dismiss Hopkins,' said Gregory, chuckling.

'That would be unfair, unjust, and, in your case, ungrateful.'

'Oh, yes, wouldn't it! When the old fellow has taught me all I know.'

So, why say it then? Even in jest?

'You will keep your ears pricked, won't you, then? And put in a good word for me when something comes up?'

'I will, of course, although there is no rush. It isn't as if Dora is—' He broke off. It would feel like a betrayal to speak of such intimate matters, even to Gregory, whose position would be directly affected by the conception of a child.

Gregory grinned at him. 'And in the meantime, I shall dog Hopkins's footsteps. Learn as much as I can, while I can.'

Perhaps Gregory was not totally spoiled. Perhaps having to work and provide for a wife would be the making of him.

Chapter Twenty-One

'I wish,' Pansy said with a sigh, as Mrs Parmenter bustled off with the day's list of tasks tucked under her arm, 'that there was more I could do to help.'

Dora wished so, too. She'd never been so tired in her whole life, even though all Mrs Parmenter was doing was running all the arrangements past Dora, so that she could learn exactly what went into throwing a house party on this scale. And it didn't help that she was getting so little sleep. Although she couldn't complain about the reason she was getting so little sleep. Toby was so…ardent. And inventive. And skilled…

'Do you know,' Pansy continued, 'what I think?'

The smile that had begun to play about Dora's lips, on thinking about how Toby was keeping her awake at night, faded. She turned her upper body, from the desk that was strewn with copies of the lists she'd just approved with Mrs Parmenter, and gave Pansy her full attention. Because if she'd learned anything about the girl, it was that she was not going to take a hint that Dora wasn't really interested. She wouldn't cease until she'd told Dora exactly what she thought, probably in minute detail.

'No,' said Dora, fixing a polite smile to her face. 'What do you think?'

'Well, I think you should take the morning off.'

Typical of Pansy to suggest shirking her duties. She was never around when there was any work she might have been able to help with, yet she miraculously appeared just as the task was done, expressing regrets and saying how much she would have loved to have done such-and-such.

'If only I could,' Dora said, rubbing at her temples where, she was suddenly aware, there was a pulse throbbing. A pulse that acted, in such warm clammy weather, as a warning, nine times out of ten, that a headache was about to descend.

'Well, why don't you? You just admitted to Mrs Parmenter that you have no talent for arranging flowers, so she must do as she thinks fit. So that is what she will be doing for the remainder of the morning. And you haven't been able to spend nearly as much time with your delightful family as you've wanted to, have you? Though I know they have been very good at amusing themselves and that they never complain, I am sure they would love it if you went over to the island to see how their fortress is coming along.'

'Yes, they would.' They had kept her up to date on their progress, at the mealtimes they shared. But it wasn't the same as actually seeing it for herself.

'And once the guests start arriving it will be much harder for you to just slip away. This might be your last chance.'

For once, Pansy was correct on all counts.

Apart from anything else, Dora had a feeling that if she stayed indoors, poring over every little detail of the plans that Mrs Parmenter, really, had well in hand, that the niggling throb in her temples would blossom into a fully-fledged headache that might lay her low for days.

'Do you know, I think you are right,' she admitted, making Pansy's face light up. She got to her feet and looked out of her sitting room window. 'It is far too lovely a day to spend it sitting poring over menus and seating plans.'

'Yes, and you can count on everyone ignoring those plans and just sitting wherever they want anyway. Have you ever been to a dinner party where everyone sat where you thought they should?'

Well, no. But then she'd never been to a dinner party of the sort Pansy meant. Not with fifty or sixty people at the table. A fair sprinkling of them with titles, too.

The very thought of it set the pulse at her temples throbbing more insistently.

'I think it will do me good to go and see what the children have accomplished on their island,' which they'd renamed The Island of Despair, after the one they'd been reading about in *Robinson Crusoe*. Their simple, uncritical acceptance of her would bolster her spirits, too, which were frankly quailing at the prospect of presiding over the impending house party. It would also mean, God forgive her for even thinking it, getting away from Pansy. Because if she was going to go all the way to the lake, to inspect the fortress the children were building, she'd have to get the pony hitched up and drive there. And Pansy was too timid to let Dora, still very much a novice, drive her even a short distance without someone else, preferably male and experienced with horses, in attendance.

And Dora had no intention of waiting around until such a somebody could be summoned, not now the notion of escape had lodged in her heart.

It was a glorious feeling to steer the little vehicle out of the stable yard, once the groom had hitched Nutmeg into the traces for her. Toby had been correct. Driving a horse, or at least a pony, was a marvellous feeling. She felt so…powerful. And free. With nobody around to demand anything from her and the ability to go wherever she wished, at whatever speed she wished, or at least could coax out of the little dappled pony. No wonder Toby was so keen on horses. They brought such an element of…fun to life. She hadn't seen it before this moment.

Learning to drive, and having him watching her every move, had been like one more way in which she had to prove herself worthy. But it was different now she was in complete control. It was…exhilarating to flick the reins and cause Nutmeg to break into a trot. And feel the breeze fanning her face, and…whoops! She hadn't tied her bonnet ribbons securely. Well, never mind. She'd collect the bonnet on the way back. Nobody was going to see her with her hair streaming all over the place, except her brother and sisters, and they wouldn't care.

All too soon she spied the tops of the trees growing on The Island of Despair, then round the next bend the shoreline came into view. She slowed the pony to a walk and drew the vehicle to a halt next to a stand of trees a short walk from the beach, so that Nutmeg could wait in the shade.

She'd done it! She'd driven herself all the way to one of the most distant parts of the estate.

Now all she had to do was get herself across the expanse of open water to the island. She'd never rowed a boat before, but how hard could it be? The children did it a couple of times most days. And she'd managed to learn how to control a pony and trap, which was far more complicated. For a boat wasn't a living being, with a mind of its own, but an inanimate object that would simply go where she directed it.

Or so she'd assumed. But it turned out that it wasn't that simple. It took her some time to work out how to get the craft to go in a straight line, rather than round and round in circles. And by the time she'd got the hang of it, she was perspiring rather freely. Although for some reason her feet felt rather cold. No, not cold, wet. She glanced down and noted in alarm that there was about an inch of water in the bottom of the boat, which had most definitely not been there when she'd pushed it out on to the lake and clambered in. That meant that it was leaking, which wouldn't be a problem if only she knew how to swim.

She glanced over her shoulder to the island she was making for, which, although she'd been rowing for some time, didn't seem to be any nearer than it had to start with. She was much nearer the shore. So it made sense to turn the boat round and head back, just in case the boat was leaking so badly it sank. She had no wish to be out in open water in such a case.

But after only a few more minutes, she realised she'd

made yet another mistake. She'd been clumsy with the oars to begin with and, now that she was feeling a bit worried, she appeared to have lost what little skill she'd so far gained. Or perhaps the boat was getting more difficult to steer as it got heavier, and more sluggish, the more water that seeped in.

Oh, why had she ever thought she could come out here on her own? Why had she ever thought she was a capable sort of woman in the first place? She couldn't row a boat in a straight line, she couldn't swim, she couldn't even arrange flowers, or a seating plan. And now not only her feet but her calves were wet. If she didn't get to shore soon, the water would be up to the little plank thing on which she was sitting and her bottom would also be wet. In an instinctive surge of revulsion at the very notion, Dora stood up.

In the circumstances, it was just about the worst thing she could have done.

Chapter Twenty-Two

'Lord luv us,' said Pawson, staring, wide-eyed at something over Toby's shoulder. 'What's the missus doing?'

Toby straightened up from his examination of the worrying amount of heat in Chancer's right fore fetlock, to see Dora, leaning on what looked like an oar, come hobbling round the corner of the path. Followed, at some distance, by her pony and trap.

His heart gave a sickening lurch. He might have known he wasn't getting things right. As he ran to help Dora, who was clearly in pain, he cursed himself for encouraging her to go out and about on her own. Ponies were notoriously clever creatures who'd do whatever it took to outwit a human, but this one had been in harness, so how the devil had the dratted creature managed to toss her out and injure her?

And why, he wondered when he drew closer, did she appear to be soaking wet?

'Dora!' Her name tore from his throat. But yet again, where she was concerned, it was the worst thing he could have done. For at the sound of his voice she looked up, saw him and instinctively held out her arms to him, and in doing so let go of her makeshift crutch, then let out an agonised cry of pain, before crumpling to the ground in a dead faint.

He wasn't even able to catch her before she hit the ground.

'Go and fetch the doctor, damn you,' he yelled to Pawson over his shoulder, as he knelt over Dora's prone form, wondering why the fellow was still standing holding Chancer's head when Dora's head was bleeding. Bleeding! Where her forehead had struck the gravel path. A cold fist seemed to reach into his gut and squeeze hard. 'And Mrs Parmenter,' he added, hefting Dora into his arms and setting out in the direction of the house. 'She'll know what to do,' he said as much to himself as to his groom.

'But... Chancer...and Nutmeg,' said Pawson, looking from one to the other.

'Damn them both,' he snarled, holding Dora close to his chest. What did horses matter at a time like this? Dora was hurt. And she was more important than a dozen horses. Even, yes, even the famous, expensive, cup-winning Bobtail. Though he would never have let any of his horses go wandering off without a groom, at the least, in attendance, so why hadn't he treated Dora to the same level of care?

When he reached the house, some instinct led him to carry her up the stairs and to their suite of rooms, scattering startled servants left and right.

Just as he was bending to lay her down on the bed, Dora's eyes fluttered open.

'Thank God,' he breathed, hauling her, briefly back closer to his heart in relief.

'Oh, Toby,' she groaned. 'Never say I fainted? Of all the poor-spirited, pathetic things to have done...'

He couldn't resist pressing just one kiss on to her damp forehead. 'I dare say you had good reason,' he said soothingly as he bent to lay her down.

'Don't put me down,' she cried, flinging her arms round his neck and clinging tight.

'No, no, of course not,' he said, past a lump in his throat at the very first sign she needed him for anything in an emotional sense.

'My clothes are soaking wet,' she added. 'You will ruin the coverlets if you put me down on the bed.'

Which dashed his momentary belief that she might be feeling some tender emotion for him.

'What shall I do with you, then?'

'J...just sit down somewhere with me and h...hold me on your lap, if you would. You don't mind, do you? I mean, you're already wet from carrying me up here...'

'I don't mind a bit,' he said, settling on the edge of a broad windowsill, which was hard on his behind, but where there were no furnishing about which she could complain. Even though it hurt like the very devil to learn she rated him less than a bedspread.

'Oh, Toby,' she said plaintively, before leaning her head on his shoulder. 'Why are you being so...kind to me? When I've been such a fool? Thinking I could go out on my own, when I can't control a pony, or a rowing boat, let alone swim.'

Because I love you, was the answer that, somewhat startlingly, sprang to his mind.

'Because you are my wife,' was the answer he spoke aloud.

'You are too good for me,' she said, looking up at him with brimming eyes. 'You should have married someone who could at the least…swim,' she said bitterly.

'No, no,' he said, appalled at the vision of having any other woman in his life. 'I don't care whether you can swim or not. Though if it means so much to you, I can always teach you.' Instantly, a vision of her standing waist deep in the lake, wearing something filmy plastered to her wet body, which was transparent from the water, flashed into his mind.

At which inopportune moment Mrs Parmenter came bustling into the room.

Getting Dora undressed, into a bath, dried and into a clean nightgown took some time and a great deal of argument, since Mrs Parmenter and the maids carrying cans of hot water seemed to think he ought not to be there. But Dora had, she told them, wrenched her ankle badly and the only way to get her into the bath, or out of it, was for someone to lift her bodily since she couldn't bear any weight on it. And he was the only one with the necessary muscle power.

'So much fuss,' Dora moaned, as he laid her down on the bed. He pulled a chair up to the bed, sat on it, and took hold of her hand. 'Why aren't you scolding me?'

'Because you don't deserve a scold,' he said, lifting her hand to his mouth and kissing it fervently.

'Oh, but I do. When you hear how utterly stupid I've been…'

'I am sure you were nothing of the sort.'

'Well, it was selfish of me to want to run off and play with the children on the island when your guests are due any time now. Only I thought it would be my last chance…'

'I don't see why. Most of the guests have been here many times before and are well able to entertain themselves. The main thing to do is provide meals on a regular basis and the cook and housekeeper do that.'

She shot him a darkling look. 'Do they all know that there are currents flowing in that lake? I suppose they do. I don't suppose, when they are rowing across in a boat that is leaking, they wonder why they are drifting along the shore instead of getting closer to it, no matter how hard they pull. And I don't suppose that when any of them get into a boat that is leaking they stand up just at the worst possible moment, either.'

From that, he understood that she'd been trying to row across the lake in a boat that was taking on water and had managed to capsize it, probably in a moment of panic. He frowned. Surely the staff wouldn't allow a boat that leaked to be left on the shoreline where anyone could get into it? They all knew that the children made a habit of playing down there. He was going to have to have words with someone about that.

'So that explains why you were so wet,' he said, putting his anger at the state of the rowing boat to one side for the moment. 'You capsized the boat.'

'I did no such thing,' she said indignantly. 'I stood there, perfectly upright, as the boat steadily sank beneath my feet, to the last possible moment. Clinging, for some reason, to the one oar I hadn't managed to lose when I was battling to row to the shore.'

'You…you must have looked very…regal…' he said, trying to picture the scene.

'Well, not for long, because as I expect you know, the lake isn't all that deep. Or at least, it wasn't at the bit where the boat finally sank. So that all I had to do, when it touched the bottom, was kick down hard and my head shot up into the air. Which I did, repeatedly, so that I must have looked like some kind of… demented march hare, bobbing up and down with the oar clutched in my hands.'

'You probably felt as if you had to hang on to something,' he mused.

'Yes, but I wish I hadn't kicked so hard. Because I did something to my ankle on some rocks and I had to crawl out of the lake, because I could not put any weight on it. Fortunately, I could use the oar as a kind of walking stick. But then, oh…' she pulled a face '…that beastly pony.'

'What did it do?'

'Well, when I got to the lake, I left the carriage under a stand of trees, so that Nutmeg could stay in the shade.'

'That was thoughtful of you.'

'Thank you. But it wasn't sensible to leave the brake off, so that, if I was away a long time and the shadows moved round, Nutmeg could move into the next patch of shade, was it? Because when I tried to climb back in, with my one good leg, the ungrateful animal just… sneered at me and trotted off! It knew I couldn't move fast enough to catch it.'

'Ah. And it followed you home when you decided to walk. In spite of the pain in your ankle.'

'Yes. Sniggering at me all the way. And then, as if I hadn't humiliated myself enough for one day, what must I do the moment you saw me, hobbling along in soaking clothes with pond weed in my hair, but faint?'

'It is more than a mile and a half from the lake to the stables,' he pointed out gently. 'And you were in agony. And had just gone through what must have been a terrifying ordeal, since you can't swim.'

'Yes, in water that is about five feet deep at most,' she said bitterly. 'And all your servants saw me.'

'Not all of them—'

'But they will all know about it by now, after the spectacle I made, collapsing like that and then you having to carry me upstairs and put me in the bath as though I am a child.'

She wasn't a bit like a child. Not in any way.

'How am I going to face your guests now, Toby?' she said anxiously. 'I am not fit to be a countess.'

'Yes you are. Every magnificent inch of you. The only Countess I could ever see presiding over my tables.'

'You are just saying that,' she said. But he couldn't reply the way he would have wished, because the children all came piling in to see for themselves if Dora really had collapsed in the driveway and had to be carried to bed, and if so, why?

This time, when she related the story, she did so in such a way as to bring out the humorous side of it all. So that when the doctor finally arrived, it was to see them all sitting round her bed, laughing.

The doctor tried to dismiss them all, so that he could examine the patient, but Toby wasn't going anywhere. He could see the children were a bit reluctant to leave as well, so he promised that the moment the doctor had left, he would come up to the schoolroom and tell them what he'd said.

Dora gripped his hand a little tighter when they'd gone.

'You will make sure they don't worry about me, won't you?'

'Of course,' he promised. No matter what the doctor told him.

As soon as the doctor had finished with Dora, she made him go straight up to the schoolroom to set the children's minds at rest. Even though he would have much preferred to stay with her, just holding her hand.

But looking after the children was what she wanted him to do and it was little enough, after all.

And she was right to insist on him going straight upstairs, he realised when he saw their anxious faces.

'There is no need to worry,' he assured them. 'The doctor says your sister has merely sprained her ankle, not broken it. And the graze on her forehead, which she sustained when she fainted, is superficial. She will need to rest, with her foot up for a day or so, but that is all.' He said nothing about the dangers of contracting an inflammation of the lungs, since Dora had not only scoffed at the notion she'd been stupid enough to swallow any water from the lake, but had also made him promise not to tell them that.

But far from seeming satisfied with what he told them, they all looked rather grave. The girls nudged Paul and whispered at him in urgent tones.

The boy cleared his throat and stepped forward. 'The thing is, sir, while we are glad that she has not been seriously injured this time, we want to know what steps you are going to take to make sure she doesn't do worse next time.'

'Next time? What exactly are you saying?' It sounded as though they were implying this hadn't been an accident. 'It was an accident. A series of mishaps. And your sister is a capable woman. I'm sure she can look after herself...'

'Yes, but we use that boat every day. And it was fine last night when we got to shore and beached it. And we saw Aunt Pansy down there earlier, messing about with it.'

'You couldn't have done.'

Paul drew himself up to his full height. 'We don't tell lies. And we weren't imagining it, either. Martha saw her, from the little window up in the attic, where we'd gone to search for stuff to use in our hideout.'

'I was keeping a lookout for cannibals,' put in Martha.

A vexed expression flitted across Paul's face. 'It was all part of our game of Robinson Crusoe. Of course we didn't expect to see real cannibals on your estate, sir, but we were using the spyglass you gave us, so there was no doubt that it was Aunt Pansy, down by the lake, fiddling about with the boat first thing this morning. And before you ask why we didn't say anything about it before, well, we didn't think anything of it until Dora told us how she almost drowned. And then we put two and two together.'

They all stood there, gazing at him expectantly. What he wanted to do, and what Dora would want him to do, was to tell them that when they'd put two and two together, they'd made five. That Pansy couldn't possibly have deliberately set out to hurt their sister.

Except…well, he'd never taken to the girl. And it wasn't only because she'd cajoled Gregory to elope with her. There was something…false about her. She said all the right things, and smiled, and yet…

And then there had been his shock to hear the boat the children played in every day was in such poor repair that it had sunk. He'd been going to have words with his outdoor staff about that, because he'd told them to make sure the children would come to no harm, no matter where they played.

And…was it a coincidence for Dora to have met with an accident the very day after Gregory had come to him, asking him what was to become of him if she presented Toby with an heir? Gregory had made him believe that he would be happy to get a job as a steward to some great house. But was he really? Who could know what went on inside another man's head?

Well, Toby would never have believed that the lad would ever have behaved with such lack of good breeding as to elope with a flighty piece like Pansy, but he had. So…was he also capable of arranging for an 'accident' to befall Dora? Before she could give Toby an heir who would cut Gregory out of the succession?

If any of that was true, there would be nowhere on earth that either of them would ever be safe from him. He would hunt them down and…

He clenched and unclenched his fists a few times as he battled back a deadly rage. Rage that anyone would dare to deliberately hurt Dora in such a sneaky, underhanded manner.

And it was his fault they'd dared. They'd seen that he hadn't been watching over her the whole time, the way he should have been doing.

'I am going to take much better care of your sister from now on, I promise you,' he growled.

'Thank you, sir,' said Paul. 'And if there is anything we can do to help…'

He looked them all over. All of their little faces, filled with concern for the sister they adored. All as determined as he that nothing bad should ever happen to her again.

'You can make sure that at least one of you stays with her whenever I cannot watch over her myself,' he said.

'As she has a sprained ankle,' said Mary, 'she will have to stay in bed for the next day or so, won't she? And whenever any of us have been ill, she has always taken great care of us, so she won't think it suspicious if we say we want to do the same for her. By keeping her company. Reading to her…'

'I could take my embroidery to her room and do it there. Get her to help me with my stitches,' said Martha. 'She likes to see us being what she calls gainfully employed.'

It would make them feel better to be doing something. And even if it was the case that their imaginations had run away with them, he, too, would feel better knowing someone would always be with her. Because now they'd voiced their fears, he couldn't help wondering…

No, surely people didn't go about trying to dispose of other people, just to stop them from providing him with an heir? Preposterous!

And yet…now they'd put the notion in his head, he didn't think it would go away. There were just too many little details that added up.

And anyway, if he didn't take measures to protect her and something terrible happened…no, he wouldn't even consider such a thing. It was unthinkable. Life without Dora…

He shook himself.

Nothing bad was going to happen to her. He was not going to allow it!

Chapter Twenty-Three

It was going to be thoroughly miserable, having to stay in her room, when the weather was so fine and there was so much to do. Particularly since she knew everything would go just as smoothly without her.

What was the point of being here at all, when they could all manage so swimmingly without her?

Swimmingly—ugh, what an unfortunate choice of word. Because she couldn't swim, could she? And no matter what Toby said about her being the only Countess he wanted, it was obvious he was just saying that to be kind. Because that was the sort of man he was. So determined to do the right thing that, from the moment he realised she'd had nothing to do with his ward's elopement, he'd insisted on making it up to her.

Although he gave every indication of enjoying their nights together, she couldn't help noticing that she was always the one who went to his room, because she clearly found him far more attractive than he found her. Because while he was handsome and attractive, she was a gangly great scarecrow of a woman with no feminine wiles and… A single tear ran down her cheek.

She dashed it away irritably. She couldn't stand females who sat about weeping and feeling sorry for themselves. Let alone ones who fainted. Although the doctor had hinted there may possibly be a good reason for that, she reflected, running one hand over her stomach. She would know in due course.

A timid tap on the door had her sniffing and swiping at her damp cheek with the back of her hand. And her mood, which had been improving on thinking about a possible baby, plunged again when she saw it was Pansy who peeped round the door.

'May I come in? I heard you'd had an accident,' she said, sidling into the room. 'That you almost drowned. Are you much hurt?' She looked round the room. 'Is Worsley not here?' She looked shocked. 'If I'd been through a dreadful ordeal like that, Gregory would never leave my side.'

Yes, but then *they'd* married for love, whereas Toby had just been determined to pay the penance for abducting her. Oh, dear, why must she keep harping on the same old grievance? The accident must have really shaken her nerves.

'He has just run up to see the children,' said Dora, defensively, 'to tell them what the doctor said and put their minds at rest.'

Pansy raised her fair brows. 'Oh? I thought I saw him going down to the stables.'

'He may have done, after seeing the children, I suppose. When I came back, earlier, I do seem to recall him and Pawson fussing over Chancer's front leg…'

'Typical,' said Pansy indignantly. 'That man always puts his horses first. The women in his life are always a very definite second. Gregory told me that he never wasted long on any of his affairs, not during the racing season, anyway. No matter how beautiful the lady concerned, none of them could ever keep him at their side for very long.'

Was that so? And if it was, did Pansy really have to repeat it? To her of all people, when she must know how insecure she felt at the way their marriage had come about?

But then that was the thing with Pansy. She appeared to be friendly, but a lot of her apparently artless little remarks were like poison darts. Many of them struck home, too, or Dora might not be feeling so miserable, and insecure, right now.

From now on, she decided, she was going to keep Pansy, and her poison, more at arm's length. Even though she felt sorry for the girl, there were limits. To start with, she'd go along with Mrs Parmenter's suggestion she employ a maid who could answer the door, if nothing else, and keep unwanted visitors out when she didn't feel up to coping with them. It was what the woman had hinted she ought to do, now she was a countess, anyway, wasn't it? Only she'd thought, hoped, she wouldn't have to change.

But in the meantime, she'd have to exert herself. Be blunt, no matter how impolite it might be.

'Pansy, I know you mean well, coming to keep me company, but I really don't feel up to talking right at this minute.'

'Oh, how tactless of me! I should have seen that you are in pain. Do you have something to take for it?'

'The doctor left some laudanum. But I don't need it and, even if I did, I should prefer to do without because it makes me feel sick and woolly headed.'

'Oh, but…well, what about some of that stuff you gave me, in the Blue Boar? That had a very calming effect on me and didn't make me feel sick at all. I could make you an infusion, couldn't I,' she said brightly, 'just the way you did for me? I know you have some of it somewhere, because when we sent the trunk back to you, I made sure everything was in it.'

That was rather a good idea. Because giving Pansy a job to do would not only make her feel useful, but would get her out of the room and give Dora some peace and quiet.

'Thank you. A soothing cup of chamomile tea would be very welcome.'

She told Pansy where to find the necessary herbs and sighed with heartfelt relief when she trotted happily out of the room. It didn't matter how many times the girl said she was her best friend, Dora simply couldn't return her feelings. Which was vexing, since she was bound to her by familial ties, brought about by her marriage to Toby's ward. Although…yes…if she was family, then she could put her in the same category as Aunt Honoria, who'd agreed to take the girls—but not Paul—during the school holidays. Aunt Honoria was not the kind of person she'd ever been able to feel all that much affection for, but for whom she always managed to muster up the requisite amount of respect and forbearance.

Just as she'd settled that in her mind, somebody else knocked on her bedroom door. But this time it was Mary who poked her head in. And when she asked if Dora minded her coming in, she simply held out her arms. Because it reminded her that she was not alone in this house, with nobody who cared. Her sisters and brother loved her unconditionally.

As if to prove it, Mary dashed into Dora's open arms like a little homing pigeon. 'Paul and Martha wanted to go and pick you some flowers before coming to see you, but I didn't want to leave you on your own that long. And also I thought I'd just check to make sure you wouldn't mind all three of us clustering round, if you are in pain, or need to sleep or—'

'I am not the kind of ill where I need to sleep. And I will be happy for as many of you as want to visit, to stay as long as you like. I have a feeling I will be growing extremely bored, over the next few days, as I have to stay put, with my foot up.'

Mary's face brightened. 'I brought a book,' she said, fishing for a small, card-covered volume she'd hidden in her skirt pocket. 'I thought I could read it to you, if you would like that, or if you wanted to sleep I could just sit quietly somewhere and read it to myself.'

'For now,' said Dora, 'it will be enough just to have you here.' She couldn't help noticing that Mary's eyes kept flicking to her book. 'You can just sit and read, if you like, while we wait for Paul and Martha to arrive, then they can't say they missed out on anything.'

And so it was, when Pansy eventually returned to the room, with a tray, that she discovered Mary curled up on the coverlet next to Dora, totally absorbed in her book.

'Should your sister really be on the bed with you?' Pansy missed the dagger glance Mary shot at her, since she was setting the tray down on the bedside table. 'It would be dreadful,' she said, picking up a cup, 'if she jarred your foot, wouldn't it?'

'I shan't do anything so careless,' declared Mary, leaping from the bed at the precise moment Pansy held the cup of tea out to Dora with the result it went flying, spattering the steaming liquid all over the bedclothes Dora had previously been so determined to keep dry.

'Oh, dear,' said Dora. 'Are you scalded?' She'd moved her own legs away from the area where most of the liquid had been spilled so rapidly that pain had gone spearing up her leg.

'No, I'm not,' said Pansy, dashing at the front of her gown, which had received a slight sprinkling. 'No thanks to this naughty girl.'

'She is not naughty,' snapped Dora, instantly defensive of her sister, not for the first time feeling like a mother tiger guarding her cubs. 'It was an accident.'

'No, it wasn't,' said Pansy. 'She did it on purpose!'

'Nonsense,' retorted Dora, pain making her finally lose her temper. 'Why ever would she do such a thing?'

'Because she doesn't like me! None of them do!'

Now would be the perfect time to have a maid to shoo people out of her room whom Dora didn't want there.

But she had never been one to lean on anyone else for support. She had, instead, been proud of being the one upon whom everyone else leaned.

She forced herself to sit up straighter and looked Pansy in the eye.

'Pansy, you need to stop thinking that everyone is against you…'

'But they are. All of them!'

'Oh, for heaven's sake!' She turned to appeal to Mary. 'Mary, please, tell her that it isn't true. That it was just an accident.'

To her surprise, Mary's expression turned mutinous. 'It was as much of an accident as what happened to you, earlier on.'

'What? What do you mean?'

'*She* knows,' said Mary, glaring at Pansy.

'It's a lie! I don't know what she means.'

Dora looked from one face to the other and perceived, from her experience of all the times she'd had to act as umpire in one of the family squabbles, that although she had no idea what the pair were arguing about, each of the combatants did.

'Would you mind,' she said to Mary in her most reasonable tone, 'explaining *exactly* what you are arguing about?'

'She did something to the boat to make it sink,' said Mary, pointing a finger at Pansy. 'When everyone knows you can't swim. And I do hate her, I do!' She flung herself across Dora's lap and burst into tears at the same time. 'I couldn't bear it if anything happened to you. I had to stop her giving you that drink.'

'Mary, what has come over you? Pansy wouldn't...'

But Pansy had gone white, placing her hands to her mouth in a gesture which *could* denote horror at being accused of such a terrible thing. But suddenly, Dora recalled how adamant Pansy had been that she go down to the lake, as soon as possible, before guests started arriving...

And she felt as if a chill hand had just seized the back of her neck.

'Pansy?' Dora had always known the girl could be a bit spiteful, but surely she couldn't stoop to causing her physical harm? 'I thought we were friends...'

To Dora's shock, Pansy fell to her knees and burst

into noisy sobs. 'It wasn't so bad when you first came here. But then Gregory said that you and Worsley were getting very warm, and that like as not you'd have a baby before long, then he went to speak to him about what to do if he was no longer his heir and I heard him say he would become a farmer. A farmer,' she wailed. 'I could not have thrown my fortune away to end up married to a farmer!'

'So...you tried to get rid of me?' As she said it, Mary cuddled even closer, putting her arms round her waist, as if to protect her. Or cling to her. And in spite of being the older, the one who'd always protected the younger ones, for once, Dora clung right back.

'None of this would have happened,' Pansy protested, 'if you hadn't come into the taproom when you did. *I* would have been the lady here!'

'Do you really hate me that much?' How could she have said, and so many times, that she was her friend, if that was the case?

'No, I don't, that is the worst of it,' said Pansy, beating the floor at her side with her fists. 'You...you are so kind to everyone. So capable. Everyone likes you and respects you. But...but you see, I *love* Gregory,' she said, looking up with tragic eyes. 'And this is all my fault. The poverty and him losing the chance to become an earl, and not even getting my fortune to live on. I've ruined him. Completely ruined him. I thought it was going to be all right until Worsley fell for you. But now...' She shook her head. And wrung her hands. 'I had to do something to prevent him from having to work for a living. Don't you see?'

'Yes, yes, I suppose I do...' Because if she were in Pansy's shoes, and someone was threatening to take away everything Worsley owned, because of something she'd done, well, heaven alone knew what lengths she might go to, to make things right for him. Oh, yes, and she knew just what it felt like to be unworthy of the man she'd married. But...

'But two wrongs don't make a right, though, do they?'

Pansy's shoulders slumped. 'I suppose you are going to tell Gregory now, aren't you, and then he won't love me any more, and I will have lost everything!'

Dora shook her head. 'No, Pansy, if you are really sorry and can promise me you won't try anything like this again...'

'Stop right there,' came a stern voice from the door.

All three of them flinched and turned to see Worsley standing in the doorway leading to his own bedroom, his face like thunder.

Chapter Twenty-Four

Toby had been listening to Pansy's confession with mounting anger. He couldn't believe Dora was on the verge of forgiving her!

Yes, he could, though, that was the trouble. She was altogether too quick to forgive people who'd wronged her—first him, then Mrs Warren…

Well, Dora might be the closest thing, this side of heaven, to a saint, but he wasn't. So, before Dora had a chance to utter words that would make the girl think she had got off scot free, he stepped forward and made his presence known.

Silence fell, apart from the soft sound of shaky sobs from Mary, who was still clinging to Dora like a limpet. He knew how she felt. He wanted to cross the room, sweep her into his arms and hold her safe and tight. So tightly that nobody would ever be able to prise her from his arms.

But that would mean thrusting the little girl aside and only a monster would do that at such a time.

Besides, it was more important for him to deal with the danger to the one they both loved.

The first thing he did was to stride across the room to the bell pull and tug on it, hard.

When he turned back, he looked again at the tableau of the three mostly silent females. Two of whom had red, teary eyes and the third...

She was gazing at him with an expression between exasperation and amusement. Amusement! When she'd just heard that Gregory's wife had attempted to kill her.

She had nerves of steel. Well, he'd learned that much during their very first encounter, when he'd accidentally kidnapped her. He'd admired her for her bravery, then. Or stoicism in the face of adversity, as he'd thought. But this was something else. Not only did she show no sign of fear of the girl who'd just tried to do away with her, but she'd actually been on the verge of forgiving her.

Or had she?

'Were you really going to simply forgive Pansy?'

'What else can I do?' replied Dora with a wry shrug. 'She's family.'

There was a knock at the door and a maid came in.

'Go and tell Spenlow he needs to come here, would you, please? And then, if you can, round up Martha and Paul.'

Pansy shuffled across the floor, on her knees, and made a grab for Dora's hands, her eyes wild. 'Please don't tell Gregory what I've done. I couldn't bear to lose him!'

Dora took a breath as if to speak, but Toby held up his hand for silence.

'You may have wormed your way into my wife's favour, but you won't succeed with me. I am most certainly going to tell Gregory what I have learned today.'

Pansy uttered a shriek.

Toby took no notice. 'It will be up to him to deal with you,' he said, implacably. 'You are his responsibility. But one thing I will say,' he said, walking across the room until he was directly in front of her. 'You will never have the chance to get anywhere near Dora again.'

Pansy let go of Dora, and made as if she would fling herself at him. He took a swift step back as she went to embrace his knees.

'Pansy,' said Dora, in a stern voice. 'You have to face up to what you have done.'

'But—but—Worsley said *you* would forgive me,' she wailed.

'Yes. If you are truly sorry, of course I forgive you,' she said and shot him a warning glance when he would have objected. 'But,' continued Dora, in that stern voice, 'you need to speak to your husband about what drove you to act in such a reprehensible way. Face up to the life you will have to live together. In short, my dear, it is time you grew up.'

Pansy howled in outrage. The door burst open and Gregory bounded in, perplexity and concern all over his face.

'What is going on? Pansy, darling, what is the matter?' Gregory went to her, his arms outstretched as though to hug and comfort her. But she recoiled, placed her hands over her face and wept even louder.

When he made as if he would have got down on the floor with her, Toby took hold of Gregory's elbow and drew him to one side.

'I had better inform you that you wife has just admitted to attempting to murder mine.'

Gregory laughed. 'Don't be absurd.' Then his face stiffened. 'If this is what has upset Pansy, if you are going round accusing her of such things, then no wonder...'

'It is the truth. And before you say anything to me that you will later regret, I suggest you take your wife somewhere private, where you can hear the whole, from her own lips.'

'That is exactly what I will do,' said Gregory, stiff with affront. He then went to his wife and gently but firmly got her to her feet, and led her, still sobbing, from the room.

It felt much quieter once she'd gone. Which was partly because Mary had stopped crying and was sitting up, wiping her eyes and regarding him as though he was a knight of old who'd just slain a dragon.

Just then Paul and Martha arrived, at which point Mary bounced from the bed. 'She confessed to the whole thing! The moment I let on we knew what she was up to.'

'You all...' Dora looked round the trio and then at him '...*knew* she'd tried to...'

'Suspected,' Toby hastily explained. 'I found it hard to credit that anyone could really want to hurt you. Nor did I think her capable of thinking up a plan and carrying it through, so ruthlessly.'

'Hah! She may look like a little fairy,' said Dora wryly, 'but she is very determined about getting her own way. She cajoled poor Gregory into eloping, don't forget. Although,' she added, in a more lenient tone, 'she isn't totally selfish. She does appear to love Gregory, as far as she is able. She was, after all, in her own muddled way, trying to undo the wrong she felt she'd done him.'

'I hope,' he said in disbelief, 'you aren't going to suggest I put this all behind me and carry on as though nothing has happened.'

'No,' said Dora, as Martha climbed on to the bed next to her and snuggled up while Paul flung himself across the foot of the bed. 'I think it might be a better idea to send the pair of them away somewhere that they can be alone, to thrash out their problems without anyone else interfering...'

'Yes,' he said. And where they couldn't interfere with him and Dora any more, to boot. 'And I know the very place. Maybush House.'

'Yes!' Paul bounced on the bed and punched the air for good measure. 'She's the kind of person who will be terrified of the rats!'

He hated to disappoint the lad by admitting the rats were a thing of the past since they'd sent in a couple of terriers, laid some traps and mended a few broken drainpipes, so he said nothing.

'And she won't have as many servants to contend with, either,' said Dora, rather more charitably. Which also wasn't completely true, because he'd instructed his man of business to deal with the staffing shortage, too.

'Right,' said Toby firmly. 'Now that that's settled, you can stop bouncing on Dora's bed and making her fear for the safety of her ankle, and get off back to the schoolroom for your tea.'

They protested, but only half-heartedly, so that before long, he and Dora were alone. And, hang it, he couldn't hold himself back any longer.

So he climbed on to the bed they'd so recently vacated and hauled Dora into his arms.

'I could have lost you,' he said with a shudder. 'I didn't know how much I'd come to love you until I saw you collapse at my feet and I went cold inside, wondering whatever I would do with the rest of my life if I didn't have you to share it with.'

'You love me?' She pulled out of his arms far enough to gaze up at him in disbelief. 'But how can you? I mean, you are so...' She waved her free hand at his face, his torso. 'And I am so...' She made the same gestures over herself, but with a grimace of revulsion on her face.

'Why can you not believe it,' he grumbled, 'when I tell you I find you beautiful?' Why could she not just fling her arms round his neck and tell him she loved him, too, the way any other woman would?

Because she was... Dora, that was why.

'Well, anyway,' he grumbled, 'the thing is, you don't need to understand it, or even love me back. I don't expect you to. I mean, why would you after the way I've treated you? And even if I hadn't, I've always known I'm not the kind of man who could make a woman happy. But I just wanted you to know, that's all.'

'Not make a woman happy? Who made you think you couldn't? Toby, you foolish man, don't you know you are the stuff of most women's dreams?'

'No, I'm not. I'm too insensitive. Rude. I... I'd crush most women...'

'Well, you'd never manage to crush me,' she retorted. 'Because I'm not like most women, am I?'

'No, you're not,' he said, making her face fall. 'But that is what makes you perfect.'

'I am so very far from being perfect,' she began. So he placed one finger across her lips to stop her running herself down, yet again.

'You are perfect for *me*. If you won't believe anything else, believe that.'

She tilted her head to one side. 'You are perfect for me, too,' she mused. 'And of course I love you back,' she said in a tone that implied he was an idiot for not knowing that already. 'Can't you see that's why I found it so easy to forgive Pansy? If it wasn't for her, we would never have met. And the thought of what my life would have been...' It was her turn to shudder and hug him more tightly.

'But we have,' he said in an attempt to comfort her. 'I mean, we did, that is, we do—'

'Toby, stop talking,' she said in an exasperated fashion. 'You know that is not where you excel.' Her lips curved into a wicked smile. '*Show* me how you feel, instead. You are very good at that.'

And so he did. Very carefully, naturally, because he didn't want to hurt her injured ankle, which took some ingenuity and athleticism on his part.

But it was worth it.

Oh, yes, for Dora, any amount of effort was *well* worth it.

* * * * *